Wildfire

Ella Moore

Copyright © 2021 by Ella Moore

All rights reserved.
No part of this publication may be reproduced in any form or by any electronic or mechanical means, including information storage and retrieval systems, without the prior permission in writing of the author, except for the use of brief quotations in a book review.

All characters and events in this publication are fictitious and any resemblance to real persons, living or dead, is purely coincidental.

D/2021/Ella Moore, uitgever

Edited by Writing Evolution
Cover design by JJ's Design & Creations

*To my family, and especially to M.
I belong with you.*

Content Notes

Before you get to reading, I'll provide you with some content notes—in case you want to know what you're getting into. I kept them as high-level as possible, but be aware that some readers may consider these a kind of spoiler.

Cursing: occasional, when needed for emphasis
Sex: several fully described consensual sex scenes
Violence: graphic fight scenes, references to torture
Other: references to enslavement

Chapter 1 - The mission

-Erisi, 1820 BC-

Erisi looked up at the fortified walls of Lucifer's palace and took a deep breath. A summons from the fallen angel who intended to rule all demons was rarely a good thing. The fact that it had been urgent and personally delivered by one of his generals made it worse.

When she arrived at the bronze outer gates, the guards took one look at Lucifer's mark on her chest and let her through. Chilled to her core by the wind whistling over the courtyard, she hurried across and climbed the polished quartzite stairs to the palace entrance.

At least the eternal rain showering Mount Roraima had stopped. If only the dark clouds would dissipate. And take the damn summons with them.

Two large demons with even larger swords waved her through the fortified doors.

Breathe. With every touch of her leather boots on the shiny floors, her breath settled into the steady rhythm she sought before battle. By the time she reached the end of the hallway and the guards stationed outside the throne room, she was ready to face Lucifer. No matter what he'd throw at her, she could handle it.

"He's expecting you," one of the guards said when she told them her name. The other one opened the bronze doors for her.

There was only one being in the large room on the other side, but that did nothing to ease her wariness. The fallen angel who sat on the throne atop a dozen marble stairs, black long hair bound at his nape, and eyes an almost poisonous green, wasn't just the most beautiful being she'd ever laid eyes on. He was also one of the most dangerous.

She knelt, head bent, and waited for his command.

"Get up." Lucifer's voice was pleasant enough as he strode down the stairs.

She straightened.

"I've heard stories about you, Wildfire Warrior." He circled her like a predator would its prey. "The demon who never turns demon, yet yields a power greater than any in their demonic form. The one who always fights alone. Who always wins."

Erisi took care not to move a muscle under his piercing stare.

"I have a mission for you." He came to a halt before her, close enough she had to look up to meet his eyes.

She tried not to show her surprise. "Yes, my lord."

Eyes narrowed, he studied her. "You will make the Arav bow to me. It's time to take power in the Indus Valley, and that demonic family will do nicely."

She nodded once. "What scout should I get information from?"

"Talk to Beelzebub."

She tried not to cringe at that name. Her fingernails cut into the flesh of her palms as she remained silent, waiting for the rest of Lucifer's orders.

"You have one chance to show me you are worth more than the other elites. Make this family mine, command them to fight for me. If you can, I will make you one of my generals. Fail..."

She didn't need it spelled out. More than once, she'd been sent on a mission to teach demonic families the value of loyalty to Lucifer. And the price they'd pay for treason.

"I will make the Arav yours to command, my lord."

Lucifer didn't bother replying as he ascended the stairs to his throne.

She left the room, barely able to refrain from running all the way back to the gate that separated the palace grounds from the rest of the plateau. As soon as she got outside, she let go of the breath she'd been holding.

A general. She could become one of the most powerful demons to walk this earth.

She'd be respected, revered. No more fighting to prove her worth. Nobody would ever touch her again. And if they did, she'd have the power of Lucifer and his horde backing her up.

A shiver shook her entire frame. *Never again.*

She crouched, steadying herself with her palm on the rough dark sandstone making up the Roraima plateau.

Never again. Well, as long as she managed to force the information she needed out of the bane of her existence. The thought of Beelzebub's handsome, arrogant face lit her up with anger.

She stood.

Deciding against flying to the south side of the plateau, she set off running, jumping over the shallow pools and uneven rock formations. It had her heart rate spike and the cotton of her long-sleeved tunic stick to her skin. Erisi relished the strong pulse hammering in her chest, the smooth movement of her limbs, and the air rushing along her face.

Once she arrived on the opposite side of the plateau, she easily scaled the rough stone wall surrounding the perimeter of the barracks and training yard. She found the recruits training on the grounds in their demonic form, gawking at her as she dropped down the other side of the wall.

Most demons scoffed at training in their human form, but she knew better. They infiltrated the human world often, living among them, influencing their leaders, and claiming their souls to create their young. Blending in was a valuable skill.

Besides, her demonic form was too dangerous to unleash on the world, bringing destruction to humans and demons alike. Destroying a piece of her soul every time she did.

Frowning at the lack of elites training, she wandered toward the low buildings at the far end of the grounds. She found Beelzebub in the one that housed the elite warriors.

A scowl darkened his face. "I heard sleeping with Lucifer has finally paid off."

Erisi ignored his baseless accusation. For centuries, the male's jealousy had driven a wedge between what they could have been. "I don't have time for your games. Tell me about the Arav."

He crossed his arms over his broad chest. "As if. We both know you don't deserve this mission."

Tamping down the urge to punch him in the face, Erisi turned away from the large demon and began packing her few possessions into a satchel. Her leather and cotton garments, the hard leather shoulderguards, and the oils and cloths she used to keep the chains she fought with in good condition.

While she wrapped her chains around her wrists and lower arms, she looked around the vast room filled with crude wooden beds and chests. There was nothing she would miss. After the betrayal from the warriors she'd once considered her family, nothing tied her to this place anymore.

She felt Beelzebub shift behind her, felt his hot breath against the back of her neck. "Lucifer is setting you up for failure, sending you into the Indus Valley by yourself. I guess he wants you out of the way."

Of course the bastard knew about the mission. As the all-important second to general Himani, who was in charge of Lucifer's scouts, Beelzebub was better informed than most elites.

"Do you want to tell Lucifer that you're withholding information on a mission he assigned me or shall I?" she asked without turning around.

His fingers dug into her shoulder, forcing her to face him. The smile on his beautiful dark face was slow and cruel. "No need to kick up a storm, maggot. I'll tell you. I wouldn't want to delay your departure. We have a celebration to get on with. It's not every day the most pathetic of the elites gets weeded out."

That's when she took note of the faint shouts and off-key singing drifting in through the clerestories. After a decade of being left out, she should have gotten used to the isolation. The twisting pain in her chest just made her a fool.

Beelzebub's smile widened, telling her he knew exactly what she felt. "You'll need to kill the head of the Arav family, Ashoka. He's a big burly angry male prone to wearing indigo blue robes as if he's a king. Even you can't miss him. You might need to kill his second, Torag, too. He's the intelligent one. They live at Dera Rawal, a fort in the Cholistan desert."

He left so many questions unanswered, but she refused to ask for more help.

She was done with the male.

"Goodbye, Beel. May our paths never cross again." She closed her satchel and left without looking back.

* * *

In the final hour of her flight east, the landscape changed to everything Mount Roraima was not. Where the steep cliffs of the tabletop mountain had towered over the golden savanna and forests at its feet, this part of the world was flat. The heavy rain and cold that reigned the blackstoned plateau were replaced by scorching heat and arid winds.

The day-long journey across the vast ocean followed by the savannas, mountains, and deserts of the mainland had only steeled her determination.

She would succeed in this mission. She'd become Lucifer's general, untouchable.

She would show the Arav what true power looked like. Subdue them. Bring them under Lucifer's command—another family for him to rule.

After traversing the green ribbon of the Indus Valley, she landed in the Cholistan desert to the east of the river. She had no trouble finding the Dera Rawal stronghold. The midday sun beat down on imposing brick walls fortified with numerous towering bastions. Its tan brickwork blended in with the ocher desert surrounding the fort. As the scorching breeze picked up strength, hot sand swirled around her ankles.

A group stood outside the southern gate. Despite their human form, the males were too tall and broad-shouldered to be anything but demons. The burliest one of all, dressed in blue robes, was indeed hard to miss. If only for his raised voice that had most of the others cower. Only a golden-skinned male stood tall, facing the head of the Arav family. She wondered if he was the intelligent one—Ashoka's second-in-command.

In the heat of their discussion, they didn't see her coming until she pushed through the crowd, stopping right in front of the shouting leader in the center. He fell silent as he stared at her.

Looking up at the male she was about to kill, Erisi smiled. "I challenge you to a fight to true death."

His dark eyebrows knitted together. "I don't

fight pathetic tiny females. Fuck off."

Erisi sighed. Was it too much to hope for an original response from any of these damn males?

Cracking her neck, she wrapped her steel chains tighter around her wrists. Blowing her black bangs out of her eyes, she straightened to her full height—which brought her to the midriff of the head of the Arav family.

"I guess you're scared a tiny female can beat your ass." Erisi kept her voice light.

By now, more demons had gathered behind Ashoka. None of them turned into their demonic form or drew their weapon. They seemed confident that their leader could handle her. Of course they would.

"Ashoka." The dark-eyed male with the golden skin and short brown hair who'd withstood his leader's anger, stepped closer. "Don't do it."

She smiled. At least one of them realized a single demon issuing a challenge could be a trap. Beelzebub was right; Torag was the intelligent one.

"Even your chiefs think you can't beat me." Erisi's smile widened when Ashoka's cheeks got darker.

The meddling demon put his hand on his leader's shoulder. "You have nothing to gain. Walk away. For the family."

Turning away from her, Ashoka missed the grin Erisi threw at the glaring chief. "Lucifer sent me to take over," she said. "A tiny female to take out the head of a powerful demonic family. Talk about an insult."

The speed with which Ashoka whipped around gave her pause. She would be wise not to underestimate him in a fight.

"Lucifer?" he roared. "Lucifer sent *you*?"

Always with the disbelief. She'd be insulted except she knew what she could do. If they knew her name, they would too. She was a legend.

Nobody ever believed it was her though. Too small. Female. Non-threatening until provoked.

It was helpful to be underestimated. Only, it did get old after a while.

"My lord, if you walk away, we can—"

She interrupted with a sweet smile plastered on her face. "See, I want to give you a fighting chance. You could kill me in this fight and then nobody could take your power away from you."

Torag still had his hand on Ashoka's shoulder, but he'd lost his leader's attention.

"You said it, I'm just a tiny female."

Damn, it stung to say that out loud.

Her strategy was working though. The male shrugged off Torag's hand and stripped off his robes. Witnessing him in nothing but a loincloth, she could understand his obsession with royal indigo. Without the robes, he looked like a giant throwing a tantrum.

He drew his sword from the sheath strapped to his back and turned full demon with a grunt. The flaming orange of his leathery wings and auburn scales that now covered every inch of his skin was so bright it hurt her eyes. The horned spikes atop his ugly head looked sharp enough to slice flesh.

Worse, a spiky orange giant throwing a tantrum.

Erisi didn't shift. She didn't need her demonic form to win this fight. Ashoka thought the odds were uneven. He was right.

Her hellfire burned brightly under her sternum, begging to be let out to play. The chains unwrapped from her wrists. They heated as her power fused into the metal, dark red licks of hellfire playing along the surface. That alone should have alerted Ashoka to the trouble he was in, but he was too far gone.

Torag's eyes widened, his gaze on her weapons.

Too late. He couldn't interfere in a challenge to true death. To do so would mean his leader lost face, which would be almost as detrimental to Ashoka's status as true death.

Power was the essence of the demonic world. She counted on the begrudging respect of the Arav family by slaying what they considered a mighty opponent in hand-to-hand combat. Anyone was free to challenge her after, but nobody would taint the honor of their family or question Ashoka's power by attacking her during this fight.

The orange giant didn't share Torag's qualms. He circled her, orange hellfire lighting up his sword. Just about enough power to warrant her focus.

His low growl turned into a roar as he charged. The fiery sword hacked down toward her neck.

Erisi dodged the blow easily, spinning to keep him in her sights as he passed her by.

Too slow to be a threat. She was almost disappointed.

His next attack was aimed at her gut. She slid sideways, out of his blade's reach. Waiting for her moment to strike.

His death would give the Arav a tiny taste of her power. She intended to make it count.

This time he charged her with his full body, head down, horned spikes directed at her chest. She went low and punched him hard in the throat, rolling away before he recovered.

Ashoka roared, throwing his head back, giving Erisi the perfect opportunity.

Two swings of her right chain. It flew through the air, wrapping around his throat. Her hellfire burned through his scales into the soft tissue underneath.

Like she knew he would, Ashoka tugged at the chain with his free hand. His grappling fingers couldn't reach the embedded links. Ample time to swing her second chain, wrapping it around his broad neck too.

She pulled both chains tight. The orange giant fell to his knees, sword dropping in the sand.

Both his hands scratched at his throat.

In the silence that surrounded them, his breathing grew louder. Rougher. Until it stopped.

His dark eyes locked with hers. His hands fell by his side.

The gathered demons shifted. Weapons were drawn. Scales, spikes, and wings filled her peripheral vision. They knew better than to attack while Ashoka lived.

She hoped Torag was indeed the level-headed strategist he was rumored to be. If he didn't hold them back once Ashoka was dead, she'd have more demonstrations to give.

Erisi pulled her chains tighter still. Her hellfire burned deeper into Ashoka's throat, but he didn't flinch. His last stand in front of his demons. No sign of surrender.

She could respect that.

Pushing every spark of the hellfire she possessed through the chains, she snapped them both as tight as she could. Ashoka's head rolled on the crimson-tainted dirt.

With deliberate movements, Erisi twisted the chains around her wrists and forearms, painting her pale skin with blood and gore.

Looking straight at the Arav's second-in-command, she stepped over Ashoka's headless body. Torag had shifted from a tall, muscled warrior into an even broader demon. Onyx wings and scales matched the darkness of his eyes. None of the demons behind him moved, a helpful testimony to how much control the imposing male had over his family.

"You belong to me now, and through me, to Lucifer. To your knees," Erisi commanded.

As one, the assembled demons looked to Torag. He crossed his broad arms over his scaled chest and stared at her. Nobody went down.

Erisi smiled. This was turning out to be much more fun than she'd imagined.

Chapter 2 – Erisi and Torag

-Torag-

He was going to die for this.
Knowing he was the only one who might be able to protect the Arav, Torag was torn between a show of strength to gain her respect or obedience in the hope she'd be lenient with his family. He swallowed hard when his eyes landed on Ashoka's head.

He couldn't give up his family to Lucifer.

"Down." The female sounded almost amused by his defiance.

Squaring his shoulders, Torag waited for the burn of her hellfire. It came a few moments later, but not where he'd expected it.

The chain sliced through the cotton of his pants and cut into the scaled skin above his knee. Even before the second chain wrapped around his other leg, the blast of fire bit into his muscle.

Torag ground his teeth and fought to stay standing. He would be damned if he submitted to a pint-sized enemy who hadn't even shifted into her demonic form.

When she smiled and both her chains heated even more, the searing pain that shot through his body took the last of his breath and thought away. There was nothing but raw skin and the sickening scent of his burning flesh.

He dropped to his knees. As he hit the rough sand, he nearly threw up from the impact.

At least Ashoka had felt it too. At least he'd die knowing the bastard had gone down in the most agonizing way possible.

It took him a moment to realize the female had pulled back her chains. They pooled by her side. Torag couldn't tear his eyes away from his skin and scales sticking to the cooling metal.

Why hadn't she killed him?

He clenched his fists. His skin was already knitting together, his demonic powers coursing through his body to heal the injuries he'd sustained. No matter how painful, her fire hadn't hit any vital organs. Which meant he'd have to wait mere moments to attack her.

He held still and waited. Given the strength she possessed, he'd need the element of surprise.

The demon's ice-blue eyes fixed on his face. She spoke in silken tones so quiet he strained to hear her. "Right now, my focus is on you alone. Try to fight me, and I will start killing, one demon at a time, until this family submits to me."

There was no doubt in his mind that she would execute her threat. Swallowing his pride, Torag stayed on his knees. His jaw hurt from the force with which he ground his teeth. When she patted him on the head, he almost bit through his tongue.

"One down. How many of you left to go?"

Raising his hand, Torag motioned for the demons gathered behind him to kneel. Relief flooded him when he heard his family members go down as one. They'd all survive wounded pride. Revenge could wait.

"Very good," Lucifer's warrior said. "Now listen carefully. The bad news for you is that I'm taking over this family. You will obey my orders. I can be very persuasive if you don't."

With patches of his healing skin still raw, Torag could attest to the strength of her dark red hellfire. He'd never felt anything as strong. Never saw anything darker than the red of his own fire when he turned demon until now. It left him wondering how much stronger she would be if she shifted from her human to her demonic form.

The hint of a smile still tugged at the corner of her mouth when she continued, "The good news is that I take my mission seriously. I will make this family thrive. If you work with me, we can show every other family what the Arav are made of. I know you have no reason to trust me yet, but you'll learn I keep my word. No matter the cost."

Torag found himself staring once more at the evidence sticking to her chains.

"Tomorrow, I'll decide about the strategy to make this family powerful again. As my second, Torag will help me figure out who I should assign to what mission. Take the opportunity to prove your worth. I expect you on the grounds inside the stronghold bright and early."

Her second? He tried to grasp the consequences of her words.

Behind him, a soft hum lingered among the kneeling demons, their hesitation palpable in the hot dry air. The ice of his new leader's gaze fell on him. The glare of the midday sun cast her in an aura of gold.

Sighing, he complied with her unspoken demand. "Do as she tells you. Be here, and tell every family member to attend the gathering tomorrow morning. Now go!"

On his knees, he waited until they'd all left, not even trying to get up. He wouldn't give her another reason to bring him down.

Her thoughtful eyes still rested on his face. "I don't understand why Ashoka was leading this family."

Torag stayed silent, unwilling to spill their history. He wouldn't give her even more power by revealing how weak he'd been in the face of Ashoka's rule.

She grinned at him. "You don't have to tell me. I will find out."

He believed her. "Who are you?"

"See, that's the question Ashoka should have asked me when I showed up. I'm Erisi."

If he wasn't on his knees already, he would have dropped when she'd mentioned her name. "Erisi?"

Some legends spread fast like lightning. The legend of the Wildfire Warrior was one he'd heard countless times in the two millennia since his creation. The warrior with fire as black as the darkest night and deadlier than anything encountered by demons before. The warrior who destroyed entire families by herself. Erisi.

Nobody had mentioned anything about a small female with an attitude and intelligent ice-blue eyes.

Erisi sighed. "Not you too."

He frowned, unsure what she meant.

"I thought you at least wouldn't underestimate the threat I posed."

His gaze dipped down to the blood on her hands before he answered. "You're the most dangerous demon I have come across in centuries. There's a reason I'm still on my knees." He lifted his eyes to hers. "I just didn't realize Erisi was a female reaching to my chest. The legends don't do you justice."

She laughed out loud. "I'm going to love working with you."

"I can't return the sentiment," Torag told her.

"Give it time. I'll grow on you."

Chapter 3 - Time for answers

-Erisi-

As Erisi strode toward the open gate set in the southern stronghold walls, Torag's demonic presence loomed behind her. Every well-honed instinct she possessed was trained on him. Any moment now his self-respect would demand he take her down.

She found herself smiling when he didn't.

Patient as well as intelligent. She liked the male already.

When they reached the sturdy gates, Erisi traced the slashes in the wood that had cracked and bleached under the relentless sunlight. Countless battles must have been fought outside these walls, and yet the visible defense of the stronghold was sorely lacking. She could only hope there were guards she couldn't see from her current position. Maybe there were some stationed on the bastions flanking the gate or on the archway above it. On the ground, only two wary demons eyed her, spears clutched in hand.

She couldn't blame them for their apprehension. They'd witnessed their leader die at her hands and their strong second submit to her.

Erisi turned to Torag, who stopped in his tracks. "Please tell me you have more guards for this gate than just these two."

His eyes narrowed and his mouth tightened to a straight line. He didn't even need to answer.

Right. "Put archers up there. At least a dozen near this gate, same at the northern one, and a couple on each of the corner bastions. We need guards who can defend from a distance." She gestured at the spears. "Those will only get you so far."

Eyes that reminded her of onyx shards met hers. He nodded once, and she wondered if he'd actually obey.

He'd better. Her presence here would attract Lucifer's enemies like flies to a rotting carcass. The dozens of independent families around the Indus Valley wouldn't take kindly to Lucifer's power grab.

She sighed. She'd have her work cut out if she wanted to secure an entire region with the help of a family woefully unprepared for attacks.

"We haven't been attacked in a century," he said, his voice rough and low.

Erisi suppressed a shiver as his words reverberated in her chest. Maybe it was the power inherent in that voice of his that had the Arav obey without question.

"Be thankful. They would have gotten inside in a heartbeat," she said. Any half-powerful family would have some warriors capable of attacking with pure hellfire while in flight, rendering even a stronghold like this vulnerable.

Torag shrugged. "Where we would kill them instantly."

"Why risk destroying a part of your stronghold in the process?" Erisi countered.

He nodded again. "Having you here will increase the likelihood of attack. I will strengthen our defenses as suggested."

Suggested? Erisi grinned at the subtlety of his defiance. No matter how reluctant, his willingness to see reason boded well for how many times she'd have to make him submit at her feet —unlike other warriors she had encountered in Lucifer's horde and beyond.

Erisi looked at the gate again. "What's up with the wood? I can't imagine it works well against hellfire attacks."

The groove between Torag's brows deepened. "It was a status symbol Ashoka insisted on."

She willed him to continue. Apparently she'd have to drag every bit of information out of him with the power of awkward silence and the occasional threat.

Finally, he conceded. "Wood is hard to come by. A few centuries ago, the winds turned more arid and the trees started dying. The gates are the symbol of our wealth and our importance to the trading in this region."

She needed to know more. So much more. Cursing Beelzebub again, she asked, "Which demons have been around the longest?"

Torag clenched his jaw and stayed silent. His eyes fixed on Ashoka's remnants sticking to her forearms and her chains. She could only imagine what he thought she wanted to do to the next family members she met. It was endearing that he thought his silence would help them.

Erisi walked over to the closest demonic guard. His spear shook harder with every step she took.

"Who has been part of this family the longest?" Erisi smiled at the demon, but he didn't look at her. His eyes were fixed on Torag's face.

"I don't know!" he blurted out.

"Try again."

The poor demon closed his eyes when she took a step closer. Erisi chuckled. "I'm not going to magically disappear. And believe me, I've tried. The only thing that helps is getting strong enough to slay the big bad monster."

The guard opened his eyes, staring at her as if she was his nightmare come true.

Erisi leaned in and murmured, "Now, who's been around the longest?"

"Torag," the demon stammered.

"Yes," came the confirmation from behind her back.

Shaking her head, she put her palm on the trembling guard's chest. Her hellfire surged. The guard staggered back from the flaring heat. It was too late though; the bronze of his chestplate melted into his skin.

"Try again," she urged.

The demon sank to his knees. He tried to get the armor away from his body, burning his fingers with every hard tug. "Please! I can't—"

Erisi wasn't leaving without an answer. "Tell me."

The air moved behind her. Stepping to the side, she pivoted and lashed out with her steel chain. It wrapped around his arm, halting the path of his sword. With barely a grimace, he switched hands. Her second chain wound around his left forearm, and she sent the full extent of the powers she could use in human form through the metal. His sword fell to the ground.

She admired his tenacity when he tried to charge her. Pulling the chains tighter, she sent another surge of hellfire through them. This time, the pain brought him to his knees.

Without hesitation, she turned and crouched next to the heavy-breathing guard, who was still trying to wrench his chestplate off. "This is your last chance."

The demon's voice cracked as he blurted out, "Divit and Gagan! Please!"

Moving to the guard's back, Erisi cut the leather straps holding the chestplate up. She ripped the thing from the demon's body and tried not to flinch at the sound of his tearing flesh. No matter how fast the male would heal thanks to his powers, she hated these little demonstrations. Hated having to be the big bad monster to get things done.

She dropped the armor to the sand and straightened.

She *got* things done. No matter the cost to her soul.

Lifting her gaze, she found Torag had once more turned full demon, his black wings wide and splendid, his sword burning bright with crimson hellfire. His power level was close to that of Lucifer's elite fighters, but he had to know she'd destroy him in a fight. He'd seen what she could do. Still, he stood strong.

"You will not touch either of them," he growled.

Torn between frustration and admiration, Erisi shook her head. Speaking to the guard, still on his knees next to her, she said, "Your leader will get himself killed to protect the two demons you named. I'm giving you a moment to tell me where they are so I don't have to bring him down."

The guard didn't even need time to think. "They stay in living quarters in the south-west corner of the stronghold."

With a low growl, Torag charged again. She dove to the side, rolled through the sand and came up behind him. Her hellfire bolt hit him in the back of the thighs. The hard kick in his lower back finished the job for her. The muscles of his damaged legs gave in, and he tumbled forward.

As much as she admired his tenacity, she had a lot to learn before tomorrow's meeting. The sun was setting. She didn't have the time to deal with him.

She picked up her chains and walked through the gate without looking back. No doubt he'd be joining her soon.

Past the gates, she stopped in her tracks. The first look at her new home excited and depressed her in equal measure. This would be her mission for the foreseeable future. A stronghold unlike any she'd seen before. But one that had holes in its defenses so big they could just as well have torn down those impressive walls.

In the middle of the stronghold, the keep loomed. A few clusters of demons were gathered around what looked like the remnants of a bonfire amid the large open space in front of the clay brick building. They averted their eyes the moment they noticed her and scurried off.

Between Dera Rawal's defense and its inhabitants, she had so many things to tackle. She'd promised Lucifer the Arav would serve him, and hell, she'd make sure they'd serve him well.

Which meant she really needed to seek out Divit and Gagan. She turned left to a row of low buildings along the southern wall and went in search of answers.

* * *

Erisi found the two demons huddled inside the farthest house to the west. The moment they laid eyes on her they started pleading for mercy.

"*Shri*, please. We were mere advisers to Ashoka. We carry Lucifer no ill will. Spare us, please."

The honorific and their pleading voices grated on her. She cut them off with a gesture of her hand that had the two full-grown, broad-shouldered demons cowering. "Just answer my questions."

"Anything," the tallest one said.

She hardly knew where to start. Maybe with the question that had been hounding her since she'd realized what state Dera Rawal was in. "How do the Arav survive? How have you not been taken over by one of the families to the north?"

The demon farthest from her paled even more. "I d-don't know what you mean."

"You have no defenses to speak of. Do you even have a horde?" She could count the armored warriors she'd seen since her arrival on the fingers of one hand.

"We do. They're collecting souls."

"All of them? How many souls are they even gathering?"

"Krish likes to go into the human villages

with a bang. They rush to make a deal for their soul after seeing family members slaughtered before their eyes."

Erisi resisted the urge to groan. *What the hell is wrong with this family?*

She had a sinking feeling. "How many souls did this Krish collect since the new moon?"

"A dozen or so," the tall one whispered.

"And how many warriors does he drag along?"

"They split in cohorts, but typically most of the hundred-fifty our horde counts," he said, his voice fading even more. She could only imagine what he saw on her face.

The sheer magnitude of stupidity left her floundering. "When does he collect the souls? Does he even wait until they die?"

A low voice behind her answered. "Whenever Ashoka told him to."

Not when they died of natural causes, like most families would. She had a feeling Ashoka had wiped out entire villages before their time. She turned to Torag and found him looking subdued and exhausted. "Why? Why would he do that?"

Torag laughed mirthlessly. "He was building up his army to fight Lucifer. He knew it was only a matter of time before your leader would turn his eye to the region and subject the families here."

Erisi looked at the male, then at the shivering advisers. "Nobody thought that was a bad idea?"

she asked in disbelief. "None of you advised against it?"

The tall demon's eyes flickered to Torag.

Of course. At least she wouldn't have to adjust her assessment of Torag's intelligence.

"Ashoka and Krish take all decisions…" The pale-looking demon swallowed. "—took all decisions about the strategy for the horde and the souls. We—we only provided information. And Torag wasn't allowed…" His voice died away.

Torag's jaw clenched hard; she could see the muscle jump.

At some point she needed to find out what had happened between Ashoka and Torag, but right now, she needed to understand how this family functioned. "What happened to the souls he collected?"

She could only hope the family had a healthy amount of them. If Lucifer intended for the Arav to represent him in the region, they'd need a healthy family with a sizable, well-trained horde and plenty of young to grow.

Torag's voice promised a world of pain when he spoke up. "If you touch even one of our souls or young, I will kill you. I will find a way to end you."

She studied him, not taking his threat lightly. When it came to this family, Torag was a force to be reckoned with. "I realize you have no idea who I am and what I value, but I would never harm a young."

The hard glare didn't diminish, but he'd find out soon enough that there were lines she'd never cross.

Looking back at Divit and Gagan, she realized all she'd get out of them was a better sense of the thousand ways in which Ashoka had screwed over his family. She had no more patience left for their trembling fear and excuses. Her voice sharper than she intended, she said, "Don't go anywhere. I'm sure we have some more family matters to discuss once I've settled in."

Their whimpered responses left her even more annoyed.

She walked outside and took a deep breath of fresh evening air.

Thank hell the temperature has dropped. After centuries on a wind-swept, cold, and rainy mountain top, the heat was a lot to take.

She turned and found Torag with his arms crossed over his broad chest and a vein pulsing at his temple.

Erisi locked eyes with him. "I have something to attend to. You're more than welcome to join. I think you may find it useful to see how I spend my nights."

She'd rather keep the strongest demon around where she could keep an eye on him.

When he followed her without a word across the stronghold toward the northern gate, Erisi smiled. Time to show her new second-in-command just how powerful she truly was.

Chapter 4 – Hellfire and fulgurite

-Torag-

As Torag followed the Wildfire Warrior, he tried to keep a cool head. Her interrogation of Divit and Gagan had painted a picture of his family that left him frustrated and unsettled. He wished he could say things were about to change for the better, but he didn't trust her or the fallen angel she served. Once more, it came down to him to protect this family.

He wished he could simply close the gates behind her the moment she ventured outside. Except there was no doubt in his mind that she wouldn't even bother flying over the wall to get him. She'd hunt down any Arav demon still roaming outside and use them to force his surrender.

The warrior halted on the training fields and observed the large keep that took up most of the western side of the stronghold. Its brick walls reached high into the night sky. Torches dotted the battlements lining the flat roof of the keep.

Without turning, she asked, "How many guards?"

"Six archers. There are two scouts who circle the stronghold and report back about any irregularities."

Erisi nodded. "Where does the chief of war reside?"

"At night, Krish is at the fire with the other family members or in his private quarters behind the keep. During the day, he's with the horde for training and missions." Torag pointed to the large building in the south on the edge of the training field, close to the gate. "The horde's barracks are over there."

Her eyes briefly rested on the building before moving to the large bonfire a hundred feet from the keep. Usually, the air buzzed with loud voices, laughter and excited shouts at this time of night. Tonight, quiet ruled the stronghold. The few demons at the fire kept their heads down.

Resuming her path to the northern gate, Erisi scanned her surroundings. Her constant questions about their defenses set Torag on edge. Having her here would paint a target on all of their backs. The more powerful Rohi in the mountains to the north wouldn't take kindly to Lucifer's warrior at Dera Rawal. Even the smaller families spread across the Indus Valley might band together to drive her out.

He clenched his fists at the knowledge they would also take over the stronghold, kill the horde, and capture the young. His nails dug deep into his palms at the thought of their young in the hands of slavers.

Anything. He'd do anything to spare them that fate, the gut-wrenching shame and the scars it etched into the soul.

Erisi had left while he was deep in thought. She'd picked up a torch and walked through the gate by the time he caught up. They reached a sandy hill north of the stronghold. Two tall trees loomed over a few of the resilient plants that had survived the ongoing drought.

The moonlight reflected on her short black hair as she ran up the incline. The dark leather of her garments was a stark contrast against her pale skin. She looked too delicate to be the Wildfire Warrior. Too easily overpowered. Too easily dominated by his much larger form. He should be able to push her against that tree, tip her chin and force her to look up at him.

He swallowed hard, willing the foolish thoughts away.

He wouldn't be another idiot who underestimated her because of her beauty, the elegance of her movements, or how tiny she was.

Shifting on his feet, Torag watched her plant the torch into the sand.

"Want to join me?" she asked as she turned to face him. "You can find my weak spots while we spar."

He just stared at her while the image of her on her knees before him flashed unbidden through his mind.

"Oh, don't look so surprised. You're all the same. Big powerful demon. Can't figure out how the hell the tiny female beat him. Needs to find her weakness so he can have her crawl at his feet." Erisi smiled at him. "You are more than welcome to try."

Torag stuffed the infuriating flicker of lust deep down where it belonged and tried to find his voice. "You've got me all figured out. I felt enough of your hellfire for one day though, so I will decline your kind invitation."

"Giving up already? You disappoint me," she drawled. Torag watched the torchlight caress her face, illuminating the small smile still playing on her lips.

Broadening his stance, he put his hands behind his back and straightened his shoulders. "I think you're mistaking me for someone who is easily riled."

Erisi's smile turned into a full-blown grin. "Suit yourself."

She dropped her painfully effective chains at the roots of the highest tree. Placing her hands on either side of the trunk, she scaled up to a thick branch. Her leather-clad legs wrapped around it, and she let herself fall backward.

Torag couldn't keep his eyes off the hard muscle of her stomach and the tattooed lines swirling across. Every time she pulled herself up, those muscles clenched, the lines rippled, and his arousal flared higher.

It should have been boring to see her repeat the movement hundreds of times. It wasn't.

He fought to keep a cool head and think through the consequences of her arrival. The threat of Lucifer's claim meant he needed all his wits about him. Somehow, seeing the precision of her movements and the inherent power of that tiny body made him lose those wits over and over again.

He needed to find a way to keep his family safe. Some way to appeal to the powerful female without succumbing to the heat that roared through his veins.

Maybe this was the time to strike. The element of surprise might be enough to use his physical strength against her before she could use her hellfire. Maybe he could save his family from her tonight.

Tomorrow he'd think about saving them from the other dangers for a family without a real leader. A family that defied the fallen angel who intended to rule them all.

He moved his hand ever so slightly to the dagger in his scabbard and unsheathed it. As soon as it was out of sight behind his back, he infused the metal with hellfire and charged. He aimed the blade at her exposed stomach.

Fate, I just need one moment. Just one.

She caught the dagger. The blade slashed open her palm, fire doused with her blood, but she didn't even flinch.

"I'm insulted you thought I wouldn't notice." Erisi dangled from the branch by her other arm, her muscles tight. Holding his gaze, she dropped into a crouch on the sand.

He braced himself for her wrath, the dread in his gut mingling with acceptance. The past millennium had taught him not to fight his fate. To submit to the pain so Ashoka's rage would quiet. He'd breathe through the agony knowing his family was safe from the anger, that he'd find a way to minimize the havoc Ashoka would wreak.

Except Ashoka was no more. And the warrior he faced would—

She tossed his dagger back to him with a half-smile. The blade landed in the sand at his feet, and he could only stare at it.

When she picked up her chains and infused them with hellfire, he clenched his jaw and waited. Now she would—

She didn't even look at him. Instead, she settled into a crouch and started what looked like the next part of her training, her chains dancing in the air, arcing and weaving past each other in a series of precise movements.

Torag stared at her, mesmerized. His gut was

still roiling, and his jaw felt tight with the anticipation of whatever punishment she'd come up with.

It never came.

The dread faded to unease, but he kept watching her. He couldn't look away from the grace of her movements and the way her muscles tightened. His blood heated at the sight.

He willed the thought away and tried to stomp the flicker of hope about what kind of leader she could be. One who wasn't ruled by rage and revenge.

He couldn't let false hope lead him. He couldn't submit to her like he'd done to Ashoka for a thousand years.

This time it wasn't a power hungry demon whose worst decisions he could curb. This time he'd have to protect his family from the demon rumored to be the most powerful of all. Worse, from the fallen angel who used the families he conquered as pawns.

And still he could only stare at her with a racing heart.

By the time the caracal's hunting call thrilled through the night, she fastened the chains around her waist and took off running. Torag followed her to see what else she could do but soon wished he hadn't. Still in human form, she led him on a merry chase through the desert. Refusing to bow to her unspoken challenge, he didn't turn either.

He'd forgotten what a pain it was to train in his human form. Sweat beaded on his brow and ran down his face. The muscles in his legs burned. Cursing the female running in front of him, he tried to channel his demonic powers into bursts of speed and found he had little left in him after their earlier fight.

Miles later, she still hadn't slowed.

He wouldn't give her the pleasure of his surrender again. The damn female had spent hours training before this. She'd killed Ashoka, and she'd made him submit. He'd be damned if he gave up before her. With a groan, he pushed himself harder.

Finally, the female came to a halt beneath the same trees they'd started from. Sinking down on the sand, she sat without moving, eyes closed, legs folded, hands on her thighs.

Bent over and gasping for breath, Torag watched her.

Her fire flared on her palms and crept along the bare skin of her arms, the red flames so dark they looked black. With every breath that moved her chest, the fire burned brighter, flaring, the flames coating her body and lighting up the night.

Torag's nails dug into his palms as he stared at a power he'd never seen before.

With a graceful movement, Erisi got up and brought her hands together in front of her chest, palm to palm. When she slammed the flat of her hand against the ground, hellfire surged into the sand with such intensity, the air around them sang.

The sand fused into a smooth, glittering surface. When she brought her other palm down hard, it shattered. She straightened, blood dripping from her hand where a few of the shards were embedded. Placing her hands together again, she took a few steps forward and closed her eyes. She punched down once more. Her damaged palm slammed hellfire into the ground, and her next move broke through the hard surface she'd created. Turning, she found the next spot of sand to burn.

Defeat crushed Torag's insides as he looked on. Her muscles worked in perfect unison to create the most spectacular display of power he had ever seen.

Erisi was strong beyond anything he'd witnessed, strong in every sense of the word. And she was only using a fraction of her actual power as long as she didn't turn.

If she wanted to use the Arav as a tool for Lucifer, there was nothing he could do to stop her.

His family was doomed.

Chapter 5 - The gathering

-Erisi-

Erisi felt Torag's eyes on her as he followed her back into the stronghold. She smiled. His demeanor had changed. He had worked hard to keep his expression blank, but there was a newfound wariness lurking in his onyx eyes.

Training through the night had been everything she needed. Her muscles ached. The healing cuts on her palms burned, but the pain satisfied her. It was a pulsing reminder that she'd pushed herself to the limit and beyond. Power sparked in her chest, fed by the rush of her training.

She was ready to take on the Arav family.

She walked onto the vast training field at the heart of the stronghold. Three large demons faced her, two of them in demonic form with their leathery wings spread. Their weapons might still be sheathed, but she didn't miss the message. The Arav tattoo on their chests showed three interlocking squares rather than two, marking them as the chiefs of the family.

Behind them, hundreds were gathered, all turned full demon. The indigo, yellow, and red-patterned clothes of the deal-makers and crafters provided a vivid contrast against the more subdued colors of the warriors' attire. She couldn't spot the young and wondered if they were shielded by the larger demons. It wouldn't surprise her to see Torag's protectiveness mirrored in this family.

The chiefs eyed her warily as she approached them.

"Are they all here?" Erisi asked.

Torag nodded to one of the chiefs who answered for him. "All but a few who couldn't get back in time."

"Good enough. Let's get started."

Erisi considered climbing on top of something to see eye-to-eye with the tall chiefs but decided it would only show her frustration. Sighing, she took a step back so she didn't have to crane her neck as much, and spoke, "I have taken over the leadership of this family. For those of you who weren't here yesterday, I challenged Ashoka and won. I made your second submit. I rule this family."

Two chiefs managed to maintain a blank look. The one still in human form glared at her, his face contorted and the muscles of his broad neck corded. She wondered if he was trying to impress her by staying in human form as well.

Turning from the fuming male, she locked eyes with Torag and made him a promise she intended to keep. "My leadership means I will take care of this family as if I was born into it. I vow to you that the Arav name will be revered."

In the silence that followed, the chief in human form scoffed. "Who do you think you are? We will crush you. We are four hundred strong against one tiny demon," he sneered.

To her right, Torag sighed. That saved her the trouble of doing it herself.

"I am Erisi. Elite warrior and Lucifer's envoy. Wielder of hellfire and wildfire. Head of the Arav family."

Apprehension rippled through the assembled demons. The murmurs started quietly and rose in volume like a sandstorm picking up force. Briefly, Erisi wondered what exaggerated legend about the Wildfire Warrior had made it to these remote parts.

The troublesome chief stepped forward, forcing her to look up. Another idiot who thought he could intimidate her with his greater height and bulk. "You? Erisi? How dare you pretend—"

Torag cleared his throat. "Krish, do you really think I would hand over the reins of this family without good reason?"

"They were never yours to hand over," the male said, his smile dark and without humor.

"And who knows? Look at the little bitch. I'm sure you'd fall at her feet if it meant getting a taste of her."

Erisi held up her hand to keep Torag back. She could practically hear him grind his teeth. He could get his revenge over the insult to his name later.

Right now, this one was for her.

"Oh, I'm definitely worth falling for. Krish? The one in charge of raiding the villages and collecting souls prematurely?" Erisi let her gaze travel over the fuming demon before flicking her eyes back up to his face. She made sure he couldn't miss her contempt.

He met her stare. "Yes."

At least, Divit and Gagan had proven accurate sources of information so far.

"You are stripped of any rank you had. Not for your witless insult but for your lack of courage in questioning Ashoka's orders that damaged the Arav family. Step back and join the horde."

Krish laughed, the sound shrill. "Even if I accepted your fucking leadership, you can't do that."

"I can do whatever I want. Step. Back." Erisi kept her voice low and calm and her muscles relaxed.

Bright red darkened his cheeks. "Like hell I will."

He drew his sword from the sheath strapped to his back. Behind him, a few others followed his example.

Torag bellowed, "Nobody else moves a muscle. If Krish wants to challenge the head of this family, that's up to him. Nobody else will be punished for his idiocy."

Most of the demons behind Krish lowered their weapons. Erisi wondered why Torag honored the traditions of a leadership challenge. It would have been a prime moment to overcome her and the threat she posed to his family.

As the chief turned demon, she focused on his tawny spikes and scales that turned his body even bulkier. She much preferred Torag's smooth onyx form over this abomination. The chains uncoiled from her forearms, glowing with hellfire. Dark flames enveloped the metal.

Throwing his head back, Krish roared.

What was it with these moronic warriors? Despite the form she was still in, she wasn't a puny human intimidated by his ugly ass and loud growls.

Taking advantage of his mistake, she wrapped her first chain around his shoulder and ribs, slicing through his wing like a knife through butter. He faltered in his battle cry.

Her second chain crossed over his chest and shoulder, hitting his other wing. Krish fell to his knees, sword falling by his side, fingers tugging at the chains. He failed to rip the metal from his flesh.

Without much effort, she kicked him over.

The next blast of hellfire through her chains had him writhe on the ground. The sickly sweet smell of burning flesh assaulted her nostrils.

The small sound Torag made had her turn to him and smile at the worried-looking male.

Behind her, the idiot scrambled back to his feet, tugging at her chains. She kept her eyes locked with Torag, and her smile widened.

As she swiveled to put the tawny asshole down, an onyx demon charged past her. Right into the two daggers Krish had infused with orange hellfire. He stabbed Torag in the armpit and forced the other dagger between his ribs.

Torag didn't even flinch. He wrapped his arm around Krish's neck, grabbed the demon's head, and snapped it to the left. The crack echoed over the silent training field.

Krish dropped.

Pulling the daggers from his body, Torag cursed. He infused each one with hellfire and nailed Krish's hands into the ground. "That will give him some time to reflect on bad life choices when he regains consciousness."

Given the power level Krish had shown, he'd be laying in the burning sun for days before his body had recovered sufficiently. Erisi grinned at Torag. She knew she liked him for a reason.

Face grim, he pushed his hand on the wound beneath his armpit to quell the bleeding. She couldn't help but notice how the blood ran along the grooves of the muscles stretched over his ribs and side.

She forced herself to look away and scanned the crowd instead, wrapping her chains around her arms. The other chiefs had distanced themselves from the fight, and most of the gathered demons kept their eyes on the ground, unwilling to provoke her.

"Now that we've solved that little problem, who should take over command from Krish?"

Before Torag could answer her, an earthy-scaled female stepped forward from the horde. "I should."

Chapter 6 – The Arav will be revered

-Torag-

His entire body stilled, muscles primed to step in between Sura and Erisi. He wished the warrior's courage had failed her, just this once. It was bad enough that he'd had to save Krish's head from Erisi's rightful wrath, though he wouldn't deny he got plenty of satisfaction from pounding the idiot's ass into the ground.

Erisi's smile at Sura didn't reassure him.

"Why you?"

Straightening, Sura told her new leader, "I know every demon here, their strengths, their weaknesses. I know how to push them to become better warriors on their own and as part of this horde. These warriors will be the steel fist required for the Arav name to be revered. Let me forge the steel for you."

Torag's blood sang with pride as his protégé stepped up, becoming who he'd always known she could be. He'd have preferred it if she'd picked a different moment though. It took every ounce of his willpower not to interfere.

"Tell them to attack me." Erisi's voice was flat, her gaze unreadable.

As Torag tensed even more, doubt flitted over Sura's face. Still, she turned, raised her blade, and shouted, "Draw your weapons—now!"

Metal sung. Crossbows were cocked.

Torag wished they had a chance. Even if they did overcome Erisi in the end, dozens of his family members would die. In a pinch, his new leader wouldn't hesitate to target the crafters and hit them where it hurt. He hoped she would draw the line at the young like she'd promised before, but he couldn't take the chance.

Drawing his sword, he infused it with hellfire. He wasn't sure yet if he would be part of the attack or stand between the horde and Erisi when it came to that. Whatever would save his family...

Sura pointed her blade forward and shouted, "Everyone with m—"

"Enough." Erisi's voice didn't waver despite the threat. The lines of her muscles were sharp with tension. Dark hellfire danced on her palms. Whatever the outcome of her command, she was ready.

Sura dropped her sword and held up her hand

to halt the horde.

Erisi let the silence linger long enough for Torag's gut to plummet.

Finally, she spoke. "Congratulations. You are the newest chief of the Arav family. Leader of the steel fist that will come down on our enemies. You will train this horde to become stronger, quicker and—" Erisi strode over to one of the warriors who hadn't drawn his sword at Sura's command. "—braver."

The hellfire on her palm touched the warrior tattoo on his pectoral muscle. His skin blistered and bled. The demon sank to his knees, whimpering.

"By the time you heal enough for that mark to be visible again, I hope you'll find the determination to be an Arav warrior. I need fighters who obey their chief without hesitation, no matter the dangers you face." Erisi's eyes scanned the crowd. Torag saw several warriors shrink back. "I know exactly who didn't intend to attack despite her command. I propose you do better next time; I don't have time for cowards."

Sura seemed to have grown a foot when she asked, "What are my orders?"

Erisi smiled at her new chief before turning to Torag. "I trust you know exactly how to make the Arav first among all families. Give your orders to your chiefs."

He stared at the small demon with ice in her eyes. His heartbeat drummed in his ears as all the plans he'd been honing for a century flooded his mind.

Hope flamed. No more bending to Ashoka's ego. No more suggesting plans without knowing if his fickle leader would ignore them, do the exact opposite, or wait for a decade before claiming them as his own.

Straightening his shoulders, Torag crushed the hope under his heel. Who knew what Erisi would do with his plans? Yet, he had no reason not to try.

Sura looked up at him with the same expression he'd seen a thousand times before. The intelligence in her brown eyes had always set her apart. The respect and admiration she showed him had his chest tighten.

Swallowing the lump away, Torag explained, "I want this horde drilled as if war is looming on the horizon. Prioritize your missions to make time for more training. These warriors shouldn't be mowing down humans to collect souls. They should be able to take out well-trained demonic warriors. Half of this horde has never faced an enemy in battle. I want them prepared."

Next to him, Erisi nodded. "I agree. I will join the training tomorrow night to see what you and the horde can do."

The skin of the newly minted chief took on a distinct grayish undertone, but she kept silent.

Erisi grinned. "Don't worry. I won't hold you accountable for their inexperience. I only want to evaluate where we stand." She turned back to Torag. "What else?"

Yerle looked at him expectantly. The chief leading the deal-makers knew Torag's mind about the lack of contracts they had left. Torag had spent enough time ranting to his friend about Ashoka's strategy—or lack thereof.

"We need new deals. A lot of them." He knew Yerle wanted nothing more. The demon lived for the sweet moment he coaxed humans into signing over their souls. He watched his friend's smile grow when he said, "I know you've not been able to keep up with Ashoka's premature collection of contracts, but things are about to change. We need to build up our reserves."

Yerle's smile faded. "Ashoka's strategy has left very little to work with in our territory. Krish eliminated too many of the villages." Yerle kicked dust over Krish's motionless form as he spat out the words.

Torag paced in front of the chiefs as he let his thoughts spill out. "Dera Rawal is sitting on one of the major human trade routes. We should tempt every single trader in every passing caravan. We should send our best deal-makers with the caravans to far-flung human cities and establish more contracts."

Yerle spoke up. "The other families won't take kindly to us making deals in their territories."

"I know. That's why our horde needs to be ready for war. We won't become the mightiest family by sitting in our own little corner. The other families won't attack us straight away over a few measly deals. By the time they realize it's a conscious strategy, we'll be ready for them." Or so he hoped.

Torag knew he shouldn't like the look of approval Erisi sent his way. He needed to ponder over her reasons for handing him power. Right now, though, he didn't care. He had the chance to shove this family into a brighter future instead of trying to nudge them along, and he was grabbing the opportunity with both hands. He would deal with any fallout later.

"Chandra." Torag turned to the last chief whose scales and wings shone coppery under the morning sun. "Your crafters need to produce more armor, more weapons. The buildmasters need to look at our defenses. Anything we can do to strengthen this stronghold will benefit us when our enemies come knocking." He looked over at the group of young in the middle of the crowd, flanked by the best Arav fighters. "We need to expand the housing for the young. Their quarters have been bursting at the seams for too long. You can recruit some of the young to help with the smaller tasks. It will be good for them to build some discipline and muscle."

Torag didn't miss Chandra's glance in Erisi's direction, waiting for her curt nod, which came soon after he stopped talking. None of the chiefs would admit it, but they had already accepted her rule. This family was used to falling in line. Annoying Ashoka on a bad day got you killed in a heartbeat. They weren't risking Erisi's wrath, knowing the stories about her power.

"We will discuss the rest of your plans later. This is more than enough to keep the family occupied for years." Erisi turned to the chiefs and the demons behind them. "You heard my second. Get moving. I want you to report to me and Torag in four days. Sura, expect us tomorrow."

His family scattered as the sun reached its highest point.

"Tell me about our territory," Erisi said behind his back. "One of the chiefs mentioned hostility from the other families."

He turned to find her ice-blue eyes fixed on him and nodded. "We have a map in the keep that will help."

They crossed the ochre sand of the training field, passed the fire pit in front of the keep, and entered the imposing building through the large wooden doors.

Inside, the air brushed cool against his skin, the dark lit by torches a welcome reprieve after the glare of the sun. A steel throne sat in the middle of the large room, surrounded by brightly colored carpets on the walls, made from the finest of wools. To his right, stone tables and benches served as a place for the meetings between the chiefs, or the occasional feast for human guests. Torag hated the meals with a passion. As a demon, he had no need for food or drink. Pretending to consume vast quantities of both while Ashoka basked in the adoration of his human guests was a waste of time. Especially because Ashoka tended to have them killed soon after.

Erisi stared at the throne. "Get that damn thing melted for something useful."

Fighting his smile, Torag nodded and beckoned her to the left side of the room where a large slab of sandstone was laid out on several pedestals. The flickering torchlight illuminated the carvings in the stone.

His new leader's eyes shone as she leaned over the crude map and ran her finger over the markings.

Torag pointed to the square within a square in the middle of the slab. "This is Dera Rawal, and here—" He followed the curving line to the west of the stronghold. "—is the Indus river."

He showed her the other landmarks: the Kirthar mountain range spanning the entire west side of the Indus Valley, the awe-inspiring Karakoram mountains to the north, and the towering Himalayas to the east.

"The strongest family in the region are the Rohi demons. They live in the Rohtas Fort. There are many smaller families living around the Indus Valley in smaller forts, but they mostly keep to themselves. The Rohi like to expand their territory through warfare. The only reason they haven't attacked us yet is because we're located far enough south. If we start expanding, they might retaliate."

"Do they attack human cities too?" Erisi asked.

He shook his head. "No. Like us, they try to win over the humans by forging alliances. At least that's how we used to do it until Ashoka wanted to expand the horde at all cost. These are the villages he took out recently."

Erisi's eyes followed his hand as he showed her on the map. At the last tap, her gaze traveled up his arm and to his face. She studied him in silence. "Were you keeping Ashoka on as a figurehead in case of attacks?"

Anger roiled in Torag's gut at the suggestion. "Do not question my integrity," he ground out.

Erisi shrugged. "Didn't think so, but I can't come up with many good reasons for a demon of your intelligence and strength to take backstage to that idiot."

He knew she wasn't going to let it go, but telling her the real reason would divulge more about his weaknesses than he was comfortable sharing.

"Do you want to hear more about the families in the region or not?" Torag asked, not liking the slight tremble in his voice.

Leaning over the map, Erisi pointed to a few structures he hadn't mentioned yet. "What are those?"

"Those are the larger human cities."

Well into the evening, Torag's voice gave out while he tried to explain Ashoka's misguided strategy, Krish's influence, and how he had tried to maintain some semblance of order within the stronghold as his second.

He hated laying out all the things that had gone wrong. His gut felt tight with misery.

With every mistake he told her about, his determination grew not to make another one.

Not to let Lucifer use his family. Yes, he wanted the Arav to be strong, to be revered. But not to serve another power hungry being.

No matter what, he couldn't trust Erisi. She served Lucifer's interests, not the Arav's.

Erisi stretched her arms behind her back, pulling his attention back to her. "Seems like you need a break as much as I do. You're welcome to join."

An eerie calm descended on him as he followed her out the northern gate to the two trees. He watched her scale the trunk and take her position on the thick branch that had served her well before.

He watched and waited. Watched her push herself to the brink, sweat dripping from her pale skin. Tried to breathe through the flickers of desire her determination and strength fired in him.

He simply waited.

Until she dropped to the sand after hours of training, panting. Then he made his move.

Chapter 7 - Unmoving

-Erisi-

The dagger buried hilt-deep into her shoulder. She nearly stumbled to her knees at the punch of pain. The acid of his fire blistered her skin and spread through her veins.

Her limbs shook with exhaustion. She struggled to dodge his charge, the first slice of his sword. Her eyes flicked to the chains she'd left at the roots of the tree. Out of reach.

Fate be damned. So fucking arrogant to think I wouldn't need them.

She gritted her teeth and pulled the dagger from her flesh. His fire hurt a lot more than she'd thought it would, a testament to his power.

He easily evaded her throw and charged again. Breathing through the pain, she dove to the side. She sneaked the short knife from the sheath in her boot. Before she could get up, his sword pierced her side.

Her body stilled from the shock. Every instinct in her demanded she transform.

She couldn't.

She couldn't risk bringing Dera Rawal down. She refused to let wildfire consume her again. Refused to lose another part of her soul.

He kept his dark eyes locked on her face as he pushed his sword deeper. For a moment she wondered why he didn't drive his blade through her chest. She'd be done when his hellfire reached her heart.

She fought the darkness that evaded her vision. No wildfire.

I can't—

Her palm clenched around the hilt of her knife. *Not yet.* She only had one chance.

It felt like someone was tearing her wide open and pouring fire into the gaping hollow. The agony exploded in her gut as the cross-guard of his sword sank into the muscles on her side.

She gritted her teeth and slung her unharmed arm around his neck in a parody of a lover's embrace, locking him to her.

His eyes widened as she plunged her blade into the back of his neck. The sound that escaped him came from somewhere deep. His knees buckled. She saw the moment he realized his body no longer obeyed.

It took the last bit of her strength to stay standing when he fell backward, the force of his descent embedding the blade even deeper into his spine.

Erisi watched the life flicker out in his onyx eyes.

She dropped to her knees and shrieked at the sharp pain of the sudden movement. Swaying, she wrapped her fingers around the hilt. If she wanted her body to start healing, the sword needed to come out before she fainted.

When she pulled out the blade in one smooth move, the agony peaked to a screaming crescendo. Erisi threw the weapon to the ground, swallowing her curses. Nothing would stop the bleeding, so she didn't even try.

Hands on the sand, she kept herself upright and tried to think.

This time she needed to sleep. It was the only way her body would recover fast enough. She was surrounded by enemies. Any sign of weakness would get her killed.

How had she made such a stupid mistake? For hell's sake, she liked how dangerously patient Torag was; she should have known better than to drop her guard.

She sighed as she looked over at Torag. Carefully rolling his body on his side, she pulled her knife from the back of his neck. That would hurt like hell when his spine mended enough for him to regain consciousness.

She steeled herself against the pain before getting up. Still she couldn't silence the yelp escaping her lips as she stood.

Body wrecked with violent shivers, the

stronghold looked too far away. She locked her eyes on the flickering torches near the north gate and took another deep breath. By the time she came into full view of the guards, she needed to get her act together.

Crimson trailed her path back. The first steps were the hardest, but the gradual numbing of her body the closer she got to the imposing walls of Dera Rawal worried her. She needed to find a safe spot to rest, *now*.

At the gate, she straightened and called one of the guards over, before gesturing toward the trees. "Drag Torag into the stronghold. You can leave him next to Krish on the training field. Close the gate when you're done."

The demon was less skilled in hiding his emotions than Torag was. She watched fear and anger follow each other in rapid succession, his lips and jaw tight, before he bent his head in deference. The guard scurried away in the direction of her training spot.

She took a deep breath and straightened her exhausted body. Feeling the blood drip down her right side, she passed the bonfire on her way to the keep. The eyes of the Arav burned on her. Nobody moved, and she thanked Fate for the reprieve.

She'd have no choice but to turn if anyone attacked her now. She could only hope the power she'd demonstrated these past few days would be enough to keep them at a distance.

Once inside the main hall, she slumped against the wooden doors and took a deep breath. At the table, Chandra and a few of his crafters had fallen silent at her arrival. She ignored them and climbed the stairs to the flat roof lined with demon-height brick walls on all sides. Elevated guard posts were positioned on each corner of the roof, covered with leather to keep the guards safe from attacks carried out from above. Perfect to shelter her while she healed.

Erisi cleared her throat. "Everyone out! Guard duty for tonight is done. Go downstairs and get your orders from Chandra. He'll find you something to do."

Her display this morning seemed to have smothered any wish to rebel, at least for now. The six guards obeyed her command without hesitation.

She slammed the trapdoor shut behind them and melted the hinges with the little hellfire she had left to delay unwanted visitors from below. Now all she needed to worry about was the sky.

She hauled herself up the steps to the guard post closest to the training field and looked out over the stronghold through the embrasure. The dry desert wind whistled through the slit in the wall and tugged on her hair, the cool night air whispering over her beaded forehead.

Maybe she'd survive the night after all. She took a deep breath and cursed the flare of agony as her lungs expanded.

In the distance, three demons carried Torag's still form onto the training field. She wondered what would happen when he woke. How hard he'd continue to fight her.

She needed to find a way to get him working with her. She needed his skills. She needed his loyalty. For more reasons than she cared to admit.

Then there was Krish.

Thinking about the crude male made the pressure behind her eyes bloom into a sharp ache throughout her skull. He possessed the kind of anger that would fester in the underbelly of this family and infect anyone still loyal to the former chief.

All of that could have been avoided by killing the bastard outright, but Erisi had no interest in cutting down members of her new family.

Lucifer would consider her strategy weak. Beelzebub would laugh in her face. She didn't care.

She planned to show the Arav that she was good for this family.

Erisi crawled against the wall, arms hugging her knees close to her chest. The pain was a pulsing heart in the center of the little ball she made. Resting her pounding head against the rough bricks, she watched Torag's unmoving body laid out on the sand.

The demon she'd sent to retrieve him stood guard next to his leader in an act of defiance she admired.

She looked forward to locking horns again with her second tomorrow.

Erisi closed her eyes and drifted off with a smile.

Chapter 8 – The young

-Torag-

A blast of fire exploded at the base of his spine when Torag tried to move.

At least he could move his upper body now.

Sweat dripped from his face as he pushed himself into a sitting position. He squeezed his eyes shut to ward off the morning light. His entire skull throbbed. He needed to get off this damn training field before the sun gained strength. Before his head burst. If only his legs would cooperate.

When the dizziness cleared enough to open his eyes, Torag found Erisi sitting on her haunches a few arm lengths away from him. Her blue eyes roved over his body, dipping down his chest to linger on his waist. He doubted she was thinking about the same thing he suddenly was, but the way she smiled had him thanking Fate he was still half-paralyzed.

Hell knew he didn't need to give the female any more power over him.

"Good morning," she said, her voice cheerful enough to worsen the throbbing behind his eyes.

He bit his response back and met her gaze. Her blue eyes were unclouded by the anger he'd expected after his botched attack.

When she stood with fluid grace, only a pink line low on her side hinted at the grievous wound he'd dealt her last night. Meanwhile, he was laid out on the sand trying not to scream.

His stomach knotted even harder. He didn't stand a damn chance. Not even with a surprise attack causing an injury that would have forced warriors twice her size to their knees.

She was too strong. The realization hurt almost as much as the blasts of agony that kept coursing along his spine.

She smiled at him. "When you're done plotting my demise, come find me. We have family business to discuss."

Torag swallowed hard as he watched her walk away. After what he did, was she keeping him around as her second?

Then again, it was only a matter of time before she found out he was less. Less than a true Arav. Before she realized she actually owned his life, to do with as she pleased.

Torag looked to his right where Krish's brown skin had started blistering after a day under the relentless sun. Even if she didn't find out from the others, Krish would tell her. The vengeful male would spend every moment of his recovery finding ways to bring her down, and Torag with her.

Torag doubted she would show Krish pity the next time he attacked her. The question was how much poison the former chief could spread before his inevitable downfall.

Torag tried to keep in the sigh lodged in his chest. If he could keep the rest of the family safe...

He tried to move his feet. The sparks flared to the point of pain, but his toes didn't move. Damn her to hell and back.

Damn himself for even thinking he stood a chance.

* * *

By the time his toes cooperated, he found Erisi observing one of their smiths working the glowing metal of a blade.

"So you can forge steel?" she asked Chandra, who stood beside her.

"Aye. Our hellfire is ideal for heating the ore to the right temperature. It's been a great help in our dealings with humans. We want 'em to fear an' admire us without divulging the full extent of our powers so they'll still be willing to close deals. Being able to smith steel while they're only capable of forging bronze gives us the edge."

"What else do you do here?" Erisi looked

around the large room. Her eyes rested on the stacks of materials stacked in their dedicated corners.

By the time her eyes found him, he felt her gaze drop to his weak-kneed limbs. Heat flushed his face when she looked up and grinned at him.

"We cut stone from sandstone and make mud bricks. With the sheer length of walls an' buildings to maintain, we need a steady supply. We also tan camel an' goat leather, but the bulk of that process is done outside the stronghold because of the stench." Chandra gestured toward the pile of leather hides in the corner of the workshop. "We 'ave other crafters who make clothing an' items with it."

Erisi pointed at a sturdy door to the right. "What do you do in there?"

Torag stiffened at the same time as the chief of all crafters.

"Nothing special," Chandra ground out.

When she stared at the male in silence, Chandra scowled. "I distill alcohol from rice meal. Nobody but me enters that part of the workshop." He straightened to his full length, all the while glaring at Erisi. "Nobody."

Last time a young tried, he'd been on tanning duty for the better part of a moon cycle. The stench had lasted many moons longer.

Erisi held up her hands and grinned at the coppery-skinned chief. "Don't worry. I won't interfere in what's probably the most important part of this workshop."

She turned to Torag and gestured at the demons working around them. "How do you assign duties to the family members? When do you pick the warriors, the scouts, the messengers, the deal-makers, and the crafters?"

Torag stared at her. *Was this a test?* She had to know the answer to that.

She arched an eyebrow.

Clearing his throat, he said, "When the young turn full demon for the first time. By then, we have a good sense of their specific talents and what they'd like to do. Once they leave the barracks, they either join the horde in the barracks for further training as a warrior or scout, or join Chandra and Yerle to apprentice as crafters, messengers, or deal-makers."

Except Ashoka had been pushing the young to join the horde, regardless of their talents and desires. The surge of relief knowing he no longer needed to fight the male when it came to the young was short-lived. Who said Erisi wouldn't do the same to build a larger horde for Lucifer?

"Do all families use the same process?" she probed.

Wondering at her questions, he shook his head. "From what I've seen, it depends on the leader and the family's traditions."

Erisi nodded, deep in thought. After a few more words to Chandra, she walked outside. "I have a mission for you," she told him without turning.

He followed her as she walked along the northern edge of the training field, waiting for her command.

"First, I need to see the young."

His heart stopped, then started pounding against his ribs with brute force. "No."

She walked on as if she hadn't heard him. He grabbed her arm.

Last night should have taught him resistance was futile, but he couldn't let her. Not when it came to the young.

Erisi glanced at his hold on her before looking up with a smile. "I'm sure you know by now that I will find out where they are. Wouldn't you rather be there to protect them from the big bad monster?"

His grip tightened. "You'll have to kill me if you want to touch them."

"I've told you before, I don't intend to harm them. I will never hurt a young. Ever." Steel edged her voice. Her eyes were as cold as ice, the earlier sparks of mischief extinguished.

He held her unwavering gaze. Hoping that she was telling the truth.

Hoping that he'd read her surprising lack of rage and revenge right. That she was the kind of leader who protected rather than punished.

He didn't know how he could stop her if she wasn't. Getting himself killed again only meant the young would face her alone. "I—"

"You made your point, Torag. I made mine. Bring me to them." Her voice brooked no argument.

She let him lead the way. With every step closer to the young's quarters, he had to work harder to breathe through the tightness in his chest.

This was a mistake. Even if he could trust her, he could never trust Lucifer's plans with the young. His jaw hurt with the force of his teeth grinding. He felt nauseous at the realization that for the first time in centuries, he had no back-up plan to protect his family. This time he couldn't sacrifice himself to keep anyone safe. She wouldn't let him.

Noises of the young's usual chaos reached them before they even got to the large wooden door. His heart squeezed. He took a deep breath and opened the door, letting Erisi through.

Inside, disorder reigned. The wooden beds, normally shoved against the walls, had been used to build some kind of fortress. Two brothers, Hiro and Ahio, were defending from the top against Mei and Khloe. Judging by the scorch marks on the beds and their bare chests, the young males were losing in spectacular fashion. Anea was tied to one of the bedposts. A fierce blush darkened her face as she struggled against her bonds. At her feet laid a collection of rocks he suspected belonged to Kaemon, and a pile of training swords. He found the chest that usually held them now harbored a shouting young.

Cursing, he knelt beside Anea and cut her ties. She almost got past him to pummel Kaemon before he got a hold of her wrist. Maybe he should have left her tied up. For hell's sake, maybe he should tie them all up himself.

"Get in line. Now!" he said loudly, trying very hard not to shout.

Nothing showed the decades and decades of work to turn them into strong and disciplined family members. You'd think they were fledglings rather than century-old young.

He saw Anea stiffen the moment she laid eyes on Erisi and slink behind a few of the other young. Hiro, Ahio, and Mei didn't seem in the least bit intimidated by their new leader, much unlike the way they'd tiptoed around Ashoka.

The fact that she was shaking with laughter might have something to do with their lack of fear. The hard knot in his chest loosened the tiniest bit.

He caught a movement in the corner of his eye. "Mei, if you don't get back in line in the next ten seconds, I will have you run laps around the training field for the rest of the day," he bellowed. "Is this the way you want to impress your new leader? By showing her how lazy, unorganized and—"

He turned as a blur dashed for the fortress. "Ahio, don't you dare!" Smiling, the young stashed the dagger behind his back as if he hadn't been about to plunge it into his brother's thigh. "Hiro, get down from there. Now."

Scowling at the lot of them, Torag took his place next to Erisi and looked at the line-up. They looked exactly like the sulking, lanky, growing young they were.

When Torag looked at their leader, he found Erisi's easy smile had melted from her face. The knot in his chest tightened again.

She spoke, her voice so soft, several of the young leaned forward to catch her words. "Listen carefully. You are the future of this family. You may be the most important demons in this stronghold."

Several of the young straightened their shoulders. Torag saw Ahio eyeing his brother, his hand inching from behind his back.

"You need to take your role seriously," Erisi continued, "You will need to train, help the crafters make this stronghold better, and learn to work together and become a team. None of that will be easy or even fun most of the time." Erisi's smile appeared again.

Torag glared at Ahio, who blinked innocently at him. The circle Torag drew in the air was enough for the young to drop his hands. The threat of laps rarely failed him.

He tried to focus on Erisi's soft voice.

"I'll give you all you need to become the best you can be. The first thing, the most important thing, will be a leader who can teach you all he knows."

Torag took a deep breath when she looked up at him. The respect shining from her eyes coursed through his body with unexpected warmth. His heart picked up its pace like he'd been the one running laps.

"Torag will continue to be your leader. He will show you what it takes to become a true warrior, what you need to do if you want to be the best deal-maker or master crafter. From today onward, Torag will be the only one in charge of you."

Mei paled, and Erisi grinned at her. "I'm sure that may mean a lot of laps around the training field for some of you."

When she turned, an explosion of chatter erupted behind her. He could only see her, the warmth in her eyes as she issued her commands.

"Get them organized. Make sure they get more living space. Train them to understand they need to obey your commands without question. If we get attacked, I want them ready to do exactly what you tell them to do. Whether it's to run and hide or to be part of the battle."

The thought of the young caught in the cross fire woke him from his daze.

She patted his arm. "I'm sure they listen better when I'm not around. They clearly know and love you."

The softness of her voice and the smile that lit up her face made him believe she thought that was a good thing. It had the hope flare again, unbidden.

Torag was still staring when she pulled the door closed behind her, just in time for Ahio's dagger to dig into the wood.

"Oh, and make sure all seventy-five of them are still alive tonight!" she yelled from the other side of the door.

Chapter 9 – The first test

-Erisi-

Twisting her chains around Sura's blade, Erisi blocked the quick attack. With one hard pull, she disarmed her warrior chief. She whipped her chain toward Sura's thigh. Rolling out of reach, the female stood with both her daggers in hand. Erisi dodged the first toss and caught the second in her palm. She sent it back infused with dark red hellfire.

"For hell's sake! It's been a damn week, and I still don't see it coming." Gritting her teeth, Sura pulled the dagger from her shoulder with a slight whimper. "Maybe I should join your nightly training sessions."

Erisi grinned and wiped the blood off her palm. "Always welcome. Torag still hasn't done anything but stare holes in the back of my head. I'd lo—"

All hell broke loose. The sound of the ram horn echoed between the walls of the stronghold. Shouts and pain-laced screams pierced the air from the direction of the northern gate.

A dozen dark forms dotted the sky. She swore. They weren't even close to ready for a demonic attack.

No matter how hard her warriors trained and how diligent her new chief of war had proven to be, they couldn't catch up with years of minimal training in mere days. They lacked the experience to face enemies who knew what to do with hellfire.

Worse, beyond a greater number of guards, the stronghold's defenses hadn't improved yet. That fucking wooden gate would be the death of them all.

Cursing Lucifer, Erisi handed Sura her blade.

The megalomaniac couldn't wait more than a few days to test my leadership?

"We split the horde. You tackle them head-on with the majority. I'll take a dozen warriors to attack the demons in the air before they eliminate all our guards," she told her chief of war.

Sura nodded, then turned to command her warriors into formation. Despite her clear orders, half of the demons didn't seem to have a clue where they fit into the formation. A few of them ran toward the northern gate without heeding their orders.

Erisi ground her teeth. She understood the instinct to charge into battle and help the guards, but they were going to get themselves killed.

She needed to nail this test if she wanted a chance at becoming Lucifer's general. If she wanted the Arav to survive this battle and all the ones to come.

The thought of her warriors getting slain, torched with hellfire... The thought of some of them meeting true death nearly made her run after the idiots.

But she couldn't.

She could only hope her horde was strong enough and their enemies weak enough to hold them off until dark. It would give the family the chance to hide, charge from the dark corners of the stronghold. Hell, if need be, she'd kill every enemy with her bare hands, one by one.

It took her everything to turn away from the warriors running toward the gate. She faced the rest of the horde instead. "If I pick you, come with me. Everyone else joins Sura."

She got a scowl from one of the warriors she'd relentlessly pushed for days.

"This is not a fucking sparring session. If you disobey orders, I will consider it an act of treason and I will find you after this battle is over." The cold focus that preceded combat crawled up her limbs and bled into the icy threat she issued. As the male cowered from her gaze, she pointed at a dozen demons who'd demonstrated precision during the training sessions.

"We need to eliminate the enemies in the sky." She looked at the crossbows several of her team carried. "I need you to take out as many as possible."

Raising their bows, the warriors fired as soon as the demons flew over the gates. Four bolts slammed into their targets. One of the demons they hit stayed airborne. The other three plummeted to the ground, their screams bloodcurdling and the sound they made as they hit the ground even worse.

Erisi punched up her shield, pushing her hellfire outward in a fiery barrier that incinerated the spears headed for her group of warriors.

Behind the broken bodies, Sura and the rest of the horde charged into the enemies who'd breached the gate. The group of flying demons circled back and charged, wings pulled back, scaled bodies aiming for them.

"Keep going," she shouted. The archers cocked their crossbows for the next attack. She dropped her shield at the last moment to let their fiery crossbow bolts through. Turning to the sword and spear-wielding warriors on her team, she ordered, "Protect our archers. Once all our attackers are on the ground, we need to finish them off. Don't underestimate—"

She caught the flash of fire in the darkening sky. Finely-honed instinct alone had her counter the incoming strike with a shimmering wall of dark-red hellfire to protect her team.

Damn Lucifer to hell and back.

One of these demons was powerful enough

to charge with pure hellfire while flying. She'd hoped her damn lord would have sent a weaker test.

Maybe she should take it as a compliment. If only she didn't fear her warriors would suffer for it.

Fuck this. She'd nail his test. And keep the Arav safe.

Dropping her shield so their crossbow bolts could get through, she shouted at her archers, "Him first! Get him down any way you can!" She turned to the others. "Can any of you throw up hellfire shields?"

"No, we've never had to use—" A spear slammed into the warrior's shoulder, dropping him to his knees. "Damn!"

Erisi cursed with him, knowing she wouldn't be able to attack if she had to shield them all. "Get behind me. I will drop the shield when you are ready to fire again." Re-erecting her hellfire shield, a dark red wavering wall of heat formed in front of them. Another blast hit, and she pushed even more of her power into the barrier. "Tell me when!"

The lead archer shouted, "Ready!"

She dropped the shield. Crossbow bolts flew past her. One of her archers went down without a word, hellfire burning through his throat.

A snarl tore the air. She looked up just as two more bolts buried deep into the demon's chest. A final one pieced his eye, turning his snarl into a scream. He dropped, hitting the sand hard.

Erisi shielded her warriors again, observing the first flying enemy to land unharmed. Crouched he waited as more of them landed. Spears and swords ready, they advanced on Erisi and her warriors.

A dozen blades and spears slammed into her shield. Their attack reverberated through her body. Gritting her teeth, she pushed her hellfire out, burning anyone close enough.

Most dropped their swords as her fire burned their hands and turned tail, retreating to the northern gate to join what remained of their horde.

"Kill them! Now!" She dropped her shield to let her warriors pass. With satisfaction, she saw them slay the fleeing demons as she strode toward the most dangerous of their enemies. He was writhing in the sand, growls escaping him. Blood painted his face crimson. He kept touching the arrow still sticking in his eye before shrieking and pulling away.

She drew the knife from her boot and slit his throat. He might not be a danger now, but she wasn't taking any chances. "Chop off their heads so they don't recov—"

The sudden high-pitched screams chilled her blood. She froze when she realized the sound was coming from the north-east corner of the stronghold.

The young.

She forgot every good battle practice drilled into her for the past few centuries. She forgot the warriors waiting for her command. She didn't give a fuck that Lucifer was most likely testing her.

She simply ran.

The barracks were cracked open. Young were fleeing in every direction. Torag was defending the entrance from five warriors; there was nobody to help the young being chased.

When one of them was struck down by a burly male, a vicious snarl erupted from Erisi's throat. "Come and get me, you bastards. It's me you need."

Her chains boiled hot with the heat of her fury. Hellfire pulsed through her veins, the thrum serving as a bass to her rage.

The attackers dismissed her on sight, continuing their hunt for the other young.

Fools.

Coming up behind the two demons closest to her, who were cornering three of the young, she wrapped her chains around the throat of the largest attacker. Her hellfire blistered his skin and sliced through with ease.

When the other demon turned, she shoved the headless corpse at him. He fumbled back. She aimed her knife right between his eyes. Rushing forward, she recovered her blade and slit his throat in one smooth move.

She hissed to the young, "Go to Torag and listen to him. He'll keep you safe while I kill every last one of these cowards."

The young stared at her, frozen in fear.

"Go!" She regretted her shrill shout the moment she threw it out, but it worked. They ran back to the building where Torag was still fighting off the remaining three demons.

Erisi turned and eyed her next enemy whose hellfire lit up the darkness of the night.

Oh, this was going to be good.

Chapter 10 – Confrontation

-Torag-

The legends about the wildfire demon didn't do her justice.

Every time the stories had been passed around the fire, Yerle had talked about the power of wildfire—black and so strong it could kill with a mere spark. Never had the legends mentioned her pale skin glowing a dark red until she looked like a goddess of war painted with blood. They didn't talk about the cold precision with which she killed, or the grace of her chains as they sliced through the air before burrowing into flesh.

Even without seeing her demonic form, Torag knew he was witnessing the most powerful demon in existence.

One by one, the young pushed forward behind him, trying to catch glimpses of Erisi's wrath. With their warmth at his back, all he felt was gratitude. They lived, unharmed. The female slaying the last of their enemies in the light of the rising sun had made sure of that.

When she approached, the rage in her eyes was still simmering. His gaze traveled down the short length of her toned body, which was covered in blood and guts. He couldn't tear his eyes away from the crimson drops falling on the sand beneath her feet, wondering how much of it was hers.

Ignoring his stare, Erisi strode into the building and was instantly swarmed by the young firing question after question at her. Only Kaemon and Anea kept their distance, watching the chaos with wary eyes. Torag knew he needed to talk to them soon. The two young had adored Ashoka and Krish. The changes in the family were a lot harder on them.

"Enough." He admonished the others. "Give her room to breathe."

The young took one step back before they resumed their persistent battering of her senses. He saw her eyes trail along their faces, saw the relief he felt too. Torag shouldered his way forward. The fatigue lining her fine features caused a pang inside his chest.

She had defended them all, without a moment's hesitation. The rage that had lit her up hadn't been about winning or proving a point to Lucifer. The least he could do was give her a moment of reprieve.

He brushed her shoulder and motioned to the

open door. Her weary smile cut right through him.

Without turning back, he told the young, "All of you, rest. Then we'll have a conversation about what happened during the attack."

As soon as they got outside, she looked up at him. "We need to talk." The rasp of her exhausted voice twisted his gut.

He gestured toward a large rock at the edge of the training field, shaded from the rising sun. Erisi sank down next to him on the rough stone.

"What happened?" she asked.

Torag cleared his voice. "We were training outside when they attacked. The majority of the young got inside the building, but some didn't heed my command."

The choice to defend only the ones inside had torn his soul. If not for Erisi, the others would have succumbed to the fate he'd fought so hard to escape a millennium ago. They would have been captured and tortured by slavers, sold to other hordes for the most horrendous purposes.

"I tried to protect the young inside. I couldn't —" He fought for breath. "Thank hell you were on time."

Erisi closed her eyes. When she opened them, he saw trouble brewing in the icy depths. "How do you train them?"

Her question was innocent enough, but he had a bad feeling. Still, he answered her. It was the least he owed her after she'd saved Khloe,

Varun, Anea, and Basha. "I teach them how to call up their hellfire and how to improve their focus so their powers get stronger and last longer. I improve their physical condition. No matter what they'll do after, they need physical strength and endurance. I teach them how demonic families function and what the world looks like. They spar every day."

"With actual weapons?"

"Wooden," he ground out, knowing where her mind was going.

Her next words proved him right. "As of tomorrow, we will raise the stakes. Pair up every demon who has control over their hellfire. We'll bring them to a point in the desert and have them make their way back to the stronghold. Everyone else will spar using real weapons going forward. The only way they're going to learn quickly is if we add pressure."

Torag stood, straightening to his full height. "No."

Erisi narrowed her eyes. "They're not prepared for an attack. Not even close. Do you think they'll learn to survive by running laps or sparring with wooden swords?"

"Eventually, they will move on to more dangerous training methods. They're not ready."

She threw up her hands. "Exactly! They're not ready, and we're running out of time."

Torag crossed his arms. He stared the fuming female down in silence.

"This was Lucifer's first test, the easiest one. He knew I could beat the attackers single-handedly if needed. But if it wasn't for me, this family would have lost a part of the horde. You would have lost some of the young. They didn't obey when push came to shove, Torag!"

He stiffened. "If not for you, there wouldn't have been an attack in the first place. You assigned me this task hours ago. Do you really think I can—"

Erisi stood and faced him head-on. "Oh, pull the stick out of your ass. I. Don't. Care. I don't care why they're not ready or who should have trained them better. I don't give a damn about what came before. All I care about is the young surviving the next attack Lucifer sends our way."

"Instead of having a rival family kill off the young, you plan to do it yourself?" he snapped.

Erisi glared at him. "Cut the drama. All I'm suggesting is to drop them in the desert and have them find their way home. I'm not about to burn them to ashes."

"The desert is crawling with danger," he argued.

"They are fucking demons, Torag. They heal. They don't need food or water. Send our best warriors to shadow them and intervene if they're at risk."

The scenarios his mind conjured up shook him to his core. "What happened to not harming them? You promised me you wouldn't harm them!"

Erisi stabbed him in the chest with her finger. "I'm trying to stop them from getting harmed by our enemies! We will prepare them for their little adventure. They will never get better if you keep protecting them."

"They won't ever trust me again if I throw them in harm's way!" His voice came out much hoarser than he'd intended.

Erisi stilled. She looked at him. She looked right through him into his soul. Her soft voice slew him. "What did he do?"

Torag pretended he didn't understand. "Who?"

She stared at him without words. The understanding in her eyes struck him in the gut. He didn't need her cursed compassion.

"Like you said, you don't care about what came before. It doesn't matter."

"Oh, but it does. I want to tear him apart with my bare hands," her voice rasped. The gleam in her eyes sent a shiver down his spine.

There were too many to count. Too many torturers he'd never had a name for.

The scars on his thighs ached. A barrage of memories made the skin on his back crawl.

He turned away from her. "I know how to take care of myself."

Every whispered word she uttered behind his back vibrated in his core. "I'm well aware. You also know how to take care of others. And they let you. They trust they won't come to harm because they know you will not let it happen."

Torag closed his eyes, waiting for her next words to cut even deeper.

"But you won't always be there to shield them, Torag. Today, you weren't able to protect all of them. Next time may be worse. Let them go so they can grow into the best they can be. It shouldn't matter if they like you. The only thing that matters is leading them to greatness, as a family and as individuals."

She didn't understand. She couldn't. Not without knowing everything that had come before.

"The answer is still no." He kept his back to her.

Erisi's voice barely rose above the noise of the demons milling around, dragging mangled bodies off the training field. "You're already a better leader than anyone I've ever met. You care. Now care enough to get out of their way."

Eyes closed, he waited for her to give him the order. It never came.

When he looked over his shoulder, she was gone.

"Fuck!"

He hated knowing that she was right.

* * *

He stared at the horizon from his position on the north-west bastion. Below him, the demons in the stronghold looked like carved figurines instead of life-sized family members he needed to take care of.

His heart pounded at his temples. The trembling in his hands hadn't subsided. Erisi's words had hit him where it hurt, stirred up too many memories best left buried.

From his vantage point, Torag watched Krish struggle to get up. One of the warriors rushed to his side to help, but even from this far, he could see the former chief flinch. Those blisters he'd seen almost a day ago would have only gotten worse with another day of sun.

The male was going to be trouble. At some point, Torag needed to have a conversation with him before he did something even more idiotic than insulting the most powerful demon alive. Another thing to add to his never-ending list of worries.

Most of the time, Torag loved taking care of the family. When the sun rose, he was happy to kick the young out of bed to teach them about demons, fighting, and life. Discussing strategy with the chiefs sharpened his mind and provided him with some much needed entertainment thanks to Yerle's antics. He loved it when family members asked him for help because he could make a difference. In those moments, he was an actual part of this family despite his past. Like he'd earned his place.

His chest tightened at the thought of almost

failing them today. His knees went weak at the thought of the young he'd almost lost.

He couldn't stop thinking about Varun dragged along in chains. How any slaver worth the name would crush Khloe's spirit. The sandstone battlement under his hand crumbled under his death grip while he tried to breathe.

He remembered.

It had been a long time since last the memories had overtaken him. He stared at a point on the horizon and inhaled shakily. Felt his chest expand and his lungs strain against the all too familiar tightness.

Breathe. One breath at a time.

He couldn't let that happen to them. He couldn't bear seeing them taken or slain. And they weren't ready.

But he couldn't be the one pushing them in harm's way. Not even when he knew Erisi was right.

Taking another deep breath, Torag tried to relax his shoulders. It didn't help. He descended from the bastion and strode toward the barracks, hoping to find Sura inside.

She looked up when he walked in. As soon as she saw his face, she dismissed the warriors she'd been talking to.

"Let me get my weapon," Sura told him. She walked over to the chest at the foot of her bed and strapped on her weapon with practiced movements.

Joining his side, she asked, "Where do you want to go?"

She knew him too well.

He led the way outside and changed to his demonic form, relishing the sharp pain of his wings breaking through his scaled skin. When they took flight, the cool winds high in the sky provided reprieve from the scorching midday heat.

Sura barreled past him, a flash of earthy scales and wings. "You're getting old," she teased.

Without a word, he pushed himself harder. The muscles in his shoulders felt like they were on fire. Shooting past the female he'd raised, he grinned when she yelled something that was lost in the wind. He could venture a guess as to what it was. She'd always liked colorful phrases. It had cost her more laps than she cared to admit.

By the time they sank down on an isle in the middle of the broad Indus river, Torag had no more energy left to panic. He leaned back, panting, and let the heat of the sand seep into his exhausted muscles.

Finally, he broke the relaxed silence hanging between them. "Erisi wants to train the young differently."

Sura's eyes fixed on his face. "I wondered if it was just the attack that got you so restless."

"She wants to send them into the desert for some kind of practical training so they'll learn faster." Torag closed his eyes and tried to even out his breathing.

"Your methods always worked fine, but that was before. It's clear she wants us all to improve quickly, and the attack was a good demonstration of why it's important we do."

Opening his eyes, Torag sighed. "If it wasn't for her, there wouldn't have been an attack."

Sura tensed at his words. "Did she—?"

"No, not her. Apparently, Lucifer sent the attackers as a test of her leadership."

"Bastard," Sura muttered.

The silence lingered for a moment before she spoke again. "No matter what, we need to prepare, Torag. And that includes the young. I know you want to keep them from harm, but taking it easy on them won't work anymore. You know it won't."

Torag didn't reply. The tension in his shoulders and the pounding in his skull returned with a vengeance.

He knew.

He also knew he couldn't do it. Erisi be damned.

Chapter 11 - Stars

-Erisi-

Torag hadn't come around.

Since their confrontation three days ago, Erisi had barely found time to think. The battle had shifted the dynamics in the Arav family for the better. The chiefs came to her without coercion. The guards no longer shivered when she walked through the gate. Still, the one demon she needed by her side to make this family thrive hadn't come around.

She replayed their last conversation over and over. Heard the crack in his voice again, and felt another surge of that feral urge to hunt down the beings who hurt him.

The darkness in him resonated with her tainted soul. But unlike her, he had found a place for others. She fought for herself, for a place in the light, as far away from her dark origins as she could get. He'd found a way to love and care. To let others love him.

She'd seen it in the young's eyes. In the way Chandra and Yerle and Sura looked at him.

In the way he defied her. He would never let her send the young into danger, even if she personally ensured they wouldn't come to harm.

He made her yearn for something she could never have.

Erisi took a deep breath and leaned her cheek against the trunk of her training tree. A slight noise made her twist around, smile on her lips. She watched a rat scurry under the bush and sighed. He wouldn't come.

Maybe it was time for her to go to him.

She wasn't surprised to find him in the young's quarters when she slipped in unnoticed. He walked amid the young-induced chaos, skin lit up like gold in the last light of day as it filtered through the clerestories. His beauty was breathtaking, but it was the slight smile as he sat down cross-legged on the sandstone floor that had her still.

The young stilled too. The shrieks of laughter and chatter faded when they joined him.

Erisi found a spot near the door to sit and folded her legs under her.

He told them to close their eyes, and she watched them obey, their beautiful faces turned to him. She obeyed too.

Maybe she'd find some peace in this meditation, in the quiet of this moment.

Unfortunately, the husk of his voice worked

like a pebble on the smooth surface of her thoughts. The ripples he caused reverberated from the base of her spine up to her hairline.

In the end, she gave up. Opening her eyes, she watched the serene focus infused in the male's entire being. His large hands laid on his strong thighs, palms up and open. His broad chest expanded with every deep breath he took. Her eyes roved the strong lines of his jaw, the relaxed slant of his lips.

The unrest nestled in the pit of her stomach turned into an ache she couldn't ignore no matter how hard she tried.

His eyes opened, and his dark gaze found hers. She sucked in a breath. For a moment, it was just the two of them.

"Erisi!" With the moment lost under the squeals of excitement, she smiled at the young charging her from all sides. Varun plonked down so close that his red-patterned tunic brushed against her upper arm. She made a mental note to talk to the young male about personal space.

Mei tackled her in a fierce hug—a blur of indigo fabric, tawny skin, and dark hair smelling of soapberries. "Erisi! When can you train with us again? Torag said we couldn't ask, but you're here, so maybe you—" Mei tried to catch her breath.

Trying to ignore the heat of Torag's gaze on her, Erisi faked a frown. "What have I told you about obeying the orders of your leaders?"

"But—" Mei tried.

"No buts." Despite the laughter she tried to push down, Erisi knew it was crucial she hammered the point home. During the next attack, the young better obey orders, or they might not survive.

Mei fluttered her lashes at Torag, and Erisi finally looked at him, her skin tingling where his eyes lingered.

"Can I please please ask her?"

Torag hummed without looking away from Erisi. "How badly do you want it? Enough to run more laps?"

Mei considered it. "Yes?"

"Is that an answer or a question?" Torag's eyes betrayed his mirth despite the straight line of his lips.

"Yes! If Erisi can come spar with us, I can run more laps," Mei all but shouted.

He conceded. "You can ask your question."

Mei almost combusted. "Erisi!"

Erisi bit the inside of her cheek to avoid laughing at the young demon. She wrenched her gaze away from Torag. "Yes?"

"Can you please spar with us?" Mei stilled while she waited, her entire focus on Erisi's face.

"I will. Tomorrow."

"The whole day!" Varun looked at her with an intense adoration that made her move a couple of inches away.

Torag growled, "You do realize Erisi leads this

entire family? She doesn't have ti—"

Erisi smiled at him, and he stuttered to a halt. She turned to the young. "I'll try."

The moment the words had left her lips, Mei knocked her to the ground as she threw herself in Erisi's arms. Erisi swallowed the pesky lump away and tried to get back up, unsuccessfully. She was certain Torag was having a great time at her expense.

The warmth in her chest left her no choice but to admit that she was having a great time too.

* * *

After he'd given the young his final orders for the day, Torag followed her outside into the night.

They walked toward the northern gate in silence. There, he cleared his throat. "Thank you."

Erisi hoped he didn't know how much power the low vibrations of his voice had over her. She rubbed the goosebumps on her arms, pretending the chill of the night air was to blame.

"For promising to spar with them? My pleasure. I love spending time with the young, and I was serious when I said I would do anything to train them—" Realizing she was rambling, she stopped herself before it got worse.

He cast her a look from the side. "That too. For not forcing my hand. For not dropping them in the desert."

Erisi stopped walking and turned to face him.

"I made you their leader; you have authority over them. I keep my word, Torag. I won't intervene unless I have no other choice."

The slow curl of his lips nearly knocked her off her feet. Erisi had seen all kinds of expressions on his striking face. Anger and annoyance at her being the most common ones, but this…

His smile was deadlier than his dagger.

Her own smile bloomed in response. "Join me? I'm going for a walk outside the walls. I want to watch the stars and enjoy the silence."

His eyes lingered on her face as she turned toward the gate. She tried to ignore the little jump in her chest when he appeared next to her, matching his stride to hers. He gave her the silence she'd foolishly asked for.

On top of a dune well away from the stronghold, Erisi dropped into the sand and looked up at him. The moonlight cast harsh shadows on the angles of his face. After a while, he sat down next to her, his long legs stretching out.

She leaned back. The night air cooled her heated skin. Thousands of fiery dots sparked in the night sky. It was a sight she usually reserved for after training, when she was too exhausted to move while her muscles mended and her powers recovered.

She often wondered if the night sky had changed since her first night of freedom, when she'd walked out of Gyasi's temple, covered in his blood, and stared up for the very first time. Had it evolved the way she had? Or had it always been the same, etched into eternity as a reminder of that fateful night?

Torag leaned back, his breath slow and even. The heat his powerful body threw off warmed her left side. Letting the sand slide between her fingers, she spoke up. "Ask me anything."

The silence stretched. *Too soon.* She'd misjudged—

"What's coming for us?" He turned, leaning on his elbow to look at her. Erisi's eyes dipped to his straining biceps before she forced her eyes back to the night sky. "You said this was only the first attack."

Keeping her gaze on the stars, she said, "I have reasons to believe that was the first of many. Between Lucifer, the families close by, and my enemies, Dera Rawal will be under siege more often than not."

His breath caught at her words, but his voice was even when he asked, "What does Lucifer want with this family? There are more powerful ones to the north he could have chosen."

She glanced at him, fighting back a smile. His intelligence never failed to impress her. "Lucifer always chooses the ones with the most potential, never those with the most power. That goes for the warriors he surrounds himself with and the families he conquers. You need to break a powerful family if you want them to bend to your will. This family was ready for change. Of course,

I had to force my way in. Blood needed to be spilled. But I only had to kill one demon to establish my rule. It didn't require an army. All I need now is patience and capable leaders around me. This family has the capacity to be great."

Because of Torag. Because of the young. Because of his protectiveness built into the very fabric of this family.

She sat up. "I won't send them to the desert. Not even if you'd let me."

Torag pushed himself up next to her. "Why?"

"I don't want to break what you've built." She swallowed and looked back up at the stars.

She felt Torag shift beside her, felt his heat at her side. In the silence, she could hear him breathing. Her own breath slowed to match his even as her heart raced.

His whisper warmed her bare left shoulder. Feverish heat zinged through her veins. "And what have I built exactly?"

"A true family."

His body went very still. Silence reigned once more, but this time there was no peace in it. Only the anticipation of words unsaid.

"Look at me."

Erisi turned her head until his beautiful face filled her vision. She swallowed hard.

"What do you want?" His words were mere whispers in the night.

Erisi could barely remember the plans she'd shaped her life around. She could swear the stars reflected in the onyx of his eyes.

"You." The word fell from her lips without thought.

Torag closed his eyes with a groan. "Fuck."

Her exhale came out on a stutter. His eyes snapped open and focused on her mouth. Desire wrapped around her like a blanket, and her hands fisted the sand at her sides.

His palm caressed along her jaw, his soft touch holding her captive. When his thumb brushed her lower lip, Erisi nearly combusted. She tackled him to the sand, straddling his waist. Her fingers twined in the silk of his hair, right before she slammed her lips against his.

With a soft growl, he angled her face so he could deepen the kiss. She forgot how to breathe. As his tongue swept inside her mouth, she arched into him. Torag's arm wrapped around her waist, keeping her locked against him.

Her power flared, and little bursts of hellfire born from desire licked her skin.

Torag stared at her. "So fucking powerful."

The respect in his voice made her knees weak. "Torag…"

He swallowed. When he lowered his eyes, she knew he'd come to his senses.

"I don't trust you, Erisi. I can't," he whispered. Still, his arm stayed around her waist, and his hand gripped the back of her neck. His mind might have caught up with the real world but neither of their bodies had.

"I know." Regret colored her voice.

She let him go.

Without a word, Torag stood and walked back to Dera Rawal. Erisi watched him go with her fingers resting on her tingling lips.

She caught his gaze when he cast one last look over his shoulder. Her breath caught, released when he continued his path away from her.

Rolling onto her back, she noticed the stars had lost their shine.

Chapter 12 - The color of hellfire

-Torag-

Torag paced in front of the southern gate, kicking up dust and sand as he went. He snapped around the moment the scout landed.

"She's been with Chandra in the workshop, talking about additional fortifications since first light. It sounds like she wants him to replace the gates as soon as possible," Sumit told him.

Torag nodded his thanks. "Let me know when she's on the move. I'll be at the west of the stronghold."

"Will do!"

Still as excited as he'd been as a young. Torag smiled as he watched the male run off.

When he remembered what he had to do, his smile faded. It was time to have a conversation with Krish.

Now a mere warrior, the male should have resided in the barracks with the rest of the horde and resumed training with them. Instead, the former chief refused to give up the status symbol of his own quarters. Erisi had ignored his petty act of defiance so far, but Torag wasn't sure how much longer she would tolerate his disobedience.

Worse, he had noticed a coming and going of warriors visiting Krish. Although the demon was still healing, he wasn't wounded enough to warrant that much concern or assistance. Torag had to stop him before he did something stupid.

He crossed the courtyard to the west. The door to the low brick building crammed between the keep and perimeter wall stood wide open. When he got closer, he felt the heat emanate from inside. Despite their thick walls, the scorching sun tended to turn the smaller buildings into ovens.

He didn't go in, but leaned against the doorpost. Krish sliced the air with what seemed to be a new sword, the metal still unblemished.

The male turned midway one of his dramatic charges in thin air, noticed Torag, and slumped, cradling his arm against his stomach. Torag didn't miss how he kicked the sword under the bed behind him.

"Get out," the male mumbled with a feeble voice.

"You can drop the act now. Twelve days is

more than enough to heal from a broken neck and some holes in your hands. Even for you."

Krish spit at his feet. "Fuck off!"

"I don't think so," Torag said, staring the male down.

The two of them had never seen eye-to-eye, possibly because of the height difference.

"What are you doing here? Shouldn't you be crawling through the dust for the little bitch?" Krish sneered.

Torag swallowed his rage. "Be thankful I didn't bring her. I'm not sure if I can keep her from ending you the next time you insult her."

"My warriors wouldn't let that happen," the male hissed.

Torag doubted those who sided with Krish would stand up against Erisi, but he wasn't about to argue with the idiot in front of him. "About those warriors, what are you up to? I know you've been getting together every day."

"Friendly visits. Nothing more." Krish stared at Torag, daring him to oppose his claim.

"I know what you're doing, Krish, and I'm telling you it won't work."

"Of course you don't want it to work. You are calling all the shots as her second. Your lapdog Sura is now in power thanks to her. Why would you want the little bitch to leave?"

He slammed Krish against the brick wall, forearm pressed against the male's throat. "Stop what you're doing. Your rebellion doesn't stand a chance."

Krish struggled against his hold, but Torag only pressed down harder.

"What are you going to do? Tell on me?" Krish choked out.

"If only you were involved, I would in a heartbeat. But I don't intend to put the other warriors in danger. Stop this before she finds out because you won't like the consequences," Torag warned.

When he let go, Krish charged.

Torag evaded the headbutt easily and brought his elbow down on the male's back. The former chief dropped with an *oof*, but rolled over to recover his sword from under the bed. Torag kicked his wrist hard and hauled him up by the throat.

Ashoka had never allowed him to train with the horde, but Torag's skills were honed through a millennium of the most gruesome training long before he'd come to Dera Rawal. Krish just kept forgetting who the stronger was between the two of them.

Torag slammed him back against the wall and held his hellfire-infused dagger to the demon's throat. "Your pride will get you killed some day."

He shoved the male away and sheathed his dagger as soon as the door slammed shut behind him. Now that he'd given Krish his one and only warning, he could move on to his favorite time of day—kicking the young out of bed.

*　*　*

Torag would have smacked anyone who told him the air could spark. Unfortunately, it was the only way he could describe what happened when she entered the young's quarters.

"Erisi!" Mei jumped up, only to sink back down to the sandstone floor under Torag's leveled stare.

He shifted his gaze to Erisi. The band around his torso tightened as her mouth curved. The echo of their kiss still burned his lips.

This is going to be a long day.

"Good morning. I thought I'd find you outside sparring." Erisi sat down in the middle of the group, her dark leather clothing contrasting with the brightly colored clothes of the young. "What are we doing?"

"Torag always teaches us what's happening outside of the stronghold before we spar. We're talking about the Rohi." Mei sidled up to Erisi, smiling at her in adoration.

"For once, we'll skip this part so Erisi can spar with us," he tried. He needed more distance between them if he wanted to survive the day.

"Oh, no, don't stop on my account. I have all day for you. I'd love to hear about the biggest threat in the region." Erisi purred the last words, her eyes traveling down his chest and stomach.

Air became a problem.

"He always starts with the boring stuff."

Varun moved next to her again, his legs brushing against hers. Torag suppressed his grin when she shifted an inch away and leveled his eyes at the young.

Catching his stare, Varun ducked his head. "I'm sorry, chief. I won't show disrespect again, chief."

Torag ground his teeth. Unless he wanted the entire group to run laps—again—he'd better get on with it. "I'm sure you can tell me all about the Rohi then?"

"Erm, there's a very bad leader. I-I-Ish-something…" Varun stuttered, his face darkening with a fierce blush.

"I was hoping the hour we just spent on the subject would have given you more relevant insights." Torag tried to keep his voice even. He wasn't sure if he should burst out laughing or bang his head against the wall.

Khloe practically vibrated as she raised her hand.

He nodded at her. "Go on."

"His name is Ishan. He's been leading the Rohi for the past three centuries and he likes torture and slaves and blood and war. We're lucky we're living far from them, because we don't like war." She beamed at Erisi.

"We didn't like war because Krish sucked. Now we have the Wildfire Warrior and we can beat their stupid asses," Ahio blurted out.

Torag reached the end of his patience. "That's

it. Out! Laps!"

Erisi didn't even try staying silent anymore. As the young filed out onto the training field, Torag crouched in front of her and waited for her laughter to die down. "Having fun?" he growled.

"More than you know." Her slow smile pierced the lust roaring through his gut. For hell's sake, he was concealing a rebellion intent on bringing her down, and all he wanted was to haul her up against him.

Torag stood before he did anything stupid.

Her smile lingered in her voice. "A little help to get me up? I've been training too hard."

As if. Unfortunately, he wasn't one to back away from a challenge. Torag held out a hand, locking every muscle to control his reaction to her touch. Their fingers brushed, and a jolt arched through him.

Erisi stood. The heat her small body generated was enough to make him go up in flames. She looked at him with a smile he wanted to kiss from her lips.

Breathe. I need to breathe.

"I need to check on the young," he murmured.

"You should."

Erisi didn't step aside. Torag didn't move.

He stared down at her, his fists clenching in an effort not to brush the bangs from her forehead. Once his hands were free, who knew what else they would do?

He took a deep breath and walked away. Like

last night, regret overpowered the heat and guilt.

Outside, half of the young pretended to run laps, while the other half loitered. When they saw his face, they all ran like they were being chased.

"Ahio!" he shouted.

"Yes, chief!" The young sounded out of breath already.

"As you were volunteering answers, care to tell me how many warriors the Rohi have? Keep running, the movement can only help your mind function."

Ahio muttered something about breath being more helpful as he passed by.

"More than we have," he finally yelled, halfway through another lap at the other side of the training field.

"Hiro, help your brother get a little more specific," Torag said.

The young just shrugged on his way past. Torag crossed his arms. "Nobody stops running until I get an answer."

"I can't remember. My mind is malfunctioning due to lack of air," Hiro shouted, only proving he had plenty of air left.

"Too bad. What do you think will happen in battle? Do you think the enemy will wait for you to catch your breath and think about your next move?"

"At least they won't ask me these stupid questions," the young dead-panned.

"Hiro, you can be my first volunteer when we get to sparring." Torag grinned at the cursing young. Demonstrating offensive and defensive moves always required a test subject. The young normally knew better than to taunt him, but it seemed Erisi was infectious.

He ignored her warmth at his back as he stared Hiro down, waiting for the answer.

Mei ran past him, ochre dust in her wake, and shouted, "The Rohi have two hundred warriors." She wasn't even out of breath. Torag guessed all the extra laps she'd done had paid off in the end.

Ahio came to an abrupt stop in front of Torag. Doubling over, he tried to catch his breath. "Can I stop running now, please? I'll remember e-ve-ry-thing there is to know about the Rohi."

Torag doubted it, but they had other things to do. "Gather around. It's time we talk about hellfire. Erisi?"

She took her place next to him and addressed the panting young. "Who has just come into their powers?" Erisi smiled at Khloe, who was waving her hand as if trying to extinguish a fire. "Show me. It's alright if it doesn't work."

The lithe young demon lowered her hand. Brows furrowed, her hazel eyes focused on her palm. A lick of pale yellow fire flickered on her skin.

"Very good, Khloe," Erisi praised.

The young beamed at her leader.

Erisi continued, "Who will turn full demon

soon?"

Mei, Ahio, and Hiro joined the dozen others who raised their hands. Despite their antics, Torag would miss all of them wreaking havoc in their quarters after they turned for the first time.

"Have you caught your breath enough to show me, Hiro?"

The tawny young demon's skin flamed in embarrassment. He called up his yellow hellfire, which glowed bright until it too faded.

"You're close. It won't be long before you turn and join the adults."

Hiro turned an interesting shade at her words.

"Torag?" Erisi looked at him with a smile.

His hellfire burnt hot, fueled by the sparks she caused with her mere presence. He let the bright red flames play over his golden skin. For once, he took his time, focusing his powers to create a line of fire along his forearm. He smiled at the murmur of approval rippling through the group. They were in for a surprise when they saw Erisi's hellfire up close.

"There are many power levels between the bright yellow of a young about to turn full demon and the bright red Torag is showing off." Her grin made his hellfire surge in response. "The color an enemy displays will tell you how much power they're packing. Don't underestimate someone with an orange or light red flame though. Someone with less power but better training than you can still win."

Mei stared at Erisi. "Can you show us yours? Please?"

The darkest red flames flared on her palm. The young were stunned into silence, their mouths agape.

Pulling a knife from her boot he was all too familiar with, she infused the metal with fire. "Pure hellfire is hard to hold onto, and the metal of our weapons helps as a conduit. In battle, stamina is as important as your power level. You need to learn to hold on. Learn how to infuse your weapons and save your strength. Powerful demons can use pure hellfire bolts but not for long. If you want to fly, you'll need even more energy to defend or attack in flight."

"Is dark red the best color?" Basha's eyes were fixed on the hellfire-infused weapon.

Erisi smiled at the young. "There is no best color. All it means is that the flame is more powerful. There is one more powerful than this —a fire as black as onyx."

Like the young surrounding them, Torag couldn't look away from the dark red flames that danced over her hands and forearms.

"Why isn't yours black?" Ahio asked. "You're the Wildfire Warrior. The legends say your hellfire should be black."

Erisi's smile faded. Her voice was soft when she answered, "Only when I'm in demonic form do I wield wildfire. I hope you'll never have to see it."

"But I do!" Varun said. "I want to see it."

He watched her inhale shakily. The need to protect her took him by surprise as it blasted through him. "Varun, st—"

Erisi stopped him with her hand on his arm and told the young male, "My demon is too dangerous. It's something only my worst enemies get to see. And you are my family now."

Torag stared at her, chest tight and mouth dry.

She smiled up at him, before turning back to the young. "Wildfire, like all hellfire, comes at a cost. The more powerful it is, the more energy it costs." Erisi extinguished her hellfire and sheathed her knife. "Try it. Take your weapon and infuse it with your hellfire. If you haven't unlocked your powers yet, we'll do a focus exercise after, which can speed up the process."

Her insistence on real weapons for the sparring session made sense now. Torag watched her walk among the young, taking her time to help each of them. For the first time since she'd arrived, her shoulders were relaxed and her smile was warm and easy. His chest tightened more.

"Who can use their hellfire to shield?" Erisi looked around the group, then back at Torag when nobody raised their hand.

He tensed. "None of them can. Nobody in the family has mastered it, so we can't teach them."

Her smile extinguished the shame of his admission. "Then this lesson will be useful to all of you. First thing you need to know, you only have enough power and focus for either more offensive or defensive moves. You cannot do both. That means your physical fighting technique is crucial for defending yourself while you attack with your hellfire. It's one of the reasons we also train combat without our powers."

She called fire to her palm, then fused it in a wall of dark red hellfire when she directed her hand outward. "All about focus. Right, Torag?" The laughter in her voice thawed something inside of him.

It turned back to ice when Erisi lowered her shield and, out of nowhere, a dagger pierced her abdomen and a spear hit her chest.

Chapter 13 - Gutted

-Erisi-

Erisi's vision swam as pain sliced through her gut. The acid fire racing through her insides and clouding her vision told her the blade had been laced with some kind of poison.

She gritted her teeth and sent a bolt of pure hellfire in the direction of her attackers. If Krish had brought his rebellion here... if he had been stupid enough to attack her amid the young, not even Torag would stop her from killing him for good.

The screams of the young cut her deep. She had to keep them safe.

"Inside! Get inside!" She forced another step forward. The spear jostled and tore something inside. She bit through her lower lip in an effort to shoot another bolt of hellfire. Panic burst in her chest at a young's shriek of pain.

Her heart battered her ribs. She tried to focus

through the blur, tried not to crumble. The agony in her gut bloomed and festered.

Was it Lucifer? Had he sent another attack?

"Erisi!"

She twisted toward the sound. "Mei, get back!"

Erisi tried to draw up her shield and protect the young female, but the world continued to swirl out of focus. Sounds distorted. She shook her head, needing to discern the blurry shapes in front of her, desperate to find out who had been hit.

Where was Torag? He needed to—

She gasped for breath. With both hands, she grabbed the spear lodged deep in her lungs. It needed to go. She needed more air before she passed out and got herself killed. Before she could no longer protect the young.

Her knees hit the dust. Darkness encroached on the edges of her faltering vision.

The force of her wildfire building inside terrified her.

No. She refused.

Hellfire blazed on her skin as she fought through her fear and pain.

"Mei, stay here!" Torag's voice grounded her. If it was the rebellion, she couldn't be sure he was on her side, but he would protect the young.

A blurry form darted toward her. "You're hurt."

"Get away from me before they attack again," she commanded.

Where the fuck was Torag?

"It's okay. Your bolt took out Kaemon, and Torag is restraining Anea." Mei fell on her knees next to her.

"You need to stay away." Erisi gasped for air. The spear needed to go, *now*. But she couldn't focus on her injuries when Mei could get attacked at any moment.

"There may be others," Erisi hissed. Only then did Mei's words register. "Kaemon and Anea?"

The young?

She didn't allow their betrayal to sink in. Instead, she wrapped her hands around the spear. If Krish and the rebels seized this opportunity, they could kill her.

With gritted teeth, she pulled hard. When the spear came out, she tilted forward and barely caught herself with her hands on the sand.

I let my shield down and I got hit. How ironic.

"Mei, you need to listen to me. Please." Erisi grabbed the young's hand. "You need to go to Torag and stay by his side. Someone's bound to attack. I don't want you in the cross fire."

Even through the blur, she could see the force with which Mei shook her head. "Nobody will touch you."

Torag shouted at the young to stay put. No doubt he had his hands full with the two attackers and the rest of the young. If she wanted to protect Mei—and herself—she needed to get back in fighting shape.

"This is gonna cost me a lot of laps, right?" Mei's voice held something between a sob and a laugh.

Erisi barked out a laugh that nearly made her pass out. "You bet. Turn around. You don't want to see the dagger come out."

Touching it was torture. Erisi closed her eyes, grabbed the hilt, and pulled. She gagged as the stench hit her nostrils.

Fuck! He hit my intestines.

She pushed her hands against the gaping wound, shivering violently when she touched her bloody insides. Gagging again, she shoved them back inside.

"Oh, Erisi…" Horror echoed in Mei's voice.

"I told you to turn around." She hadn't looked down yet. She wasn't keen on seeing the mess she'd already had the pleasure of touching.

Biting through the agony, she fought her body's instinct to sleep so she could heal faster. At least her vision was clearing now that the poisoned blade was gone.

Hand still pressed tight against the hole in her gut, she scanned her surroundings. She couldn't see Torag, but she could hear him bellowing orders inside the young's quarters. A few demons were herding young inside.

What worried her more were the warriors at the edge of the training field. A few were trying to get to her, but they were held back by three burly males she knew had been visiting Krish.

She cursed her earlier decision to observe the brewing rebellion rather than act on it.

Krish appeared with more warriors in tow. Her throat went dry.

Another one of Lucifer's damn tests would have been easier than this mess.

"Mei, for the last time, you need to go! I'm about to be attacked," she hissed to the young.

When Mei stood her ground despite Erisi's command, she shouted, "Torag! Get her out of here! Now!"

She didn't dare look away from the smirking former chief as he turned into the tawny, ugly-ass demon he was. "Torag!" Her voice sounded shrill.

"Right here." Torag's low voice came from somewhere close behind her.

She exhaled in relief. "Mei needs to go. I have a little problem I need to fix."

Krish charged with his sword drawn. Several warriors followed.

Mei screamed.

The young's tawny skin turned reddish brown. Spikes ran up her arms to her shoulders and neck. She dropped to her knees and wings ripped from her back. Panting and shaking, Mei dug her claws into the ground as her body twisted, grew, and changed to her adult form.

Erisi tore her eyes from the transformation. With Krish's attention diverted, she focused on pouring the little hellfire she had left into the spear she'd pulled from her body. Her heart dropped as the flames flickered out. She'd used too much energy. She didn't have enough to fight. Krish would—

Mei stepped in front of her, her leathery wings awkwardly dragging through the sand, her movements stiff. "Stay away from her, you big lumpy nitwit!"

Before Krish or Mei could make another move, Torag stepped forward. He pushed the young female behind him with a warning growl.

Mei tried to fight her way around him.

"For fuck's sake!" Torag snapped as he hauled her back. "You're no match for a grown demon. Stay back."

After pinning her with a glare, he turned to address Krish. "You damn idiot! Why would you attack where the young may get hurt?" His voice echoed over the training field. "Proceed and I will burn you alive. This time, I'll make sure you don't recover."

The warriors behind Krish took a step back from her fuming second-in-command. And another. Krish scowled at the males, his eyes flitting across the faces of the gathered demons. When it was clear nobody would stand with him, he dropped his sword and held up his hands in surrender.

Spear firmly planted in the ground, Erisi's fingers clenched around the wood to stay standing. She felt the eyes of every demon on the field burning into her. They were waiting for her retribution. The unwritten laws of the demonic world were clear; failing to kill the head of the family once you attacked meant true death.

She'd have to deal with the young. And with Krish, though the idiot could wait now that he no longer posed an immediate threat.

Her grip on the spear tightened even more. She refused to kill the young, no matter what they'd done. She knew it would cost her. Now more than ever, she needed to show strength. Instead, she was showing everyone her weak underbelly.

When Torag faced her, his eyes betrayed his despair. He knew the rules; he knew what she was supposed to do.

"Bring them to me." Her legs were shaking, the spear barely holding her up. The pain was maddening.

A little longer. I need to stay upright just a little longer.

Torag ignored her order. "Please, Erisi. Kaemon and Anea were Ashoka's protégées. They probably had some misguided notion about avenging his death. If you need to punish anyone, it should be me for not warning you about the rebellion. I beg you—"

Shaking her head, she murmured to him, "Stop incriminating yourself in public before I have to do something about it. Remember my promise about the young."

Hope flared in his onyx eyes.

Behind him, two warriors dragged Kaemon and Anea closer, followed by a sombre-looking Sura. The young male was still unconscious, blood blooming on the cloth someone had wrapped around his stomach. Anea was a shivering mess with her eyes fixed firmly on the sand. These were the demons who had almost brought down the legendary Wildfire Warrior. She'd have laughed if it didn't hurt so damn much.

Erisi turned to Torag and spoke loud enough for the crowd to hear. "As their chief, you will need to decide on a fitting punishment. My only condition is that they both live by the end. I propose you make an example out of them."

"Thank you." Torag's voice came out so softly it barely reached her ears.

She turned to Krish, who stood shackled between two warriors. His sly grin told her everything she needed to know.

He thought her weak. They probably all did.

She would show them weak. She'd make sure the Arav wouldn't forget who they were dealing with.

"Sura, I have a task for you and your warriors." Erisi struggled through the surging pain to keep her voice loud and even.

Her chief stepped forward, awaiting her orders.

"Nail Krish to the outside of the south gate. Post guards with him so nobody gets the brilliant idea to help him. I need him writhing and ready for my wrath tomorrow morning."

Sura swallowed. "Understood."

The two large warriors grabbed Krish by the shoulders and hauled him away, ignoring his struggle and infuriated bellows.

Biting through the agony, Erisi crouched and picked up the bloodied serrated blade she'd pulled from her stomach. She had big plans for the vicious little thing.

The Arav would learn the hard way.

Chapter 14 - Evisceration

-Torag-

At first, Krish's screams had made the blood freeze in his veins. For two long hours every morning, it would be the only sound heard throughout the stronghold. A week in, the screams made Torag cringe. Now it just pissed him off. Two weeks into this mess, he wasn't sure who he wanted to strangle first—Erisi or Krish.

Even in the workshop, as far removed from the southern gate as he could get, Torag heard every agonized howl as if he was standing next to them. He pretended to observe the smiths forging steel, grateful for the clanging of the hammer on the metal.

Torturing a demon was effective. They felt as much pain as mortals but they healed fast. It meant Erisi could repeat the same process day after day without killing the object of her wrath. It wasn't an unusual punishment for severe crimes like treason, except most demons would have gotten bored by now and killed the traitor for good. Torag had a feeling Erisi would keep this up for a while.

With every scream piercing the air, Torag was reminded that he was partly to blame for the suffering of a family member. No matter how little he liked and trusted the male, he should have stopped Krish when he'd had the chance.

The doubts caused by his torn loyalties ate away at his soul. His instinct was to protect his family, but he was no longer certain about what was best for the Arav. He was still trying to decide if having a strong leader like Erisi outweighed the danger she attracted.

It didn't help that Torag still couldn't see what Lucifer had to gain by subduing the Arav instead of the Rohi. But Erisi's instinct to protect Mei despite the risk... The mercy she'd shown her young attackers... How she'd protected him when he'd confessed knowing about the rebellion... He didn't know what to think anymore.

Erisi was a different leader than he'd expected. One he could respect and follow. One he could learn to trust with time.

If Krish had taken over, life wouldn't have gotten better. Much like Ashoka, Krish only cared about power. Once more, he'd demonstrated his priorities when he'd attacked amid the young, risking Mei's safety for a chance to kill Erisi. Maybe he could have challenged Krish for leadership after the male had disposed of Erisi, but Torag wasn't convinced the furious former chief would have allowed a fair challenge.

Beneath all that, an unexpected and infuriating thought messed with his mind. Torag knew he wouldn't have allowed anyone to touch Erisi. Even if the young hadn't been around.

He didn't want to examine that particular motive too closely for fear of what he'd find.

When the screams finally stopped, Torag left the workshop to check on the young. He stopped in his tracks when someone shouted his name from behind him.

He turned to find his friend smiling at him. "Yerle."

"Aren't you joining the crowd for our daily spectacle?"

Torag ground his teeth. "No."

"It's quite educational really. Her evisceration technique is an art form. Truly—" The admiration in his friend's voice told Torag he wasn't the only one who'd been won over by their new leader, even though she'd gotten to them in very different ways.

"I don't want to hear it." Even a millennium later, Torag remembered the agony of having his guts torn out by a grinning Ashoka. That had been the last time he'd tried to run.

Yerle joined him when he continued on his way to the barracks. "I'm still wondering when she's going to end Krish."

Torag swallowed the bile away. "It could be months. She's using him as an example. Once he's gone, the memory is going to fade fast."

"It's working. As far as I can tell, the rebellion is as good as over. Krish's closest friends are still plotting to free him and continue what he started, but they're not getting any traction."

Torag was glad for it. At least he wouldn't have to protect more family members from their poor judgment.

"I need your advice," Yerle told him.

Torag waved him over to the large rock next to the barracks. They sat side by side like they'd been doing for millennia. The sun burned high in the sky and warmed his cramped muscles. The tension caused by Krish's screams started to seep from his limbs.

"Erisi has handed me free rein of the dealmakers, traders, and messengers."

Torag leaned back and looked over at his friend. "I know."

"It's terrifying," Yerle admitted.

Torag grinned at the awe in his friend's voice. "Oh, come on, I'm sure it's not that different from executing Ashoka's orders."

Yerle dug his elbow in Torag's side. "Shut up. I don't want to be the next one nailed to the gate. Help me."

Torag knew Erisi wouldn't punish anyone with good intentions even if they failed. He wouldn't let her. For the past millennium, he'd worked too hard to abolish torture as a training technique for the young and warriors. In the end, only enemy spies, invaders, and demons who committed treason suffered torture, sometimes followed by true death.

Still, he understood Yerle's fears. In all the years they'd been with the Arav, his friend had simply done his best to keep up with Ashoka's and Krish's killing sprees. Now he had the opportunity to accomplish so much more.

Sometimes it was scary to take an opportunity and run with it.

"You know what you need to do. All your wildest dreams we used to talk about? Make them happen. They're exactly what this family needs."

Yerle sighed. "Dreams were fun until I had to drag them into real life. I want to succeed, Torag. I want to show her I'm worthy of the power she's handed me."

"You know you are. Walk me through your plans."

All Yerle needed was someone to talk to. For centuries, his friend had shared his dreams and plans with him as they'd sat by the fire at night. There was no doubt in Torag's mind that Yerle was capable of bringing the Arav deal-makers and traders to greatness.

"So I was thinking we need to work on two fronts. Souls and resources. Souls will make sure this family stays healthy in the long run, with a steady supply of young demons. No more reaping before natural death if we can avoid it. We let the population of our territories recover and breed." Passion poured from his friend's every gesture, making Torag smile. One more sign that Erisi might be better for this family than he could have ever hoped.

"Resources will help us gain power with the human leaders in the region. I'm thinking it would be helpful to be the voice whispering ideas into the ears of the local chiefs in large cities. We could offer them our protection. Same for the human warlords to the east and north. Need a whole legion of humans willing to sign over their souls? Easy when their lord tells them to, right?"

Torag nodded. "Sounds perfect. What do you need me for?"

"I have no idea where I'm going to get the souls or the resources. It's all nice in theory but now I need to—" Yerle gasped.

"Breathe. First you need to breathe." Torag thumped Yerle on the back. "You'll be fine."

"I need ideas."

"We've been talking about new sources of souls for a long time," Torag reminded him.

"You mean where we target traders and infiltrate some of the larger human cities through their trade caravans?"

Torag nodded. Closing his eyes, he basked in the warmth of the sun.

"That's all good and well, but I don't want to send the majority of my deal-makers off for months at a time. I can spare a few but not that many."

Torag let the challenge sink in for a moment. "Why not give the trade caravans a reason to stop right outside our gates then?" he asked.

Yerle perked up. "We build them an outpost. Well-provided and guarded so they all want to stop here. In return, we negotiate lower prices for the resources we need—wood, salt, ores. Then we top it off by seducing them into signing over their souls. You are brilliant!"

Opening his eyes, Torag shook his head with a wide grin. "All your idea. For the resources, you'll need to talk to Chandra and figure out if we can grow the number of steel weapons and tools we can make."

"We position our steel tools and weapons as some kind of sorcery. It wouldn't be hard to convince humans who've only ever seen bronze before. And sorcery's well worth giving up your soul for, isn't it?" Yerle grinned, his teeth flashing white in his brown face.

Getting up from the rock, Torag stretched his limbs. "You're going to do great."

He smiled at the excitement in his friend's amber eyes. They'd survived slavers by standing united. Together, they would survive this too. They might even thrive in the end.

Before he left, Yerle said, "Come spend time

with me at the fire tonight. Unless you're too busy strutting around like a peacock in mating season."

Torag bristled. "What the hell are you talking about?"

"Oh, come on! Every demon in this stronghold has taken a bet on who will dominate who first. My bet is on her."

Lust slammed into Torag like a punch of hellfire to the chest as he imagined a tiny female caged between his arms against the wall, staring up at him, pleading—

He growled. "Get out of here before I show you how I can make any damn demon in this stronghold submit. Including Erisi."

Yerle roared with laughter as he walked away. "You wish."

Closing his eyes, Torag stifled a groan. Damn right he did.

***

Mei skidded past him, leaving dust in her wake. "How much longer do you want me to pretend I'm exerting myself?"

"Until you can't talk because you need all the air in your lungs to run." Torag crossed his arms over his chest and glared at her.

Her transformation to full demon meant she was stronger and faster in human form as well. The laps she'd been running every day for the past two weeks were a breeze for her.

Torag didn't care. It was the principle of the thing. Putting herself between two powerful demons, for hell's sake.

His mood darkened even more. Tonight, Mei would leave the young's quarters. While Sura had assured him she'd take care of her new recruit, the muscles in his jaw cramped with the force of his anxiety. Reckless with the abandon of youth, Mei wanted nothing more than to impress Erisi and Sura. Doom scenarios had been playing through his head all night.

He watched her run laps for hours on end, telling himself it had nothing to do with the gnawing in his chest. *Nothing at all.*

When Erisi appeared next to him, covered in blood, Torag nearly jumped out of his skin.

"Still having her run?"

"Last time. She's part of the horde now." It hurt to swallow his worries down.

"So this is your way of saying goodbye then?"

The warmth in her voice was reflected in her smile. Unable to stop the curl of his own lips, the tightness in his throat and jaw eased somewhat.

The mirth now dancing in Erisi's eyes had become rarer with every day that had passed, as had her visits to the young. The betrayed hurt he'd seen in her eyes when she'd looked upon Anea and Kaemon was now shielded by an ice-blue layer of frost. The only one able to thaw her was Mei.

"Hi, Erisi!" Mei hug-tackled her.

Erisi seemed to be getting used to it. At least she was still standing. "Have you said your goodbyes?"

Mei nodded. "Only one left."

She tackled him, her arms going around his neck. Taken by surprise, he slammed into the dust with the laughing demon on top of him.

"I'm gonna miss you, Torag." Mei's muffled voice came from the vicinity of his chest.

No words got past the lump in his throat. Pushing himself up, he hugged her back.

"You'll still see me every day." He wondered who he was trying to convince.

"But you won't make me run laps anymore. Who knew I'd miss that?" she murmured into his skin.

Torag swallowed. "Make Sura suffer."

Drawing back, Mei grinned at him. "You know I will."

Erisi held out her hand to help up a beaming Mei. "I'll personally deliver you to your new place. They're waiting for you."

He remained seated in the sand, watching their backs until they disappeared into the barracks. The tightness in his throat returned, and no amount of swallowing helped this time.

The ram horn sounded.

Torag was on his feet and in demonic form before the last sound faded. A few hard thrusts of his wings got him airborne and to the south gate. Sura faced the guards with wings spread and teeth showing as she growled, "How in hell's name did that happen?"

"They came out of nowhere. They killed Irit and Jiera. By the time we heard Krish scream, they were already in the air."

Erisi landed behind them, her chains glowing a dark red. She stared at the empty gate, where bloody patches of Krish's skin were still nailed to the thick wood.

"Who? Who took him?" Erisi demanded to know.

A shivering archer fell to his knees. "Forgive us. We didn't—"

She broke off his rambling with an impatient swipe of her hand. "Cut it out. Who did this?"

"The Rohi demons took him. They killed the guards Sura had posted and ripped Krish from the gate before we could stop them."

Torag swallowed down the urge to curse. The most powerful rival family in the region had gotten its hands on an enraged demon with insider knowledge.

Things just kept getting better and better.

Chapter 15 - Mistakes

-Erisi-

Mistakes. She'd made so many mistakes. Erisi took a deep breath and let the chill of the early morning air clear her head. The haunting cry of a caracal drifted up from the desert. She watched the horde spar on the training field below. The dance of their hellfire-infused swords lit up the shadows of dawn, and the occasional crossbow bolt lit a fiery path through the sky. The view from the roof of the keep was the reason she spent her time here instead of in her private quarters.

The guards knew the drill by now. When she appeared, out of breath from her nightly training, they vanished with a curt nod. It gave her the precious peace she needed before facing another day as leader of the Arav.

Erisi turned to check if she'd melted the lock of the trapdoor. For a while, she'd foregone that safety measure.

For a while, she'd felt this could be her home rather than a mere mission.

So many mistakes. Erisi rested her forehead against the brick walls of the guard post and breathed through the thoughts banging against her skull.

She knew better than to pretend she belonged.

Letting the young into her heart had left her vulnerable. Even now, she couldn't stop caring about Mei and the others. Every demon in this stronghold knew her soft spot, and now a powerful family outside of these walls knew it too. She'd become what Torag feared most—a danger to the young.

With Krish gone, very few Arav would even think about hurting the young. But the Rohi demons would. Just like Lucifer and Beelzebub would have used the young to force this family to its knees.

She hadn't been able to. Still couldn't. It made her weak.

Erisi knew better than to care. She knew how dangerous she was to those she cared about most.

Thoughts of Lyx rose unwilling. Her throat tightened as she recalled Gyasi dragging the frail young into the temple. How she'd hidden her soulful brown eyes behind sleek dark hair. The way she'd hugged herself tight had woken every protective instinct in Erisi, even though she hadn't been much older and just as powerless against Gyasi's torture.

Now, every time she looked at Mei, she saw a fleeting reflection of that young female she'd failed to protect.

And Fate, she'd tried to protect Lyx with everything inside of her. Every time their bastard lord and master had chained Lyx down to tattoo the black blood into her skin, she'd begged to take the young's place. She'd taken the burn of the needle and the bloodcurdling agony without a sound, terrified he'd turn on Lyx if she failed to cooperate.

Too often he'd used the moment she passed out as an opportunity to subject Lyx to the same torture. But she kept volunteering because sometimes she lasted long enough for him not to hurt the female.

Sometimes she'd wake to Lyx holding her hand, unhurt and eyes brimming with a love that made her feel alive, happy even, for the briefest of moments.

How had she forgotten? For a little while, she'd drowned out the knowledge that happiness came at a cost she wasn't willing to pay again.

Maybe because of Torag's courage in caring and letting others care about him. Somehow he bore the terrible cost it came with. She wasn't that strong. Not anymore.

Her hands balled to fists she pressed against her roiling stomach at the memory of that night.

Of Gyasi laughing at Lyx's screams while she struggled against the chains. The coppery taste in her mouth, the warm traces of blood dripping down her wrists as she tore her skin fighting to get to the female.

That had been the first time darkness encroached on her vision. Even the fear of Gyasi's retribution if she turned couldn't stop her demon taking over. And like so many times after, she didn't remember a thing.

Until she woke with broken chains hanging from her wrists, dripping with blood. Nothing remained. The bed Lyx had been chained to was gone, pelts and furs scattered, scorched and bloodied. There were ashes. Nothing but ashes.

Her soul felt as shredded as it had then. Knowing she had been the one... In the end, she had been the greatest danger to the young she would have given her life to protect.

Just like she was fast becoming the greatest danger to the young in this stronghold.

She could barely breathe at the thought. They'd need to protect themselves. Because if she failed... if she lost control over her demon again...

Never again.

She couldn't love like that again. She wouldn't be as arrogant to think she'd be the one to protect them all. The only one she could protect was herself.

Becoming Lucifer's general... knowing nobody, nobody would ever touch her again and live to tell the tale. Knowing she wouldn't need to rely on the dark destruction of her demon, but would have Lucifer's horde behind her...

It had been everything she'd wished for when she'd stared at the stars outside the temple. With broken voice, she'd sworn on those broken chains that she'd survive, no matter what, before she'd wrapped them around her arms as a bloody reminder of her failure and her oath.

She ran her fingers over the metal circling her forearms. They were still with her. A silent promise. *Never again.*

But she was breaking that promise. She had cared a little too much. And endangered them all because of it.

The only damn thing she could do was to make this family as strong as it could be.

They needed to be ready to face the Rohi. To face Lucifer.

To face her demon if she ever lost control.

The shivery exhale brought her back from the past. Into the present where she had things to set straight.

She descended the ladder to confer with Chandra on the lower floor of the keep. The master builders had worked out a way to shield the guards on the bastions from attacks from above, while other workers were adding a floor to the young's quarters to give them more space. The progress soothed the lingering unrest in her gut a little.

By the time the sun had fully risen, Erisi was heading over to the warriors outside. When she arrived on the training field in the middle of the stronghold, she found the majority of the Arav sparring while Sura shouted her orders loud enough to be heard.

The moment she noticed her, Sura walked over, her dark hair sticking to her brow. "Erisi," she said, brushing the dust from her hands.

Erisi acknowledged her with a nod. "Sura. Are they ready?"

"They're never ready for you, but that's part of the fun I guess." Her war chief grinned at her. She was the only warrior here smiling about what she was about to do. Again.

Turning to the warriors, Erisi readied herself for the daily beat-down she called morning sparring.

* * *

Later that night, Torag approached as she hung upside down in her usual tree. Erisi reached for the dagger in the scabbard around her thigh.

He held up his hands. "No ambush this time."

His sword was still sheathed, but she'd be damned if he surprised her again. Erisi hauled herself up on the tree branch and looked at him. Even from her vantage point, he was impressive in height and width. She sighed in envy.

"Want to come down so we can talk?" The

light of the torch she'd planted in the sand cast shadows over his grave face.

"Not particularly," she told him.

Leaning against the tree, he looked up at her. "I went to the barracks this afternoon."

"Mmmhm." Erisi played with her hellfire, trying very hard not to look at his beautiful face.

"Do you think burning a quarter of our horde to the point where they need the rest of the day to recover is the way to go?"

She should have known he'd get involved. "The ones who'd practiced their hellfire shields as commanded didn't get burned. I'm hoping it'll motivate the rest of them to train harder," she informed him.

The Arav needed the ability to use their hellfire shields. By now, they'd mastered the technique, but it required constant training to turn it into a reflex.

Unfortunately, several warriors seemed to think practice was beneath them. She'd shown them why that way of thinking was dangerous during sparring this morning.

"Erisi…"

She grinned at the exasperation in his voice. "Torag."

"Our warriors live in fear of you. Is that what you want to achieve?"

"Yes." After her near defeat, that was exactly what Erisi needed her warriors to feel whenever she approached them. Enough fear to discourage them from rebelling. Enough fear to light a fire under their asses and have them train until they dropped, so they'd be ready for the next attack.

Enough fear to never let their guard down around her.

Torag looked up at her with a knowing look in his dark eyes. "How much of this is anger management?"

Erisi sighed. "Most of it is aimed at improving their skills quickly, but I admit, I don't mind the outlet for my frustration."

"Let me give you another outlet," he offered.

Fire surged in her gut at his words. She climbed down from the tree and landed next to him in the sand.

"I'm intrigued." Erisi coughed to mask the crack in her voice at the thought of the perfect outlet. She remembered the tight muscles of his arms and chest under her fingertips. She ached to explore every groove chiseled into that tall body.

"I volunteer as your sparring partner. You can beat me into the ground if you go easier on the rest of them."

This is a bad idea.

She stared at him. "You're volunteering as a living shield for the warriors now?"

"Who says I won't be able to beat you?" The corner of his mouth tipped up. Her legs grew weak.

Such a bad, bad idea.

"I know what you're doing," she told him, biting her lip to hide her smile.

Torag took a deep breath. "Part of me does want to protect my family from your wrath, but that's not the reason I'm volunteering. I need to get stronger too. If we want to have a chance of winning against the Rohi, we all need to be at our best." He held out his hand. "Deal?"

Erisi grabbed his arm. "You have a deal. Don't expect me to go easy on you."

The firm grasp of his large hand on her forearm fanned the ember in her chest into a blazing fire. His laughter turned it into a dark red inferno.

The moment he let go of her arm, he unsheathed his sword. With a wide grin, Erisi dodged his attack and called up her hellfire on her palm. He was about to find out how the warriors felt during sparring.

Heart racing with anticipation, she studied his fluid movements. When he targeted her right side, she dodged to the left. One step forward got her close enough to run her fingers up his broad chest.

He stopped in his tracks and stared down at her. Her palm slid over the muscle of his shoulder. Then she smiled and let her hellfire flare. Just a little. Enough for him to retreat with a hiss.

His slight grin warned her just in time to evade his strike. She rolled, coming up behind him. Before he could turn, she closed in on his back and ran a trace of light hellfire along his spine.

He shivered violently.

Again, he recovered faster than she anticipated. His elbow landed in her gut, and she barely avoided the punch he threw at her face as he turned.

She caught his hand and put her other on his chest, pushing enough hellfire out to make a lesser male flinch. He held her gaze, eyes smoldering and that gorgeous smile of his turning her legs weak.

Which was the moment he choose to hook her legs and slam them both in the cooling sand. Panting, she looked at the male beside her, who rubbed the burns on his shoulder and chest with a smirk. When he locked eyes with her, stars reflected in onyx.

She wasn't done making mistakes. Not by a long shot.

Chapter 16 - Souls alight

-Torag-

Torag dodged Erisi's chain but couldn't avoid the second one. As the fiery metal links closed around his upper arm, he bit back a curse.

She kept changing the rhythm and pattern of her movements. Even a week into their nightly sparring, he hadn't figured out how to avoid the acidic burn of her hellfire on his arms and legs. Every time he dropped his shield to attack, she hit him hard. The one lesson he'd learned was to get up fast after being slammed down.

As he rolled over onto his haunches, he caught a glimpse of the toned muscles of her stomach. He stopped in his tracks, mouth dry and heart pounding. It earned him the bite of her chains as they wrapped around his upper body.

They sparred for hours, only stopping when the first light of day closed in on them from the east. Leaning against the trunk of the closest tree, Torag tried to catch his breath and assess the damage his body had sustained. Every part of him hurt.

Erisi wrapped her chains around her arms, breathing hard. "This was fun. Now let's see if my warriors have gotten any better since yesterday."

"I believe we had a deal."

She grinned at him. "We do. I'm no longer using my hellfire to beat them during training."

Torag sighed. Having warriors limp around the stronghold waiting for their broken bones to mend wasn't much better, but he'd take it for now. The horde even had a competition going to see who could stay standing the longest while sparring with Erisi. Their fear had given way to fervor as their skills had grown. Any pain Erisi inflicted on them was now followed by her praise about their progress.

As she'd predicted, she was slowly growing on all of them.

Torag watched her brush the dust from her toned arms. He swallowed hard, but his throat stayed tight at the sight of her. He focused on swiping down his sword before he sheathed it and tried very hard not to let his thoughts run wild.

They walked back, sand swirling around their heels. The breeze picked up and brought a hint of the day's heat with it.

She gazed up at him when they reached the north gate. "I'm looking forward to beating your ass again tonight."

Clenching his jaw, Torag watched the small demon saunter to the training field. He wasn't the only one; the four guards who should have been looking for dangers outside of the gates were also focused on her.

He stared them down. They scrambled to resume their positions.

Inside the fort, near the barracks, he ran into his best friend. "Still being dominated by our lovely leader I hear." Yerle grinned widely as he bumped Torag's shoulder. "This bet is all mine."

"Shut up," Torag said, drawing his hand over his face. He needed the element of surprise. If only his shield would respond faster, he'd stand a chance. Erisi had taught him how to strengthen it so it blocked most of her hellfire, but he couldn't win by staying behind his shield. If he was able to drop it faster, she might not see his attack coming.

"—sacrificed a goat to the gods of rain."

Yerle was staring at him by the time Torag registered his words. "What the hell are you talking about?"

"I've been talking nonsense to see how long it would take for you to catch on. It took you a dragon, three goats, and the gods of rain to notice," Yerle said with a broad grin on his face. He side-stepped Torag's half-hearted swipe. "All kidding aside, it's time, Torag."

"For a sacrifice to the gods of rain?" Torag

eyed the sand dunes outside of the gate. Parched shrubs had taken the place of once lush date palms and mango trees. A decade ago, the winds had turned hot and dry and had stayed that way ever since. "I'm sure it is."

Yerle barked out a laugh. "If only they existed." His face went serious. "It's time to feed the souls."

The unrest Torag had released during sparring returned with a vengeance. "I know."

"You need to bring Erisi."

Torag sucked in a breath. "I—"

"The greater the powers we feed the souls with, the stronger the young will be. We need her powers, and you know it," Yerle insisted.

He did. "If I bring her to our souls, I'm handing her everything."

"You stopped Krish for a reason, my friend. You know she's good for this family. She is the leader we need. We're closing more deals. We have demons from other families asking to join us. We're stronger, faster, and better organized. The Arav will be revered just like she promised."

For once, the amber eyes of his friend were grave. Yerle knew how much it cost him to trust Erisi with the young and the souls. Finally, he voiced the doubts lingering in his mind. "She's still a danger to us all. With Krish in the hands of the Rohi, it's only a matter of time before they attack."

Yerle countered, "They will attack no matter

if she's here or not. The only difference is that we have a chance of winning if she leads us."

Hearing his friend say what he'd known all along, Torag felt his shoulders sag. "I'll take her today."

* * *

Few demons got to witness the splendor of the sulfuric caves deep below the stronghold.

Despite the swirling anxiety in his gut, Torag couldn't help but smile at the wonder in Erisi's eyes. Her fingers trailed over the gypsum formations in the gallery they were walking through.

"This is—" Her voice faltered.

Torag walked ahead, leading the way through the maze of corridors. "Welcome to the hidden wonder of our stronghold. This is the Cave of Souls."

"You're taking me to your souls?" she whispered.

He turned to her when she halted. "I am. We need to feed them. Several of the souls are ready to turn into fledgling young; they need energy to complete the transformation."

Panic bled into the ice-blue of her eyes. Of all the emotions he'd expected to see, this hadn't been one of them.

She snapped around to retrace her steps. "I need to get back above ground. You can't take me near your souls."

The finality in her broken voice made him

reach for her. "Erisi."

She walked on.

Going after her, he put his hand on her shoulder. "Erisi."

She stopped but didn't turn to look at him..

"You are our leader. Your powers will create young stronger than we've ever had before. You need to feed the souls."

"Better to have weak young than to risk burning them all to nothingness." Erisi's eyes were fixed on the rock below her feet.

Walking in front of her, Torag tipped her chin up so she would look at him. When she did, the pain in her eyes punched him in the solar plexus. Even though he didn't understand her hesitation, he recognized her protectiveness. Warmth washed over him as he told her, "I wouldn't take you there if I didn't trust you with our young and souls."

Warmth spread in his chest when he realized he was speaking the truth. Somewhere along the way, he'd learned to trust her.

"It wouldn't be my choice, Torag. I would never hurt any young, I would never extinguish souls by choice," she whispered.

"Then why are you afraid you will?"

Erisi closed her eyes before she answered, her voice hoarse. "My wildfire comes at a cost. It takes over my body, mind, and soul. I am destruction incarnate." She was shaking hard, and it took all his strength not to wrap around her and protect her from the pain. "If the souls feed on my powers, who knows what it will trigger? If I get lost to my demonic form, the souls you keep in these caves will be forever gone."

Finally, he understood. He understood the tight reins on her control, her need to tame her anger, and her refusal to turn. Her choice to walk away out of fear she'd hurt the souls erased his last doubts. "You won't turn. The souls take the edge off your powers. They won't fuel your hellfire."

Erisi took a deep breath and confessed, "I wouldn't know. I've never been part of a family, so I've never seen the souls they keep. My master bought me from a slaver right after my creation. After…" She closed her eyes for a moment. "Then I was alone until I joined Lucifer's horde."

Torag took her hand. "Come with me."

"I told you—"

"You know me, Erisi. You know I wouldn't do anything to endanger this family. Come with me."

Torag didn't let go of her hand as he guided her through the caverns. Only he knew the way to the souls, where to dodge low-hanging boulders, and where to squeeze through narrow crevices.

He watched her apprehension shift to awe as they walked into the main room. White-blue lights flickered through the darkness, illuminating the ceiling, which dripped with stalactites.

Calling up his hellfire, Torag ignited the tar in the gully in the walls. The flames flared along the edges of the cave, displaying its grandeur.

Erisi's fingers let go of his as she walked deeper into the room, her neck craned back to take it all in. She twirled around like a giddy mortal and smiled at him, joy fused in every cell of her being.

Torag stopped breathing. The last stones of the crumbling wall he'd built around his soul came crashing down.

He took a step toward her, drawn by the incandescence of her eyes.

So were the souls.

The white-blue lights circled closer to the greatest source of power in the cave. The first soul who brushed Erisi's skin drew a dark red flame from her. Just as quickly as it had appeared, her hellfire was absorbed, turning the light of the soul brighter. Erisi's breath stuttered as her eyelids dropped. The bliss on her face drew him in even further. Torag took another step toward the female who set his soul on fire.

The lights caressed her skin, her hair. They landed on her fingertips when she extended her hand to touch them. As her powers fueled the intensity of the souls, Torag watched her muscles relax and the color of her hellfire lighten. The air hummed around them.

Erisi turned and looked at him. Even the ice of her gaze had melted into the clear blue of water.

"Torag," she whispered, her voice thick with emotion.

His soul filled his entire being with light as if it fed on her powers too.

He took a final step forward until her skin brushed his, setting it on fire.

Chapter 17 - Wildfire

-Erisi-

Her soul sang in harmony with the soul-lights dancing around the cave. She looked up at the male who'd trusted her with this miracle. No words would do justice to the sparks igniting in her chest. Erisi didn't even try to find them. Standing on her toes, she wrapped her arm around his neck and kissed him.

This time, there was no hesitation. Torag hauled her up against him, his groan caressing her lips. His arm circled the small of her back as he devoured her. Their teeth clashed in their desperation for more, for everything. She climbed his strong body, wrapping her legs around his waist, relishing the way his fingers dug into her ass to pull her even closer to him.

His skin was warm velvet over steel muscle. The smokiness of his scent took over her senses, and the rasp of his stubble only added to her soul-deep hunger for more.

Breaking away, Erisi gasped for breath. The smile on his beautiful lips morphed the raging fire into molten lava—slow-flowing and impossibly hotter still.

"Torag—"

He cut off her breathless whisper with a languid kiss that had her melting into him. Her heart stuttered before resuming its pounding.

The souls fluttered close by, attracted to the flares of hellfire her desire for Torag stoked.

He rested his forehead against hers. His arm around her waist kept her plastered against him, his hold strong and tight. She kissed the corner of his mouth when he smiled.

"I need to take you away from here," he murmured against her skin.

"Mmhm." She pressed a kiss on the strong line of his jaw, burying her fingers in the silk of his hair. "I don't see why."

He laughed. The low rumble in his chest turned her mouth dry.

"These are the souls that will turn into the next generation of young. It feels odd to ravage their future leader here."

Erisi didn't share his concern. "Ravage, you say?" She brushed her lips over his.

Torag kissed her hard, his hand on the back of her neck keeping her locked against him. His power turned her on even more. She understood why the Arav relied on his strength; it was so tempting to do the same and melt into his arms.

The slow slide of his body against hers as he let her down was torture.

Taking her hand, he pressed a kiss onto her knuckles before lacing his fingers with hers. Erisi blamed the tears she was barely able to hold back on the souls. The feeding had siphoned her power until she felt dizzy with joy.

Now her hellfire was pulsing under her skin, strong and steady. Its strength grew with every kiss, every touch of the male's fingers.. She looked down at the way his large hand engulfed hers and felt the heat flare. Maybe it wasn't a bad idea to leave the caves.

"Let's get out of here." His low voice caused the now familiar shiver to run down her spine.

He pulled her through the maze of caves and galleries. She raced to match his long strides, giddy with the way he looked at her, needing to get to a place, any damn place, where those strong hands would be all over her body again.

When they got to the passage underneath the keep, Torag pressed her against the wall. She nearly drowned in the onyx of his eyes as he closed in. His lips moved hot and demanding over hers. Giving in to the longing pulsing through her body, she trailed her hand over the ridges of his muscles. Along his broad shoulder and bare chest.

His arm wrapped around her waist and pulled her to him. She groaned against his lips, drowning in the bliss, the feel and scent of him, the way her body craved his touch. She needed more, so much more.

They both froze when Yerle called out both of their names from above.

"Erisi, Torag, I don't know if you're there, but I can't get into this damn place." The mechanism of the levers above them clicked but didn't budge. "You need to get back to the surface. We have unexpected visitors."

The note of fear in his voice spurred them into action.

Erisi waited for Torag to unlock the mechanism before climbing the ladder. As soon as they entered the cellar under the keep, they found Yerle pacing the room, worry etched in every line of his face.

"What's wrong?" she asked.

"A damn big demon showed up with a group of warriors. We didn't dare attack him; he claims he's been sent by Lucifer, and his warrior tattoo confirms he's part of Lucifer's horde."

Her stomach sank. She had a sneaking suspicion about who'd just shown up. "Did he mention his name by any chance?"

"Beelzebub," Yerle told her.

Erisi cursed. Torag's hand brushed her shoulder, and for the briefest moment she allowed herself to lean into his strength.

"I take it you know him," Torag said.

"Oh yes, I do. It's going to get messy." She took

a deep breath and looked up at him. "I want you to take the lead over the family. I'll need all my energy to deal with this pain in the ass. Don't let him rile you up, no matter what he says. The bastard is very good at getting in your head." *And even better at messing with mine.*

Erisi picked up the chains she'd left at the cave entrance and straightened. When she got her breathing under control, she climbed up to the keep and walked over to the training field. Torag and Yerle followed closely behind her. The bane of her existence stood in the center, arms crossed, surrounded by a dozen of Lucifer's elite warriors.

"Beel." She let the chains coil at her feet in open threat.

Beelzebub smirked down at her. "Erisi. I thought I'd come and visit."

She huffed. "Cut the crap. What do you want?"

"Nothing much." The dark-skinned male looked around the stronghold, his gaze lingering on the Arav behind her. "How are things progressing here?"

"Does that question come from Lucifer?" She lacked the patience and the will to play Beelzebub's games today.

"No," he admitted.

Erisi raised an eyebrow and waited for the real reason behind his visit.

Beelzebub scowled. "Fine. In that case, this order does come from Lucifer. Erisi, I challenge you to a fight for leadership over the Arav demons."

The commotion behind her hardly registered over the buzzing in her ears. She fought to keep a straight face. "Why did you bring the warriors?"

"They won't interfere in our fight. I brought them to secure my leadership once I beat you and send you to Lucifer, bleeding and crying."

She doubted Beel would play fair. Her gaze flickered over the warriors. He'd brought the ones who hated her. Those who'd tried to kill her and failed, time after time.

Shifting on her feet, she asked, "You don't intend to kill me then? I'm surprised. You were always looking for an excuse to end me."

Beelzebub's smile was as cold as ever. "Lucifer's orders. He has plans for you."

"I guess that means I can't kill you either." *Too bad.*

Beelzebub barked out a laugh. "As if you stand a chance. But no, Lucifer and my general still need me. Do you accept my challenge, little one?"

His old endearment stung.

She knew what Torag was going to say before he even took a step forward and murmured her name. "Erisi—"

Shaking her head, she held up her hand. "Don't, Torag. I accept your challenge, Beelzebub."

Beelzebub's stare shifted to her swollen lips, and a bitter smile unfurled on his face. "Ah, I see you've wrapped him around your little finger. A solid strategy, sleeping with the enemy. Does he know it's a thing you do?"

Rage punched up her stomach. She barely held onto her sanity. "Jealous, Beel?"

Next to her, Torag growled. Erisi would have rolled her eyes at the two males, but she had to watch Beelzebub's every move. She knew how he worked, and this distraction was playing out exactly as he'd planned.

Infusing her chains with hellfire, she moved into a fighting stance. "Torag, no matter what happens, don't believe a word he says."

Beel attacked, his sword aimed at her right shoulder just like she knew he would. When she dodged and charged, he evaded the chains she tried to wrap around his knees. She hated how easily they fell back into their fighting routine despite decades of bad blood between them. He caught the next swipe of her chains with his sword and pulled hard, throwing her off balance.

His blade nicked her upper arm. She blasted a hellfire bolt into his thigh, forcing him back.

It only took him a moment to recover. He threw up his shield to catch most of her next hellfire bolt. She knew he would target her left side moments before he even took a step forward. They were locked in a dance they both knew the moves of, unable to break the other's rhythm.

Beel grinned at her and turned demon. Umber

scales ran from his shoulders to his wrists and plated his upper body. His hellfire darkened, turning a darker red than the fire she wielded in human form.

Her heart pounded at her temples. Sweat slickened her palms. He—

She could take him without turning. She had to.

He dropped his shield and blasted out dark red hellfire. Twisting away meant the fire didn't hit her in the chest but blistered her shoulder instead.

She fought the darkness back. Her demon was right there, pulsing at the core of her. Demanding her survival.

Her dagger didn't even penetrate the scales on his chest. Her hellfire sizzled out in his much more powerful shield. She wanted to wipe that fucking grin of the male's face.

The grin that told her he knew she wouldn't turn. He'd never seen her demon.

She couldn't—

She couldn't turn. There'd be nothing left of the Arav by the time her demon was done.

She'd win, but at too high a cost.

Her body slammed back with the impact of Beelzebub's hellfire. The skin of her stomach burned to a raw bloody mess, the fire burrowing deeper into her flesh with every passing moment.

If she didn't survive, Beelzebub would rule.

She gritted her teeth and forced herself to keep moving. She blasted one hellfire bolt after another. Some got past his shield, but none of the wounds she inflicted phased him.

Torag would die. Beel would make the male crawl before he ended him.

She couldn't face the thought.

Couldn't…

She threw up her hellfire shield just in time to catch Beelzebub's next attack. Every bolt he drove into her shield forced her back. Another step. And another.

Her shield wavered.

Beel charged her like a bull, crashing through the weakening flames of her shield. His sword slid into the flesh underneath her collarbone.

His clawed fingers closed around her throat. Black dots bloomed before her eyes.

The stench of his breath hit her.

"Turn. Erisi, turn!" Torag sounded far off.

Her demon surged, the darkness spreading through her limbs. She fought to keep her mind clear.

She couldn't…

But if she didn't survive, Beelzebub would destroy them all.

Maybe…maybe she could protect…

Mei cried out, and Erisi's chest ached at the pain in her voice.

She gasped for breath, her fingers scratching at Beel's claws. Fighting through the black haze,

Erisi choked out, "Torag!"

To her left, she heard Torag shout her name.

The growing strength of her wildfire allowed her to tear free and kick Beel in the gut. Hands clasping the burns on her throat, she tried to control the darkness long enough to warn him, "Keep them safe!"

She could no longer see. The dark was everywhere...

His voice broke through. "I'll make sure Lucifer's warriors—"

No! He didn't understand!

She forced out the words. "K-keep the family safe... from me. Get them away from me, Torag!"

Chapter 18 - Unleashed

-Torag-

Torag couldn't tear his eyes away from Erisi. Her ice-blue spikes and scales darkened as black fire flared along her body. Her clothes ripped. The intricate tattoo of a tree reaching from her hip to her chest now seemed alive, the black lines swirling and shimmering. Her midnight-black wings arched back as she tackled Beelzebub.

The large demon went down flailing. His eyes were wide and his face twisted. His fear infused Torag with a bone-deep satisfaction. The possession in Beelzebub's eyes when he'd looked at Erisi had enraged Torag. The thought of her burning the bastard alive made him happier than it should.

Beelzebub rammed his foot in her gut, forcing Erisi back. Black fire erupted all around her, spurring Torag to move. Even at the distance he was at, the wildfire's heat burned his skin.

He shouted his commands to the chiefs behind him. "Sura, Yerle, Chandra, get the family to the keep. Defend them from the warriors. I don't trust they won't interfere even if Beelzebub loses."

Torag refused to go. She was his leader. As her second, he would stay by her side during this challenge. And should she fall, he would take on Beelzebub.

The thought of her lifeless body, the possibility that he'd never see her eyes light up with glee again as she challenged him... His hand clenched around the hilt of his sword, his fingers cramping with the force.

She blasted wildfire into Beelzebub's shield. It barely held under the first bolt. The second got through and hit the male in the chest. The next one in the gut. Beelzebub dropped his weapon and used both hands to hold up his shield.

It flickered and faded as soon as she shot another bolt through his defenses.

The air wavered with the heat Erisi generated, forcing Beelzebub even farther back. Torag finally saw the full scale of her power, the demon she truly was, and it took his breath away. She was the easy smile at the young and the evisceration of her enemies. She was the twirling beauty among souls and the wildfire of destruction.

Erisi took to the air, her black wings filling Torag's vision. Pure wildfire bolts rained down on Beelzebub. He went down with a howl, clawing at the hole where his intestines used to be. Torag wondered how long he would need to recover from that.

"She's beating his ass. Good. I didn't feel like joining the rebellion against the bastard she's fighting. He doesn't look like the fun kind of leader." Yerle landed next to him.

"I told you to—"

"—defend the family from the warriors. Chandra is in charge of the keep. We thought we'd be more useful here, where we can kill them if they try anything." Sura grinned at Torag.

Heart pounding, he grappled for words. If the warriors didn't attack them, Erisi very well might. She'd told him to keep them safe. "No! Back. You need to go back."

"And miss all the fun? No way." Sura stared at Erisi's demonic form in the air. "Thank hell she didn't turn during our sparring. I'm not sure we'd have a horde left."

When wildfire shot toward them, Torag pushed Yerle out of the way. The sand where he'd just been turned hard, shiny and brittle, the heat scorching.

"She doesn't know friend from enemy in her demonic form. You need to go."

The scream that tore from Beelzebub's throat made him whip around. The male was writhing in the sand, hands still against his gaping gut. A chunk of his thigh was torn off, the flesh raw and blistered. Blood drenched the sand beneath him.

Lucifer's warriors tried to dodge the wildfire Erisi still rained down as they ran to Beelzebub's side. One of them fell. When Erisi went in for the kill and swooped down on the warrior, the others dragged Beelzebub away from the field, behind the barracks.

Yerle took wing, followed by Sura. "We're going after them. You try reasoning with our fearsome leader."

Of course they'd ignore his command. Torag's mind reveled in the ways he would punish them for their disobedience. Then, a shout behind him made his blood run cold. "Can we attack yet?"

No! His gaze snapped up to Erisi. Her black eyes turned to him and Mei.

"Run!" Torag shouted as he took to the sky and threw himself into Erisi's path, hoping to capture her attention.

He did. He narrowly escaped her blast of fire. The few flames that hit his arm burned with the power of hell, forcing him into a tumble. Struggling to regain control over his wings, he kept shouting for Mei to run.

Erisi called another bolt of wildfire onto her palm. Heart in his throat, he watched his true death take shape. He shielded with every bit of power he had in him.

She'd taught him how.

And now her wildfire would kill him regardless.

She raised her hand, and every muscle in his

body clenched. Her gaze shifted to something on the ground behind him. He twisted around. Swords drawn, Lucifer's warriors approached in formation.

His heart dropped. Did Yerle and Sura—

No!

Hoping Erisi's attention would stay on the warriors, he tucked his wings in and let himself fall. The ground rose to meet him. Spreading his wings just in time, he landed hard on his feet in front of them.

"Erisi vanquished your leader," he shouted, desperate to end this soon. He needed to get to Yerle and Sura. *Now*. "You know the rules of a challenge; you need to leave."

"Beelzebub left us with very specific instructions in the unlikely event of his defeat." A red-scaled demon infused dark red hellfire onto his sword. The telltale sound of a crossbow being cocked sounded behind the male's back.

Drawing his sword, Torag infused it with hellfire. He knew he didn't stand a chance against one, let alone all of them. It didn't matter. He refused to let her face these cowards alone.

He charged the red-scaled male who led the pack. The warrior caught his first high-handed strike but couldn't avoid the second blow. Torag's blade bit deep into the male's side. Pulling back his sword, he rammed his elbow in the warrior's face. He struck the same side and pushed all his power into the metal, burning the male's flesh.

His back exploded in a ball of agony. All around him, warriors screamed, shouted, dropped to the sand.

Torag went to one knee, sword still clenched tight.

The warrior he'd been fighting was writhing on the sand. Black fire burned the other warriors.

More bolts rained down on all of them.

I need to get out of here.

He bit through the torture of burning skin and muscle in his back and stood. A group of archers aimed their crossbows at the sky.

He couldn't get to them in time.

He wouldn't be able to save her.

"Erisi!"

The wildfire demon's eyes snapped to him. He realized he'd distracted her at the wrong moment when three crossbow bolts infused with hellfire hit her in the chest. Then another three.

She twisted toward her attackers and roared. Wildfire flared all over her body, the flames growing.

There was no escaping the fire she threw down this time. Torag scrambled to get away from their torched enemies, the heat, and their bloodcurdling howls.

Torturous pain pulsed through his burned back as he watched the warriors turn to ash.

When Erisi crashed to the ground, he knew he was next. Her chest was heaving, still skewered with bolts. Her body was covered in severe burns and gaping wounds. She held herself like a cornered beast, every muscle in her crouching body tense.

He lowered his sword to appear non-threatening. Maybe—

A sudden blur darted past him, causing Erisi to bare her teeth. He reached out, but Mei dodged his grasp. "Mei!"

She ignored him, her hands held out. "Hi, Erisi, do you recognize me?"

The ice-blue demon growled at her, her arm pressed against the worst burn on her abdomen. The wounds weren't healing.

Slowly inching forward, he put his hand on Mei's shoulder and hissed, "Back away. She's about to attack. You can't reason with her before she turns back. I don't know if she understands more than instinct in this form."

"Her instincts will tell her I'm her friend." Stomping on his foot, Mei pulled away and ran toward Erisi.

He cursed and scrambled after her. Erisi drew black fire on her palm, ready to attack.

Desperate, Torag shouted, "Erisi! Don't!"

Eyes shifting to him, she fired the bolt at him. When the wildfire bit into the flesh of his thigh, Torag went down to one knee. He watched the stubborn young shuffle closer to Erisi with small careful movements, and there wasn't a thing he could do.

"You did well. You defended us all from that

idiot." Mei's voice was soothing. "I'm here. Your family is right here. We're good now. Come back to us."

Erisi turned her attention to Mei, and Torag feared the worst. He lurched forward, dragging his leg behind him, fighting through the pain.

Instead of the fire he'd expected to take in the chest, he caught Erisi as she turned human and went down. Her pale skin was flushed, her breathing rapid and uneven.

Agony burned in the ice-blue depths of her eyes when she opened them. "Did I—"

She passed out in his arms.

Torag held her lithe body close. She was pure power, and all he could think about was how much he wanted to protect her.

Chapter 19 - Family

-Erisi-

The stars sparkled in the dark sky above her. Erisi tried to lift her head to take in her surroundings but dropped back down when her muscles locked in an agonizing cramp.

Had she—

She squeezed her eyes shut. Had she hurt them? She remembered Mei's scream, Torag… The family had been right there when she turned.

Did I—

She swallowed the bile down and opened her eyes, trying to think. The air was too warm for her to be at Lucifer's base, so she must have beaten Beelzebub. That didn't mean the warriors hadn't taken over the place.

That didn't mean she hadn't—

Her chest ached. She grappled for the tiniest bit of hope. Maybe Torag had taken back leadership. If she'd killed all their attackers...maybe he'd finally taken his rightful place.

Except, Lucifer wouldn't stop coming after them until he'd realized whatever grand designs he had for the region.

Needing to rise and face what she had done, Erisi tried moving her legs. She'd barely shifted them when excruciating pain nearly knocked her back out. Wildfire always destroyed her body, but this was particularly bad. She must have used all of her powers.

"Took you long enough."

The gruff words made her heart jump. He lived.

"Did I—" She swallowed and tried again. "Did I hurt the family?" Closing her eyes, Erisi waited for the answer.

"You didn't kill anyone from the family." Torag's voice sounded soft and close by.

Relief crashed over her in a cooling wave, extinguishing some of the flaring pain.

Then she realized he hadn't answered her exactly. Which gave her all the answers she needed. She had hurt someone. "Who?"

Torag remained silent for a long moment. "It doesn't matter. Don't you want to know the outcome of your fight?"

First, she needed to know who she'd hurt. The faces of every demon in the family flashed before her eyes.

A hazy memory struck. *Mei*. She'd heard Mei's

voice. She...

Pain burned through every inch of her when she pushed herself up. Torag sat cross-legged on the roof of the keep, watching her.

"I hurt Mei, didn't I? Please tell me I didn't hurt her."

The calm on his face shifted to concern when she got up, only to immediately collapse. Her muscles were unable to take her weight. He was with her in seconds, his strong hands supporting her failing body.

Erisi fought his comfort. She needed to know first. "Torag..."

She didn't beg for anything, ever, but she was willing to beg now.

"You didn't hurt Mei," he reassured her.

Erisi collapsed against his chest and tried to breathe. When she felt the tension in his body behind her, she looked up and found his onyx eyes carefully blank. His lips were stretched in a tight line.

Moving away, she sat up and turned to face him. "What did I do to you?"

Torag shook his head. She put her hand on the warrior tattoo on his chest, the straight slashes etched into his golden skin.

"Please, Torag. I need to know," she whispered.

"So you can beat yourself up about it? No. You never meant to harm me, so it doesn't matter."

His undeserved forgiveness was like balm to

her tattered soul. She blinked to clear her vision.

"I take it we won't be sparring tonight?" Laughter laced his voice.

Erisi smiled through the tears she was still fighting. "I'm giving you a break. I know I was being hard on you."

"I finally have a shot at winning and you back away?" Torag's grin took her breath away for all the right reasons. When his smile faded, she mourned its disappearance. "You won the fight. You blew holes in the bastard big enough to fit a sizable rock in."

Beelzebub was lucky her demon hadn't finished the job and killed him for good. "Let me guess. His warriors attacked?"

Torag nodded. "They did. You burned them to ash. Yerle and Sura fought the one who guarded Beelzebub's body. They wounded him, but he got away."

She was glad one of them had escaped her wrath. Despite everything, the deaths of the warriors she'd fought alongside for centuries left deep marks on her soul. Killian, the golden-haired archer. The one who had made her laugh until he'd ambushed her together with Beelzebub. Junia, the dark-skinned warrior who'd tried teaching her to fight with a weapon other than her chains and had failed miserably. Catrin, the fastest flier. Ruel, Beelzebub's best friend. The one who'd held her down when Beelzebub had carved his anger into her skin.

Their betrayal didn't diminish the grief over their deaths.

Torag's low voice cut through her memories. "Beelzebub is in our prison, failing to recover from your attack. I was itching to kill him, but Yerle reminded me Lucifer wouldn't be happy."

Erisi smiled at the ferocity burning in his onyx eyes. "You made the right call. I'll personally deliver Beelzebub to Lucifer and give him the news. I don't trust the conniving shit not to twist the story about who won or lost." She took a deep breath. "What happened after?"

"After you turned back and collapsed, I brought you here. I thought it'd be the place where you'd feel safest when you woke up. I know you spend most of your nights here."

Erisi looked at the male who continued to surprise her. Her fingers traced the shadows the torchlight cast on his face. Her thumb followed the strong line of his jaw to the curve of his lips and turned his breath into a sigh.

She voiced another question that had been running through her mind. "Why didn't you take over while I was down?"

Torag caught her hand in his and pulled her closer. "I'm your second, for better or for worse. You're what's best for this family."

He tipped up her chin and claimed her lips. The heat had Erisi melting into the strength of his embrace. Torag's arm circled her waist to pull her tight against his chest. His taste sparked a hunger that she fed by running her fingers along the slope of his broad shoulders to his back.

She froze.

Thick scars ran along his right shoulder blade, marring the smooth skin her fingers had expected to find.

"Oh, Torag." Erisi couldn't stop a tear from escaping. It burned across her cheek. "I'm so sorry."

"It will heal. Apparently, wildfire takes a while to recover from." His thumb brushed the tear away, his smile soft.

"I don't understand how you can forgive me so easily. I hurt you. Badly."

His arm around her waist kept her close. His eyes demanded she didn't look away.

"You're family now. We protect each other. I got hurt in battle while you protected this family. Now let me protect you from the guilt you shouldn't be feeling."

While her heart took flight, her mind came up with thousands of reasons how being part of a family made her vulnerable, with a thousand more ways she would hurt them even without wanting to.

His kiss made her forget all those reasons, even if only for a little while.

Chapter 20 - The fire

-Torag-

Torag looked up from the flames to find Erisi on the roof of the keep, her face lifted to the stars. The shouting and laughter of his family around him echoed in the night sky, joined by the occasional high-pitched chattering of striped hyenas roaming the desert. Stories of deal-makers and warriors returning from their missions flowed around him. There was no hierarchy here, no need for commands. Aided by Chandra's eye-watering brand of alcohol, banter flew back and forth, and flirting turned into demons disappearing into the night. His family bonded here.

Tonight, like every night, Erisi stayed away.

This time, she wasn't even watching them from her position on the keep. She was pulling away. His fingers clenched around his cup. He'd seen it happen the moment she realized she'd hurt him.

Once again, he cursed Beelzebub. For a moment, he had hoped...

She had let him in. In the caves, she'd let him see the whole of her and it had been everything he never knew he needed. Someone strong, brave enough to share her pain. Someone who saw his darkness and still looked at him as though he was whole and strong. Someone he could trust with this family.

Even the wildfire demon she was terrified of had protected them all. Her sheer power left him in awe. The pain he saw in her eyes made him want to wrap around her, protect her.

He set down his cup.

"I'm going to get her," he told Yerle, straightening from his spot and dusting the sand off his indigo dhoti.

"I'm so winning this bet." Yerle pumped his fist in the air. "You're right. It's time for our hot little leader to join us."

Torag stilled, glaring at his insolent friend. "Careful..."

"This infatuation of yours is giving me so much to work with, my friend. You have no idea."

He took a step toward Yerle, who backed away with a big grin on his face. Sighing, Torag threw up his hands and turned toward the keep.

Yerle shouted behind him. "The latest bet is when the both of you will finally collide. I'm giving it two more days."

His friend's laughter behind his back made

him smile. When he looked up at Erisi, longing flared. Four days ago, he'd gotten a taste of their fire when they were in the caves. Now it consumed him, day and night.

Heart racing, he entered the main hall of the keep. He climbed the ladder to the rooftop and smiled when he found the trapdoor open. She had never needed words to make her intentions clear.

When he joined her on the north-eastern guard tower, Erisi didn't turn around. He moved close enough for his skin to brush against the soft leather on her back.

For a beat, silence reigned. Then she leaned against him with a small sigh.

Locking his arm around her waist, he kissed her neck and murmured, "Contemplating the stars again?"

Erisi huffed. "Trying to figure out how to get Beelzebub to Lucifer. The bastard is still dropping in and out of consciousness. I've never seen him take so long to heal."

"I'm guessing you'd never punched a hole in him with wildfire either."

She craned her neck to look up at him. "You'd be right."

The laughter in her blue eyes warmed his chest. His fingers caressed the slope of her arched throat, causing her to shiver against him.

"Join us."

Her eyelids shuttered. No reply came other

than her quickened breath.

He put his mouth against her ear and whispered, "You are family too. Join us, Erisi."

The little sound that escaped her lips made him hungry for her taste. When his teeth grazed her earlobe lightly, she turned around and punched him in the chest. "Play fair."

He caught her wrist in his hand and tugged her closer. Her eyes were alight with the same fire he felt. "Are you complaining?"

Torag didn't give her time to respond; he knew the answer. Her lips were warm and firm beneath his. Her moan echoed in his chest. Burying his fingers in her short black hair, he tilted her face to deepen their kiss.

When the whistling started down below, Torag broke away and sighed. "I think we've changed the odds on their cursed bet."

Her lips curved against his cheek. "Want to give them something to look at?"

Grinning, he turned demon and pulled her tight against his body. His mouth fused with hers as he took off, her legs locked around his waist.

Erisi was breathless with laughter by the time he landed close to the fire. "You sneaky demon. I didn't mean that."

He shrugged. "We gave them something to look at, and I got you to the fire. Win-win."

The smile on her face faded as she looked at the rowdy demons around the fire.

He held out his hand. "Come with me."

The touch of her fingers gave him goosebumps. When he found a spot close to Yerle and Sura, he felt their eyes burning on his and Erisi's laced fingers.

Yerle murmured, "Damn, I may have taken the wrong side of the bet on who will dominate."

Sura elbowed him in the ribs.

"I'm so glad to see you here." The war chief smiled at her with genuine warmth, and Torag felt the tension seep from Erisi's grip.

Leaning forward, Yerle said, "I was regaling everyone with our adventures against Lucifer's warriors."

Sura groaned. "I told you to shut up about that."

"See? She doesn't want the family to know she saved my ass."

Torag bit the inside of his cheek at Sura's thunderous expression.

"Next time, I'm letting them roast you alive," she snapped at Yerle.

Torag sank down next to Erisi, who had already settled cross-legged on the sand.

"She was like a dragon, fierce and fiery." Yerle gestured to the sky. "He ran like the coward he was. After he set my legs on fire, that is."

Erisi shook with silent laughter. When Torag smiled at his friend, Yerle wasn't looking at him or the other demons listening to his story. His amber eyes were fixed on Sura's face, his expression intent.

Torag had a hard time hiding his mirth. *Ah, the possibilities for revenge are endless.*

Erisi's leg brushed against his. Her hand rested on his knee while she talked to Sura.

The flames of the fire had nothing on the warmth exploding in his chest.

This was his family. This was where he was meant to be.

Chapter 21 - Life

-Erisi-

"Over my dead body!" Crossing her arms, Erisi steeled her heart to withstand Mei's pleading. "I did it once. I'm sure I can do it again." The dark-eyed demon blinked with an innocence that had Erisi rolling her eyes.

"So I heard. How many laps did Torag make you run after you approached an out-of-control demon who could have burned you to ash?"

Mei stared at the sunrise from their vantage point on the roof of the keep and pretended she didn't hear the question.

"Mei…"

The female shrugged. "He wanted me to run around the stronghold until you woke up. Sura overruled him."

Erisi stilled. "She did?"

"Yeah. She had me transform to demon and back until I passed out instead. Much worse."

The glint in the young's eyes told Erisi that the punishment had done nothing to quell Mei's impulses.

"You do know why they're punishing you, don't you?" Erisi asked.

"For disobeying orders."

Because they care. They all did.

Erisi swallowed and braced herself for the harsh words she needed to deliver. "You can't disobey orders if you want to be a warrior. A single order can make the difference between victory and defeat in battle. Disobedience can get an entire horde killed. For hell's sake, Mei, I could have killed you!"

The tear that rolled over Mei's cheek almost slew her. Her stomach roiled. She could have killed Mei. Instead, she'd almost killed Torag. His wounds had only now healed, a week after the battle.

Erisi admired Mei's bravery when she straightened her shoulders and tried again. "I understand. That's why I want to train with you. We need to know if I'm always capable of luring your demon back to human form. That way, we can make it part of our battle strategy."

Erisi almost smiled at the impassioned plea. The young demon had a point, but it didn't matter. "Absolutely not, Mei. I won't risk killing you."

"We can ask Torag to protect me in case something goes wrong."

Erisi shook her head. "So I can kill the both of

you? No."

"He told me to ask you," Mei said with a sweet voice, the glint in her dark eyes betraying her mirth.

Oh, so he sent Mei my way.

"Because he knew I'd say no." She'd get her revenge during sparring tonight.

A guard burst onto the roof. "Torag asked to get you. The souls should have transformed."

Erisi's heart jumped at the news. "We'll finish this conversation later. I understand you want to help, and I'm grateful." She hugged Mei close. "Now go and try to obey Sura."

Erisi ran. She skittered down the ladders.

Out of breath, she arrived in the cellar of the keep. She'd been asking around about the souls: how long it would take for them to transform, how many of the souls would transform at once, what they would look like, what they'd need right after their creation.

Chandra had told her it usually took a week. They'd find a few young demons in the cave, naked and scared, without any memory of their former life and death. He had a theory about why they looked like human teenagers when they came into existence. According to him, their 'tiny little powers made 'em about as useful as fecking human brood' so it made sense to him they looked that way.

Yerle thought fledglings were a test of the family's patience. Only demonic hordes that managed not to kill their irreverent, stubborn young before they turned full demon deserved to grow.

Erisi had been sure that last theory was utter bullshit until she'd had to stop Ahio from burying a dagger into his brother's eye after a dispute over whose hellfire was brighter. Yerle's theory might deserve some credit after all.

"Fuck!" In her excitement, she had a hard time remembering the sequence of the levers that would grant her access to the caves. The rock remained unmoving, keeping her from the miracle she wanted to witness more than anything in this world.

She rested her forehead against the wall and sighed.

"Having trouble?"

His voice sent a shiver down her spine. She cursed her body for betraying her. *Again*.

"No, absolutely not. I was just catching my breath. I thought you'd already be down there."

Torag smiled at her and pushed the dozens of levers in the right sequence without hesitation. The rock moved back to reveal the ladder going down the caves.

"I was waiting for you. I should have known you'd run straight here." The warmth in his eyes told her what he thought about her impatience. This was exactly why she hadn't asked him directly about the transformation of the souls. Soon, she'd have no reputation left.

Erisi descended first, the satchel of clothes she'd readied for the new young tight in her hand. As soon as Torag got down, he pulled the levers to close the entrance.

She understood his paranoia about the access to the souls. They were the future of this family. Only Torag, herself, and Chandra, who'd created the access mechanism, knew how to get in. Most of the Arav knew the caves ran under the stronghold, but they had no idea where the entrance was located or where the souls were exactly.

Torag took her hand. She'd gotten used to his need to touch her. For a demon who'd always been without family, it hadn't come naturally.

She'd discovered his touch made her entire body come alive. The strong grip of his fingers fueled the hunger she still hadn't been able to satisfy. Heat spiraled through her at the memory of his kiss the last time they were here.

"Focus, Wildfire."

She smacked her grinning second on the arm. He'd taken to calling her Wildfire, claiming it fitted her personality perfectly. She should just name him Giant. It hurt her neck to look up at him.

If only the view wasn't so enticing.

The beautiful cave formations couldn't hold her attention. By the time they arrived in the gallery with the floating souls, she could hardly breathe. For the first time in her existence, her powers had brought forth life instead of death and destruction.

Torag's hellfire lit up the cave, and Erisi's eyes fastened on the three shivering young huddled at the far end. When the smallest one lifted his head, the ice-blue of his eyes struck her like lightning.

She sank to her knees.

The souls in the cave danced around her, drawn to her skin. They lit the jagged edges of her soul. They showed her in stunning clarity what she'd failed to see so far.

She belonged.

Here.

The pain, the loneliness, Fate had led her here.

The young male stood and came to her, his gaze never leaving her face. When he stood before her, his cold pale hand touched the hot tears on her cheeks.

Erisi closed her eyes. When she opened them, the two young females had joined too. Despite the different colors of their skin and the differences in height and build, they were united by the color of their eyes, the same shade of ice-blue she'd seen reflected in water.

"Welcome to this world. From this moment forth, you belong with us." Her voice came out strong. She was surprised at the capacity of her body to function despite the scrambled state of her mind.

Dazed, she got up and turned to find Torag on his knees, staring up at her. When he laid his hand over his heart and bent his head in reverence, she knew she'd do anything to protect the Arav. To protect these young.

To deserve the male in front of her.

With trembling hands, she gave the young demons cotton kurtas and trousers to warm their icy skin.

Torag must have read the concern on her face. "They'll warm up once their powers kick in. They need to recover from the transformation." The touch of his fingers aided his hoarse voice in comforting her. "Let's bring them up."

A cold pale hand closed around hers. Blue eyes overflowing with trust looked up at her.

She swallowed. "Yes. Let's introduce them to our family."

* * *

Erisi looked on as her family surrounded the fledglings. The young demons had lost all fear. Wide-eyed with wonder, they stared at the buildings, the demons, the midday sky, and the sand.

When Chandra prodded the biceps on the young male, she had to restrain herself from growling.

"Easy, tiger." Yerle nudged her shoulder. "He means well. He's trying to spot potential master crafters and get first pick of the fledglings. Chandra believes in starting them young."

Thankful for the diversion, Erisi snorted. "At least I get Torag's protective streak now."

She had the urge to teach her young how to fight, only to then make sure they would never ever need to use their skills.

Yerle smiled, a hint of sorrow lining his face. "He's had millennia to practice that streak. He's the only reason I'm alive."

She turned to her chief. "You grew up with him?"

Doubt flitted over his expressive face. "Maybe you should ask—"

She clenched her fists. "I did. He refuses to tell me who I should be hunting down."

When Yerle inched away from her, she realized her palms were coated in dark red hellfire. Closing her fists, she tamped down her rage. "You need to tell me what happened, Yerle. He never will."

"You're right. He won't. He believes his past makes him unworthy. He can't see himself the way we see him." Her chief's voice was laced with sadness.

"Help me," she pleaded. "I can't— I can't let him continue believing that. I've always wondered why he never took charge while it's clear he's led this family for the longest time."

She looked at her smiling second and found all three young gazing up at him with adoration in their eyes. It wasn't just the color of their eyes they'd inherited from her it seemed.

Yerle was grinning at her when she recovered from her distraction. "He'll need to be the one to tell you. But don't worry. If you keep looking at him that way, he'll tell you anything you want to hear. I promise."

He evaded her half-hearted punch and walked away with a little wave, leaving her alone with her thoughts. She pushed her palm against the black branches tattooed on her chest, against the tightness that clenched around her heart.

She couldn't tear her eyes away from her young. Lives powered by her fire.

If only she could be sure her wildfire wouldn't be what would end them too.

Chapter 22 - Past and present

-Torag-

"I'm going to agree with Mei's proposal."

Torag was sure he'd misheard Erisi. His loss of focus cost him. The fiery length of her chain wrapped around his ankle. Still reeling from her words, he went down on his back, gaining a splendid view of the night sky.

"Time out." He struggled to catch his breath. "What the fuck are you talking about?"

Erisi got down on her haunches next to him. The resolve in her eyes told him she wasn't joking, and his heart fell.

"You were supposed to talk her out of it," he protested.

He'd expected some savage payback for sending Mei her way. Not this. Never had he expected she'd go along with Mei's reckless plan.

She looked down at the sand. "I told her no, but I've changed my mind."

"Hell no!" Torag jumped up, towering over

her. "How can you—"

Her pale skin looked ashen in the moonlight. "You'll need to restrain me before I turn."

She was shaking so badly she had to hold herself up with her palms on the sand. Registering her pain, he faltered. "Wildfire…"

The keening sound coming from her lips cut him deep. He dropped to his knees next to her, unsure if he could touch her.

Her skin flared with hellfire, and her eyes were wild when she looked up at him. "Leave me."

He shook his head. There was no way he was leaving her like this.

"Torag, you need to go. I don't know if I can—I don't want you to see…" Erisi buried her head between her arms on the sand and cried out in pain.

The touch of his hand on her shoulder made her scramble away from him. He recognized her anguish. It had been centuries since bouts of panic and flashbacks had haunted Yerle, but he remembered what he needed to do.

She was panting, her back pressed against the trunk of one of the trees, her arms wrapped around her knees.

"Look at me, Erisi." He infused the calm authority he'd cultivated for his friend into his voice. "Look at me. Nothing else. Just me."

When she did, his heart broke for the fierce warrior. He'd known for a while that there was hell in her past. The look in her eyes told him it was worse than he'd thought.

She whimpered. "What if I turn on you? I'll kill you too."

"You're here. You haven't turned. You won't hurt me. And if you do, it's fine. It's my choice to stay here with you."

Erisi barked out a laugh. "It's fine? You'll be fine when I burn you to ash?"

It was a good sign that she could still laugh, no matter how much bitterness was buried in the sound.

"Some of us are just asking for it," he told her with a half-smile, his eyes never leaving her face.

Instead of the responding smile he'd hoped for, Erisi burst into tears. "I killed her, Torag. There was a young demon I needed to keep safe from my master, and instead, I killed her."

Watching the gate to her soul inch open, he resisted the urge to ask more. When the silence stretched between them, he let it.

"These young..." She struggled to find the words. "I made them. My powers. Something good came from me, Torag. I need to protect them."

Warmth spread across his chest at the fierce conviction in her trembling voice.

She continued, "If my demon can't be controlled, I can't stay in this family. I can't risk everyone w-whenever my urge to...protect m-makes me turn. Either you and Mei get my demon under control, or I need to go."

"I can't let Mei near you when you're in demonic form." Regret colored his voice. "I can't, Erisi."

Her laugh mixed with a sob. "I know. Ever since we brought the fledglings into the stronghold… I get it. I'll rip anyone who touches them to pieces."

"It's not just that," Torag admitted. Erisi had let him see her pain. Maybe it was time to do the same. "There's a reason being protective is core to who I am."

Erisi sank to her knees in front of him, mirroring his position. Her red-rimmed eyes locked with his when her fingers touched his trembling hand.

Torag closed his eyes to escape the questions in her ice-blue depths. He couldn't face the contempt or pity he feared. Not from her.

"I don't remember the family I was born into. In my first year as a fledgling, slavers raided our family home. They took me and a dozen others. None of the other young survived the first year of…training. They whipped me in shape for two centuries." He forced air into his lungs, drawing courage from her touch. "When I got strong enough, I led the escape of twenty other captives. They caught us and killed everyone but me. My punishment lasted for a century."

A tear splashed on his hand. Torag caught another on his thumb and stared at the symbol of her pity. His gut twisted.

She whispered his name, making him look up. There was no pity in her eyes; rage flared instead.

He could live with rage. It's what he still felt whenever he let the memories overtake him.

Her knees touched his when she moved closer. Her quickened breathing warmed his thumb when he ran it over her lips.

Numb. He felt numb when he continued, "The second time I escaped, I led a group of ten, including Yerle. We lasted a decade wandering the wilderness before we got captured by other slavers. Turns out, it could get worse. They turned us into mercenaries for sale. Enduring pain was one of the skills they taught us. They'd flay us alive, days on end." The memories were seared in his mind, in the skin on his back, chest, and legs. "Once we healed, they started all over again. I never got away from them. Not for lack of trying. Every time I tried, they branded me and punished me. When I was a thousand years old, they sold me and Yerle to Ashoka when he needed more demons to capture Dera Rawal. Apparently, they warned him I was a runner. When I tried, he ripped my guts out, again and again, and let me fester for a year, strung up in the middle of the stronghold. That was the last time I tried. I decided to play along. In the end, it wasn't too bad."

"You had to submit to your torturer for a millennium, and you're telling me it wasn't too bad?" Erisi's hands curled into fists, extinguishing the dark red flames flaring on her palms. "At least I burned Gyasi to a fiery death... even though I killed Lyx in the process. It was the first time I blacked out." The numbness morphed into something hot and molten when Erisi ran her knuckles along his jawline. "I want to stay."

His heart expanded. "I want you to stay."

"Then help me. Restrain me before I turn. Test if I can get loose. If I can't, we can try to find out what works on my demon."

She was shaking again. He pulled her onto his lap, his hands cupping her face. "At what cost?"

"I can't... Being restrained is bad. But not as bad as it would be to leave you all behind." Erisi bit her lower lip. "Not as bad as leaving you behind."

Torag kissed her until the shaking subsided. He didn't stop until she arched against him, his name a breathless whisper on her lips.

The heat in their kiss burned him, purged him, like the wildfire she was.

They'd find a way, because she needed to stay where she belonged.

Right here, with him.

Chapter 23 – The rock

-Erisi-

Arms crossed, Erisi stared at her nemesis in the sweltering prison cell. The big demon's head rolled back and forth, his black skin glistening with sweat. For weeks now, Beelzebub had been dropping in and out of consciousness.

Something was off.

Dark brown eyes focused on her, agony burning in their depths. "Please…"

She froze. In the centuries she'd known him, not once had that word passed Beel's lips. Something was definitely off.

He groaned. "I can't take the pain. You need to —"

She saw the whites of his eyes before he dropped back to the dust, hands pushed against his stomach. When he turned half-demon, wings and claws appearing, she prepared for battle despite knowing the prison cell should hold him.

Instead of turning on her or the guards, his claws raked over his stomach. Blood welled from the cuts, splattering the floor of the cell with crimson red. She watched in morbid fascination as Beel dug into his guts and pulled out a rock.

"You little fuckers." She cursed her chiefs to hell and back before turning to the prison guard. Behind her, she heard the thud of Beel's body hitting the floor and assumed he'd fainted again. She also knew this time he would heal a lot faster. "Get me Sura. Now!"

The guard paled at the expression on her face and ran to get his chief.

When Sura walked in, her face looked innocent as a fledgling's, confirming Erisi's suspicions.

"Whose idea was this?" she demanded to know.

"I don't know what you're talking about. What happened?" Sura asked.

Erisi pointed at the fist-sized rock covered in blood and pieces of intestines in wordless accusation.

Yerle walked in behind her chief of war. "Did he throw that up? It doesn't look very healthy."

Despite her mounting temper, Erisi noted Yerle seemed to appear everywhere Sura was. She crossed her arms and glared at her chiefs. If only it was physically possible to stare them down.

Yerle shrugged. "He deserved it."

"So you did this?" She slammed her palm against her chief's chest and noticed how Sura tensed from the corner of her eye.

Yerle didn't even look at her, glancing at Sura instead. "I did. If you need to punish anyone, it should be me."

With a sigh, she took a step back and tried to get her rage under control. This whole family had the bad habit of protecting one another.

Not that she could blame them. Last night, she'd almost torn a demon's head off for growling at Arren, the blue-eyed male fledgling, when he'd nicked the warrior's dagger. Protectiveness was damn contagious.

She glared at her chiefs. "The moment I find out who's actually responsible for this mess, they'll pay dearly."

Sura bowed her head, but not before Erisi caught her smile. Throwing her hands up, she stomped out of the prison building, temper flaring as hot as the midday sun burning down on her.

There were so many things she was supposed to do. She needed to consult with Chandra about the fortifications they were adding to the stronghold. Once she was able to look at Yerle without wanting to burn him, she needed to talk about the pending alliance with a local human chieftain. She wanted to check on the souls in the cave and spar with the young. At some point, she needed to swallow her damn pride and confront

Anea and Kaemon about their attack. Their punishment was coming to an end, and she needed to instill some valuable lessons about learning to aim and setting realistic goals about which enemies to attack.

Yet none of that could happen before she let off steam. Not punishing Yerle for something she knew he hadn't done meant her rage had nowhere to go.

The meeting with Lucifer was weighing on her mind. For weeks, she'd been thinking through the best strategies. The longer the surviving warrior's twisted story festered in the ears of her leader, the more likely that Lucifer would think her a traitor evading her punishment. Now it seemed she could have delivered Beelzebub a whole lot sooner if not for her chiefs.

Erisi shouted in frustration at the vast, empty expanse of desert she'd reached. The trees on her usual training spot threw small spots of shade on the burning sand. She climbed a tree and started the first cycle of exercises she intended to repeat as often as it took.

When darkness fell, the chill in the air cooled the sweat covering her body. Upside down, Erisi saw Torag approach hours before their usual sparring time. She guessed he'd heard what had happened.

Good, she could use another outlet. Her exercises were not helping, even though her muscles ached with strain and her powers were almost exhausted.

"Are you done yet?" He leaned against the trunk of the tree and looked up at her, his face blank and his muscles relaxed.

She wanted to break that damn control. More than anything, she needed his passion, the fire that flared in his eyes before he shoved it down.

She climbed down the trunk, landed on her feet next to her second, and licked her lips. "I'm going to deliver Beel to Lucifer tomorrow. Alone."

His eyes narrowed a smidge. "No."

"You seem to have forgotten your place." Surely she could find a way to rile him up. "As far as I know, I'm still the leader of this family."

"As leader, your place is with your family, ruling them. You can't go off on your own and get yourself killed." Torag took a step toward her.

Erisi raised her eyebrow. "Are you suggesting I should take my second with me and leave this entire family leaderless?"

"You take the fucking horde." Another step forced her to look up to see him fighting for control over his temper.

"Much better. I'll leave you to defend the young. Maybe the deal-makers can negotiate a truce when the Rohi show up," she taunted.

Torag scowled. His arms were crossed over his broad chest, only drawing her attention to the definition of his muscles. *Damn him for being hot even when he's sulking.*

"You can't protect me from this, Torag. I need to hand-deliver the big bastard."

"No. You're not going near that fucker alone." The line of his jaw tightened as Torag bit out the words.

"Are you talking about Lucifer or Beelzebub?" she asked.

The last name made him growl. Ah, yes, he was cracking alright.

"What? Afraid I'll fall for his incredible charm?"

Once had been more than enough.

"I don't like the way he looks at you."

Erisi noticed the simmer of rage in his onyx eyes. "How does he look at me?"

"Like you belong to him."

She put her hand on his chest, relishing the warmth of his skin under her palm. "I don't belong to anyone but myself."

His glare didn't diminish. "I should just put that fucking rock back in his gut," he snarled.

With a loud curse, Erisi shoved him. He barely budged. "That was your doing?"

Torag shrugged. "Maybe."

"You cost me valuable time! I could have delivered him to Lucifer and been done with him weeks ago!"

She wasn't playing anymore. The fight boiled inside of her, itching for release. She slammed both her palms against his rock-hard stomach and pushed. He laughed, kicking her bad temper into overdrive.

She planted her elbow in his ribs and stepped to the side, slamming her knee into the muscle at the back of his thigh when he staggered forward.

Torag attacked, not pulling his punches. She loved that he never treated her as anything less than powerful.

When he knocked her back, her spine connected with the trunk of the tree. Before she could move forward, his body slammed against hers.

The fire in his eyes took her breath away.

This. This was what she needed.

Chapter 24 - Demon domination

-Torag-

His blood boiled with the heat of their fight. The only outlet he could think of, the only way to appease his mind, was to give in to the temptation he'd been fighting for so long.

Torag needed Erisi as much as he needed his next breath. He needed the feel of her skin under his fingertips, her taste on his lips, her smell embedded in every cell of his body.

He grabbed her hand and dragged her with him.

She resisted, trying to break free from his hold. "Where do you think you're going?"

Right, maybe I should inform her about my intentions.

He cupped her face in his hands and kissed her until every thought drowned in passion.

"Inside. Somewhere private. Anywhere." His mind had trouble preparing the words his mouth was supposed to deliver.

Judging by the rise and fall of her chest, Erisi wasn't in a better state. She laughed, the sound breathless and light. "Catch me." She took off running.

He knew he'd never catch the well-trained warrior. Not like this. So he cheated.

He turned demon and took flight, going after her. Before she reached the gate, he swept her up in his arms. Higher he pushed himself, into the night sky and toward the stars. Her arms held on to his neck. Her legs wrapped around his waist. Throwing her head back, Erisi laughed.

He looked down at her, taking in every detail. He wanted to remember the joy radiating from her eyes. He wanted to bottle the explosion of happiness in his chest. Needed to etch this feeling into the fabric of his soul.

One last thrust of his wings pushed them even higher in the sky, before he launched backward into a drop.

Erisi yelled in delight, her grin wide. Adrenaline whipped through his body as they spiraled down. Needing to taste the joy in her laugh, he kissed her.

The heat of her embrace almost made him forget to break their fall. They landed with an audible thud in front of the small brick building he rarely used. He preferred to spend time with his family at the fire or in the barracks. Now, he was more than grateful for the privacy of his quarters. He wanted her all to himself.

The moment they touched down, Erisi broke free and ran. Grinning, Torag pursued her. By the time she rounded the side of the building and reached the stronghold walls, he'd grabbed her by the waist. Her wicked smile had him thinking she'd allowed herself to be caught. He would've been insulted if not for the fact that she turned in his arms and tugged off her cotton top.

Her teeth dug into her lower lip as she dropped the garment into the sand. Her tattoo pulsed with hellfire, the lines swirling over her rippling muscles, leading his eyes right up to her breasts.

He stopped breathing.

It didn't surprise him when she charged and knocked him down before he could get air back into his lungs.

She straddled him and smiled. Before he could touch her, she captured his hands and brought them up above his head, pinning them to the sand.

Fuck, she—

The thought never got the chance to take hold. Her mouth came down on his, hot and demanding. When she groaned with the same pleasure coursing through his veins, he flipped her under him and took over. His tongue swept into her mouth.

Her taste drove him crazy. Her body was pure heat against the chill of the sand under the night sky.

In the distance, he heard the shouts of his family around the fire. He wondered if they knew someone was about to win the bet.

All thoughts vanished when her fingers tightened in his hair. When he arched his head back, Erisi nipped the skin of his throat, then licked the sting.

He ran out of patience. No more waiting. He wanted nothing between them; he needed her under him, naked and writhing, right now. Tearing himself away from her, he got up and held out his hand in a wordless invitation.

She took it without hesitation.

He shoved the wooden door to his quarters open, slamming it against the wall. Erisi smiled at him when he tugged her inside. Giving up his fight for self-control, he hooked his arm around her waist and pulled her against him. The feel of her muscles, her distinct lack of softness, turned him on. The confidence in her eyes fanned the embers into full-blown flames.

He tilted up her chin and kissed her. Their lips clashed. Her teeth raked over his bottom lip. He tasted the blood and got even harder for her.

Torag buried his fingers in her hair, unwilling to leave an inch of space between them.

She attacked his mouth, her lips hard and urgent on his. Her nails dug into his shoulders as she took the upper hand. Conquered him.

He'd be damned if he let her. Not this time.

He pushed her against the closest wall and pressed the full length of his body against her. His mouth slammed down on hers while his fingers dug into the muscles of her ass, bringing her closer. The friction was driving him insane. It was heaven and hell and not enough, not by a long shot.

He let go of her mouth. His teeth grazed the side of her neck. His tongue traced her collarbone until his kisses led him to the top of her breast. Her heart raced right under her skin, thrumming against his mouth. He kissed her there.

His fingers traced the underside of her breasts before following the branches of the tree tattooed on her skin up to her nipples. Erisi's hips arched against him when he brushed his thumbs over the hard tips.

Hands on his neck, she climbed his body and wrapped her legs around his waist. With a little grin, she tightened her thighs around him, grinding her core against his rock-hard cock. He took his revenge by rolling her nipples between his fingers until her eyes fluttered shut.

When she opened them again, the fierce fire that always lit her eyes was enhanced by a longing that turned his knees weak. Torag laid her down on his bed, the furs and silks sliding against her skin. He stood and took off his dhoti, the only reason he wasn't buried to the hilt in her right now.

Her heated eyes caressed his skin like a physical touch. She bit her lip when her eyes landed on his hard length. "Fuck me."

"Don't think so," he drawled. "I'm not done with you yet."

"Oh, I think you are." She stood on the low bed frame, for once on eye-level with him. His eyes were drawn to the curl of her swollen lips, the pink blush on her pale cheeks.

She stripped and threw her leather pants to the side, standing before him in all her bare beauty. Mouth dry, he pretended not to be affected by the sleek lines of her legs or the junction of her thighs, which was darkened by little hairs he longed to touch.

Dropping to her knees on the bed, Erisi ran her hands over her flanks up to the sides of her breasts. She arched her neck back as she ran her hands down between her breasts and over the toned muscles of her stomach. Transfixed, Torag stared at her fingers when they dipped between her legs, stroking inside.

Her smile turned devious when she raised her glistening fingers to her mouth.

Torag moved before he even realized he'd planned to. He grabbed her wrist and rumbled, "Oh no, you don't."

Her taste exploded in his mouth when he licked her fingers, sucked on them until she moaned. She tasted like ginger and heat and everything Erisi.

He didn't let go of her hand when he used his body to press her down on the bed. His fingers laced with hers over her head.

Bracing himself on his other arm, he simply looked at her. His racing heart ached with longing. The slow smile gracing her lips nearly did him in.

Locking her free arm around his neck, Erisi pulled him down to her. Within a few beats of his pounding heart, the sweetness of her kiss turned wild. She hooked her leg over his waist and rolled him under her in one smooth move, her lips curling under his mouth.

"You little—" he started, only to be quieted by her sinking down on his cock. "Fuck!"

"Mmhm, yes." She moved, causing them to groan in unison. Her tight heat around him made it hard to focus.

The moonlight filtering through the clerestories lit the graceful roll of her hips, the slight bounce of her breasts. His fingers dug into her ass as he pulled her back onto him.

She went slow. Torag reveled in the tantalizing slide of her flesh against his. She lowered her body over him and tasted the skin of his chest. When her teeth grazed his nipple, he almost came right there and then. His movements turned erratic while he fought for control over his desire.

"More," she whispered against his skin, her breath calling goosebumps to life. "I want all of you."

Torag let his head fall back and gave in to the fire, his hips pushing up whenever she came down, meeting her thrust for thrust until it was no longer enough.

Rolling, he pinned her under him and slammed into her to the hilt.

Erisi threw her head back. "Fuck, fuck, fuck."

Drawing back, he waited for her eyes to lock with his before thrusting into her again. He needed more with every fevered stroke. He devoured her lips—teeth clashing, tongues matching the rhythm of his thrusts.

Her muscles tensed under his hands as she came apart. Her nails raked along his upper arms, and her heat tightened around him. Her sigh turned into a moan, into a low-pitched whine against his lips. He inhaled every sound and fucked her harder, faster. His muscles ached from the strain, his body slick with the heat they generated.

"Torag." His name on her lips was what turned fire into full-blown explosion.

He was struck by the ferocity of his release, blinded by the bliss spreading through his entire body.

"Erisi." Her name was a desperate plea that whispered past his lips.

The sweet slide of her body against his made

shivers run down his spine. Her fingers rested over his pounding heart.

He covered her hand with his and hoped.

For her. For everything.

This wasn't enough. It never would be. He needed everything from her.

So he rested his forehead against hers, bodies still entwined, and hoped.

Chapter 25 - Lucifer

-Erisi-

"I need to go." Erisi made a feeble attempt to get out of Torag's arms.

"No." Her skin against his lips muted his voice, but the determination was still clear as rain.

The light filtering in from the clerestories told her it was well into the morning. She sighed and turned to face her second.

His onyx eyes were locked on her, his mouth tight. "Stay. Let him rot in that cell."

Momentarily giving in to the temptation he posed, Erisi kissed him until his lips were supple and warm under hers. Then she tore herself away and got up before he realized her intent.

Turning away from him in an attempt to catch her breath, she bent to pick up her clothes. As she straightened, he tackled her against the wall. His arms braced her from the impact. His breath was hot on the back of her neck, his fingers painfully tight on her waist.

Welcoming his intensity, Erisi leaned her head against his chest and dropped her top. "Torag…"

She reached back and pulled his hips against her. Her breasts scraped against the brick, her sensitive skin lighting with blissful twinges of pain. Desire exploded in her core when his teeth nipped her earlobe.

"Stay." He sank into her heat with a smooth thrust, drawing a moan from her parched throat.

Damn, the male knows how to move…

Torag hooked his arm around her waist. She braced her palms against the wall, pushing back to match his pounding rhythm.

His hand moved between her legs, and her knees almost buckled from the pleasure he evoked. He didn't slow, fucking her right through to another building peak.

Needing to see she affected him just as much as he did her, she turned in his arms. The intensity of his dark eyes, the way his gaze dipped to her mouth took her breath away.

Torag's fingers gripped the back of her neck. The kiss he laid on her was wild and fevered.

Running her hands along the muscles of his chest, she reached his broad shoulders. She held on. For once, she didn't need to be strong. She trusted him to carry her if needed.

When he drove back into her, she saw the hunger, the craving she felt in her bones, reflected on his face.

His fingers collared her throat without pressure. His breath warmed her ear when he whispered, "You come back to me, or I will hunt you down. Wherever you are."

Swept away by his ferocity, blinded with pleasure, she came apart in his arms.

* * *

It took her a day and a half of flying to reach Mount Roraima with an infuriated Beelzebub in tow. Her hellfire-infused chains around his wrists and neck probably had something to do with his rage.

Breathing in the cool air, Erisi took a moment to look at the dark sandstone plateau she'd left behind a few full moons ago. A shiver ran the length of her body. It no longer felt like home. Too cold.

Behind her, the clank of Beelzebub's chains and his muttered curses interrupted her thoughts. At least he'd given up on trying to fight her outright after a few hard lessons along the way. She turned her gaze to the polished quartzite walls surrounding Lucifer's palace before moving toward the only entrance to her leader.

The guards stared at her as she led Beelzebub through the gate like a snarling dog.

In the middle of the courtyard, the large demon pulled on his chains and barked, "Fuck this! Leave me some dignity!"

Erisi lifted an eyebrow. The memory of his boot on her throat when she'd lain at his feet, bloodied and broken, was vivid even centuries later. The sneers of the warriors who'd been surrounding them still rang in her ears.

Beelzebub fell silent. He knew revenge when he saw it.

Their steps echoed in the hallway to Lucifer's throne room, punctuated by the rattle of her chains. Cold wind cleaved through her marrow. She'd always wondered if Lucifer liked his guests shivering at his feet.

The guards to the throne room opened the doors without a word. At the bottom of the stairs leading up to Lucifer's throne, Erisi knelt and pulled Beelzebub down with her.

"I see you brought me a gift. I like the ribbon." Lucifer motioned for her to get up as he looked down from the top of the stairs.

After months of speaking the Arav dialect, she needed a moment to find the right words in Minoan. "I'd like the chains back, but the gift is all yours." She shoved Beelzebub forward, infusing the tiniest bit of hellfire into her touch. "Or should I say I'm returning this gift to sender?"

So much had changed. Last time, she'd been desperate to prove her worth to the fallen angel. Now all she wanted was to return to her family.

Lucifer studied her. "You did well. You brought the Arav to heel. You passed the test I sent your way. Too bad even that wasn't enough to draw out your demon. I'm glad Beelzebub managed."

Erisi's stomach cramped at his interest in her demon.

Beelzebub huffed. "Bringing the Arav to heel? She sleeps with the second to get him to obey her."

The calculation in Lucifer's gaze made Erisi shift with unease. *Thank hell I didn't bring Torag.*

"I heard an interesting account from the warrior that managed to return," Lucifer said. She waited, nails digging into her palms. "He claimed you were out of control, that you attacked the warriors without provocation and used your wildfire to kill them all."

It was impossible to read the expression on Lucifer's face. She straightened her back and lifted her chin. "The wildfire part of that story is true. They tried to kill me after I beat Beelzebub. My attack on your warriors was warranted."

"Good." He descended the stairs. "His obvious lies got him thrown in my dungeons for a long time to come. Getting in the way of your demon seems like a dumb thing to do. I don't need fools in my horde."

The deathly green of his eyes narrowed. Erisi knew she wasn't going to like what came next.

"I want you to stay by my side. I need your demon with all of its powers here, not in some far-flung stronghold another elite can control for me."

The air seemed to grow thinner and hotter. Erisi evened out her breath before she spoke. "I'm training to get my demonic side under control, my lord. I don't believe I'm ready to fight at your side. Right now, I'm as dangerous to allies as enemies."

Lucifer ran his palm over the dark stubble on his jaw. "You can train here."

"I need demons I trust to help with the task. After the incident between me and the other elite warriors, I no longer have those here."

He was well aware of what had happened even though he hadn't intervened.

The moment Lucifer smiled, she knew she'd made a mistake. She'd shown her hand, and Lucifer always exploited weaknesses.

Paralyzed by the green poison of his gaze, she awaited his verdict.

Finally, he turned away and said, "Fine. I gave you my word that succeeding in this mission would get you rewarded, so I can't fault you for wanting to finish it. Return until further notice. I will be in touch."

Erisi didn't trust her ears. Or rather, she didn't trust her leader.

When she didn't move immediately, Lucifer barked, "Dismissed."

Leaving Beelzebub at Lucifer's feet, she left the throne room.

She had a family to get back to. A family to protect from whatever he was truly planning.

Chapter 26 - Restrained

-Torag-

Yerle cursed when his back hit the ground again. "If Erisi doesn't return soon, she won't have any chiefs left."

"Get up. Less talk, more fighting." Torag circled his friend. If he didn't get this gnawing frustration out of his system, he'd burn the next young who threw a temper tantrum alive.

Yerle crouched in the sand under the trees of the training spot, trying to catch his breath. "Seriously, I'm not a training dummy you can use to take out your sexual frustration."

"You might as well be with the defense technique you're showing. I think you need to ask your lover to demonstrate some moves. Or are you too busy learning a different *technique* when you seek Sura out?" Torag taunted.

Yerle growled and attacked, his sword reflecting the late afternoon sun. Torag let him close in. When he attempted to slice Torag's side, he kicked Yerle in the ribs, wrapped his hand around his throat, and slammed him down on the sand.

"Do you two need counseling?" Her honeyed voice hit Torag in the heart.

Taking advantage of his distraction, Yerle kicked him in the knee, causing Torag to drop in the sand in front of his leader.

"Erisi. Thank Fate. Your second was facing mutiny with the temper he's been sporting since you went away," Yerle told her.

Glaring at him, Torag wished frying his friend's ass with pure hellfire was an option.

"Thank you for the entertainment." Erisi grinned at Yerle. "Now you need to get the hell out of here."

Yerle rubbed his palm over his bruised ribs. "Why wou—" His eyes widened. "Oh. Never mind, I'm gone."

Torag only had eyes for Erisi. She was in one piece. From the black bangs falling in her ice-blue eyes to the scabbard tight around her leather-clad leg, she was as fierce and beautiful as ever.

"So this time it was you who needed some anger management, mhm?" she teased.

Torag watched her unwind the chains from her wrists and take her fighting stance, her eyes sparkling with glee. His heart picked up a faster rhythm as he got to his feet and fell into position.

She charged. The hellfire sparks hitting his skin helped him focus. He pulled up his shield to protect himself from the blow of her chains, then dropped it to bring his sword down on her shoulder. His weapon met her chain mid-air. Erisi kicked him in the gut, forcing him back. The bark of the tree bit into his skin upon impact.

She stepped forward until her chest brushed his. The metal links of her chain brushed his legs. "I've missed you."

"Good," he murmured, staring down at her lips. "It would have been awkward if I'd been the only one."

He caressed his fingertips along her bare arms down to her wrists. She arched into him with a low moan, and he reversed their positions. Pushing her against the tree, he pinned her hands above her head. Her chains dropped to the sand. Eyes sparkling, she smiled up at him.

Torag bent down and kissed her, savoring the moan he drew from her lips. Only when he strained for air did he let go of her.

She licked her swollen lips. "You need to chain me to this tree."

His body went up in flames before he caught the flash of fear in her eyes. He fought his desire, trying to understand. "What are you talking about?"

"I need to get my demon under control. Now. I don't trust Lucifer."

He let go of her wrists and brushed his thumb along her cheek. "What happened?"

Erisi leaned her head back against the tree

and closed her eyes. "He wanted me to stay by his side. Despite the legends, I don't think he knew the full extent of my powers before. Having one of his warriors witness my wildfire firsthand... " He caught the tremor in her voice. "I've been trained by his generals. I'm bound to him by a blood oath. I've proven my loyalty to him by taking over this family. He's forged me into a weapon he can use."

Tingles worked their way up Torag's spine. He cupped her face and forced her to look at him. "But he let you go. That must be a good thing."

"I made a mistake, Torag." Her jaw clenched, the muscles working against his palm. "I told him I needed to get my demon under control and that I needed demons I could trust to do so."

He stilled.

Erisi swallowed hard. "Lucifer knows what this family means to me now. He knows leverage when he sees it."

Breathing in her scent, he rested his forehead against hers. "Now what?"

"Now you chain me to this tree so I won't hurt anyone when I shift. You try to get my demon to turn back. That's the very least we need to control."

"How bad is this going to be for you?" He needed to understand.

Erisi's eyes told him before she answered. "Bad."

Her voice broke on the word.

He wanted to protect her from the pain, but right now she needed his support more than his protests. Torag had no doubt Lucifer was dangerous to her. She needed to tame her demon, to control the powers she possessed so she could beat whatever Lucifer sent her way.

Maybe more importantly, he wanted her to embrace who she was, every facet of her powerful being. The fear her own demon evoked in her made him ache for her.

Torag picked up her chains and took a deep breath. Erisi put her hands behind her, circling the trunk of the tree.

With every tug of the chains around her wrists, he felt like he was stabbing himself in the heart.

"Are you fucking kidding me, Torag?" she hissed.

He put his forehead against the trunk and waited for the words he knew were coming.

"Do you think I can't get out of this weak-ass restraints of yours? Tighter. You chain me to this tree so I'll have to pull it from the ground if I want to get free, do you understand?" Erisi growled.

He pulled the chain tighter. The keening sound from her lips nailed him to the ground.

"Don't you dare stop," she bit out.

Torag tightened the second chain around her legs. When he was done, he dropped to his knees in front of her.

Erisi looked down at him with tears in her eyes. "You do not, under any circumstance, unchain me before I turn back. Do you understand?"

With that, she turned into an ice-blue demon who stared at him without recognition.

* * *

The sun had set and risen, and still the demon fought for freedom.

Deep grooves scarred the tree she was chained to. Crimson welled on the wounds her wild movements had torn into her own scales and flesh. Still, his hoarse voice had not reached her.

Crouched in the sand in front of her, Torag had tried to coax her demon for hours, to talk her down from the frenzy. She'd almost bitten him when he'd tried to touch her.

All her demon wanted was to get Erisi out of the situation that terrified her. To be restrained, out of control, and close to a powerful demon who could hurt her. He tried not to take it personally but failed.

He needed her trust, but he knew the ice-blue demon wasn't rational. Every jerk of the powerful muscles was spurred on by instinct.

And her instincts told her he was a danger to her.

Bowing his head in despair, Torag finally gave in and left the wild demon behind.

He stormed into the barracks to find Mei, then

dragged her outside.

"What's happening? Torag, why are you covered in blood? What—"

He had no voice left, nothing left to say, until they reached the tree.

"Please. Please, help her. I can't—" He dropped to his knees and put his forehead against the burning sand. More than anything, he wanted to free Erisi from the pain she was in.

Mei's voice was soft and sweet. "Hi Erisi."

The demon didn't stop thrashing. Despair spiraled through Torag's body until he felt dizzy and disoriented.

"It's alright," Mei murmured. "You're safe with us. Let me get those chains—"

"No!" Torag jumped up, holding the young demon back. "You can't."

Mei scowled at him. "Torag! The reason you can't reach her is because you've restrained her. You've caged the most dangerous being alive and expect her to roll over? Seriously?"

"She made me promise not to free her."

"I don't give a damn. I didn't promise a thing." She tried to push Torag out of the way.

"No." He positioned himself in front of Erisi, protecting Mei from the Wildfire Warrior. Protecting Erisi from the guilt that would eat her alive.

"Torag, you know I love you, so take this as a sign of that love. You're an idiot!" Mei shoved him. "You need to free her."

Torag knew she was right, but he couldn't let her do it. If Erisi hurt anyone else, she'd disappear into the night and never come back. She would never forgive herself if she killed another being like she'd killed Lyx.

"She's almost out of power, Torag," Mei said in her sweetest voice. "Her wounds are no longer healing. Her hellfire has faded from black to dark red. You can take her on if need be. She's used all her energy. Free her!"

"Fuck!" he shouted into the silent desert. The fact that Erisi didn't react to his raised voice made him realize Mei was right.

Desperate, he tore the chains from her bleeding body. She collapsed against him, still covered in ice-blue scales. When she stared up at him, no recognition lit the darkness of her eyes.

Mei crouched down next to them. She reached over and caressed Erisi's face. "We'll take care of you. You're safe."

The dark eyes closed. Her cramped body relaxed in his arms.

It took another hour before she turned back to the small pale female he adored. Carrying her motionless form, he walked through the gate to his living quarters.

There he waited for the moment she woke, to tell her he'd failed her.

Chapter 27 – The final test

-Erisi-

Even days later, everything hurt.

The slightest movement burned. Erisi's shoulders and neck were cramped to the point of feeling like solid rock.

Worse was the grief obliterating her insides. Her demon was well and truly out of control. The only being able to get through to her was a young demon. Now that she realized being bound didn't work, she refused to put Mei in danger again, no matter how adamant the fierce warrior-in-training was about wanting to help.

She still hadn't talked to Torag about what came next. His murmured regrets in the night, the touch of his strong hands, his kiss had taken the place of the conversation they needed to have.

The distrust of her demon, her unwillingness to submit to the large powerful male stood as a wall between them. He blamed himself. She saw it in his eyes.

Her demon was damaged beyond repair, beyond Torag's powers to help and protect.

Biting through the pain, she got up from the furs strewn on Torag's bed and tore herself away from his scent. She was done feeling sorry for herself.

Pulling open the door, she was blinded by the midday sun.

"Erisi! You're awake!"

Despite herself, she smiled at the excitement in Mei's voice. She loved the young for the lack of pity or concern shining from her dark eyes. "More or less."

Mei skipped along with her as she walked toward the training field. "Torag is biting everyone's head off. Yerle is trying to steer him away from the family before someone gets hurt."

Erisi didn't know whether to smile or cry. She took a deep breath. "How is your training going?"

"Good. I pinned one of the older warriors yesterday. He beat my ass afterward, but it was fun while it lasted."

Pride swelled in her chest. She stopped and reached over to brush a strand of sleek black hair from Mei's face. "You're going to be the greatest warrior alive if you keep this up." She infused steel in her next words. "If you stay away from out-of-control demons who can kill you."

Mei shrugged. "I'd do it again in a heartbeat."

Another reason why Erisi loved her. The unapologetic way in which Mei cared healed some of the wounds the past had inflicted on her soul. "I'd better—"

The ram horn sounded, punching her heart into overdrive. "To the horde, Mei! Obey Sura."

She took off running toward the training field. When she skidded to a halt, she was relieved to see the sole intruder was already restrained.

Torag had his hand wrapped around the throat of a demon. "Who sent you?"

"Luci—" The gargled sound told her the demon couldn't breathe, let alone speak.

With a sigh, she ordered, "Let him go, Torag. I need to know what my great leader has cooked up now."

The red-skinned demon dropped to the sand, hands around his bruised throat. "I have orders to deliver this message to you and you alone."

Pushing down the sinking feeling in her gut, she motioned for the demon to follow her to the roof of the keep, where she dismissed the guards.

"Speak."

The messenger lifted the hem of his cotton shirt to pull a piece of parchment from a small satchel. He handed it to Erisi, who unrolled the message. A faint copper smell rose from the crimson slashes on the parchment. Erisi shook her head at the dramatic flair. Her leader had clearly spilled blood to convey his message.

I have a deal with the Rohi. When they attack to-

gether with my warriors, you will let them take over and return to me.

The sky crashed down on her head, the weight keeping Erisi from breathing.

She fought to stay standing, refusing to show weakness to Lucifer's errand demon.

"Go! Get back to that bastard!" Erisi hissed at the messenger.

Despite the fear on his face, the trembling male stayed rooted to the spot. "I can't! He told me he needed your hand burned into my skin to ensure you'd seen the message."

Bile rose in her throat as she pushed her hellfire-coated palm onto the chest of the messenger. She was thankful for his stoic acceptance of the pain.

As soon as her hand left his skin, the demon took off into the clear sky. Erisi went to her knees, fist against her mouth to silence the screams lodged in her throat.

She'd seen it in the greens of his eyes, the whirring of Lucifer's devious mind when he'd realized the truth about her demon and her love for this family.

Lucifer wanted her absolute loyalty. He wanted to see her destroy this family, her one weakness, before he made her general.

This was the final test.

And she chose to fail.

Chapter 28 – One last time

-Erisi-

Erisi watched Torag cross the training field. The love coursing through her was bittersweet. Finally, she'd found what she never realized she was looking for.

She belonged. With him. With the Arav.

She'd finally found the strength to care. And it was about to be taken from her.

She couldn't give Lucifer what he wanted. The price to become his general was too high. Even if it meant no longer having to rely on her demon to survive.

She'd believed that she would never take an innocent life in the throes of wildfire again. That she would never hurt like that again.

The pain that was tearing her limb from limb as she looked at Torag told her otherwise. No matter what choice she made, she was going to destroy herself in the process. If she stayed, Lucifer would decimate this family to get to her.

And if she left—

She swallowed hard, but the knot in her throat only grew.

Saving them all was the only way forward. Now she needed to figure out how. By combining his elite forces with the large Rohi family, Lucifer had made them nearly unstoppable. Throwing in Krish, who knew this family and stronghold inside out, just sealed the deal.

Torag slowed his approach when he saw her face. "What's wrong, Wildfire?"

Her smile felt taut. "Nothing. I'm thinking through our strategy." She pushed away from the wall of the keep she'd been leaning against.

"You always are." His fingers brushed the bangs from her forehead, and she relished his touch.

Erisi turned her face into his palm with a small sigh.

"You know you can tell me, right?"

"I will. Just not right now." She needed this peace before she shattered it all. She needed the connection with the male who made her feel everything she didn't know she'd been missing for centuries.

Her palms traveled up from the ridges of his stomach to the muscles stretched tight over his ribs and higher. Her fingers laced behind his neck.

He bent down and met her lips in the sweetest of kisses. It was as if he felt she didn't need fire in this moment. She shook with the force of her silent sob.

Torag kissed the salt of her tears away and rested his forehead against hers. "My l—Wildfire. Talk to me."

The ache thundering in her chest expanded a thousandfold. The pressure against her lungs restricted her breathing. Her heart bucked under the strain.

She ran her fingers along his temples to the dark stubble on his jaw. "I need you."

The lazy smile on his beautiful face shot straight to her core. "You have me."

For now, she did.

In that moment, she decided to give him everything she was. Everything she could never have been without him.

When she took his hand, he followed her to his living quarters without question.

Erisi wished she had the patience to tease him into a frenzy. She wished she had the elegance to seduce him with grace.

Instead, she slammed the door shut behind them and pulled off her cotton top. When he reached out to her, she held up her hand. She didn't want to lose the little courage she had left.

Eyes fixed on his face, she stripped off her tight leather pants and stood before him, naked in every sense of the word.

Judging by the look on his face, she'd somehow accomplished the frenzy without patience or grace. Her hellfire reacted to the hunger etched in the tightness around his lips. Dark red flames ran over her skin haphazardly, erratic like her breathing.

The step she took toward him cost her. The next one was harder. She fell to her knees in front of him.

The stutter in his breath broke the intense silence between them. She'd have smiled if not for the tears she was fighting.

Her fingers hooked over the edge of his pants and pulled them down, her thumbs brushing the powerful muscles of his thighs and calves as she did. The heat he fueled in her made sweat roll down her bare back.

Yep, I should definitely start calling him Giant.

Erisi licked her lips and let her eyes slide up from his arousal to his face. Desire flared in his eyes. The muscles in his neck were corded, his hands fisted by his sides. Much like herself, he looked about ready to burst, and she hadn't even started.

She trailed her fingers back up, this time exploring the inside of his muscular legs. Smooth skin gave way to a series of rings high on the inside of his thigh. The scars were mirrored on the other side.

"Don't—" His voice came out broken and breathless.

Erisi was ready to give all of herself to him, to let him past every shield she'd erected, but she was not letting this go. "What happened?"

She touched the metal that had been forced into his skin, the rough edges nearly concealed by scar tissue. Ten bronze rings—five on each side of his body.

"I escaped ten times."

Throat tight, she remembered his brutal account of the past. He tensed when she touched the lowest ring. "Does it hurt?"

"No. It's just—"

She kissed the raised skin. Ran her tongue up over the first ring to the second. Torag shuddered.

By the time she reached the ring highest on his leg, his fingers were laced in her short hair. She moved to his other leg and kissed her way up his thigh. The fingers tightened, the slight tug on her scalp adding to the sensations bursting in her chest. This time, she didn't stop at the highest mark on his flesh. Butterfly kisses brought her up to his arousal.

"Wildfire..." His voice caressed the endearment.

She gripped the base of his cock and ran her lips along the length of him. Once she'd tasted him to her heart's content, when his legs started to tremble, she gently led him to the bed and kissed her way up his heated skin to his stubbled jaw.

"Remember how I said I don't belong to anyone?"

His lips brushed over hers. His hand on the back of her neck kept her from escaping his gaze when she broke the kiss.

"Yes," he whispered.

"I think I may belong with you."

Hellfire flared in his eyes. The tender moment spiraled into something else entirely.

Torag rolled over her, his biceps straining to keep his bulk from her smaller body. He devoured her. Her sanity fled as their fused fire burned through her. His fingers laced with hers, trapping her hands over her head as her body bowed with pleasure.

There was no fear of being captured this time. Of being restrained. Only trust. As she looked into his eyes, she knew he would never hurt her.

The warmth of his mouth moved to her throat. He nipped her pulse point, then soothed the sting with his tongue, causing a rush of heat to flood straight to her core. He traced the branches of the tree etched into her skin. The shivers born from his caress reached down to her toes. When he let go of her hands and moved lower, Erisi bit the flesh of her arm to smother her cries. His tongue dipped into her navel and trailed down.

His large hands kept her hips locked against the bed while he tasted her. She jerked at the touch of his lips. Her toes curled into the furs; her nails dug into her palms as she fought for control. She'd wanted to pleasure him, and here he w

—

Her body bucked, then melted against him when his tongue found the perfect spot. He kissed her there, lazily lapped at her core until she tipped over the edge and fell headlong into bliss. He didn't stop his slow exploration, and she shivered beneath him. She ached with the sensations, wanting to escape the sweet torture, wanting it to last for all eternity.

He found his way up her body, and her fingers laced through his hair, needing to hold on as she gave in.

By the time he kissed the corner of her mouth, she was dazed. The hunger in his eyes hadn't abated. His hands lifted her hips and as her legs hiked around his waist, he thrust into her in one slow slide of perfection.

He stilled. Her heart pulsed in her core and in every cell of her skin touching him. She arched against him, pleaded with him to move.

When he drove his hips into her, she cried out. She held on.

One last time.

***

Torag traced the lines of her tattoo, the roots leading his fingertips from the curve of her ass to her sides and the muscles of her stomach. His palm slid up the trunk of the tree reaching over her ribs, up into the thinning branches between her breasts. Her hellfire flared under his touch, and with it, the lines of her tattoo turned dark red.

His kiss on her hip bone sent a buzz through her satiated, aching body. Erisi moved against him, her fingers loosely twisting in his hair.

"This must have hurt."

She closed her eyes for a moment. "More than you realize. This was my punishment, my ten bronze rings," she whispered.

Torag's head snapped up from his lazy exploration of her body. "What do you mean?"

She bit her lip. The resolve in his onyx eyes told her she wouldn't escape his question. "He didn't like my powers. He hated it when I turned. Looking back, I-I think he was afraid."

Torag's growl reverberated in her chest. "What did he do?"

"Every time I turned—" She swallowed. "Gyasi had... He had this black blood. Bottled. I don't know where he got it from. He'd fill an etching needle. It burned. It burned so badly. Every time I turned, he'd finish a part of the tattoo. At times, he forced me to turn, just so he could punish me. I think he wanted to finish his masterpiece. And then Lyx came and I... I volunteered so she wouldn't have to go through it too."

Torag pulled her into his arms. Their limbs entwined. His mouth fused with hers until she could no longer tell where he ended and she began.

When he broke the kiss, he traced his thumb

over her swollen lips. "Nobody will hurt you again. I promise, my love."

Overcome, achingly raw inside, Erisi kissed him to hide from his all-seeing gaze.

It wasn't as if he could protect her from what she was about to do.

No matter how hard he tried.

Chapter 29 - The Rohi

-Torag-

The happiness flooding through Torag's veins when he saw Erisi at dusk was short-lived. The tightness around her lips matched the anxiety in her eyes. Finally, she spoke the words he'd feared hearing since the messenger had shown up two days ago. "We need to talk."

His heart dropped. He'd known something had been weighing on her, and it looked like he was about to find out what it was. When she led him to their sparring spot, away from the eyes and ears of their family, he knew this wasn't going to go well.

Her fingers traced the grooves her demon had torn in the tree's trunk. "We need to hide," she whispered, her voice trembling.

Out of all the things he'd expected, never did he think he would hear those words from his fierce leader.

She turned to him. "Lucifer has made a deal with the Rohi."

"What?" He could only stare at the quiver of her bottom lip.

"Lucifer has sent his elite forces to help the Rohi take over this stronghold. The scout I sent out just got back. Lucifer wasn't bluffing. They're almost ready to attack. We have less than two days before they'll be at our gates."

He tried to unclench his fists and even out his voice. "How many did he send?"

"Seventy-five of his elites. Added to the two hundred warriors of the Rohi …"

Torag barely heard her hoarse voice over the ringing in his ears. He held onto the tree to stay standing as despair crashed over him. Almost three hundred well-trained warriors against the hundred-fifty in the Arav horde. He'd seen the damage one elite could do in the battle with Beelzebub. Now they needed to face—

Torag shook his head. "This can't be it. We can't just run." He waited for her to come up with a plan. He needed her to tell him she knew how to handle this, just like she'd handled everything else that had been thrown at her.

It was the despair in her eyes and the slump of her shoulders that did him in. Erisi's lack of fight told him there was no hope.

Still, he tried. "We have the advantage of the stronghold. Surely, we—"

"All of Lucifer's warriors can attack from the

sky with pure hellfire. The stronghold works against human armies and the typical demonic family, but it won't stop Lucifer. The only way we can ensure the survival of this family is by hiding."

Panicked thoughts flooded his mind. "What about the souls?"

"I'll ask Chandra to destroy the access mechanism. You told me there is another longer path to get to them, right?"

"Yes, but what if the Rohi—"

Her hand on his chest stopped the words from spilling out. "Does Krish know how to get to them?"

"No." He'd never trusted Ashoka's favorite chief. Ashoka didn't care where the souls were as long as they yielded new warriors. And as the demon with the strongest hellfire in the family, it had been Torag who had fed the souls. Not even Yerle knew how to get to them. Chandra could open the mechanism but didn't know how to navigate the maze.

"Thank hell," she breathed.

Torag could barely think. The Rohi would show no mercy. The scouts hadn't spared details about the forts the Rohi had razed in the north—the unspeakable horror the corpses had attested to and the screams of the shackled young they'd dragged from their homes. The thought of his family in the hands of slavers was too much to take.

This stronghold only mattered because it held his family. They needed to save them at all costs. Even if it meant hiding.

That's what they told their chiefs when they called them to the roof of the keep at midnight.

It's what they told their family on the training field, under the rays of the morning sun.

Chandra was in charge of moving the tools of his master crafters to the caves located a few hours flight to the south-west, away from the Rohi who would advance from the north-east. Yerle and his deal-makers would move the treasury and as much of the trading goods as possible. The horde would defend all of them during the trek, especially the young.

In a daze, Torag shouted orders as he prepared the young for their journey. He hadn't taken a deep breath since Erisi had broken the news. His shoulders strained under the weight of the responsibility of keeping them safe. When he crossed Erisi during the madness of preparations, he saw the same strain etched onto her face.

He grabbed her wrist and pulled her against him. "We'll be fine, Wildfire. This family will survive. We will make sure they do."

Swallowing, Erisi nodded. He brushed the back of his fingers along her jaw. "I'll see you in the caves."

"Torag..." She looked like she wanted to add something, but then shook her head. "Good luck.

I'll see you there."

* * *

Torag watched the sun set from the cave entrance in the Kirthar Range. Behind him, the Arav settled in the galleries and caves spread deep into the mountain. He heard Sura give her orders. Deeper into the cave, something crashed and Chandra cursed loud enough for the echo to carry.

Even before Erisi spoke, he felt her warmth at his back. She sounded as exhausted as he felt. "They're safe."

Something about her words fanned the embers of unease in his chest. All day he'd felt like he had missed something, but the blow of the news and the rush of their departure had stopped him from digging deeper.

When he turned to her, he found her face bathed in the golden rays of the setting sun. His heart stuttered.

He pulled her in front of him and circled his arms around her, relishing her heat against his bare skin. She rested the back of her head against his collarbone and sighed.

The thought struck him like lightning. Slowly, he let go of her and stepped back. She turned to him, eyes glistening with unshed tears.

"Why? Why would Lucifer tell you before the attack?" Torag swallowed and stared at her, hoping he was wrong. "Why, Erisi?"

A tear crept down her cheek unchecked, liquid gold in the last rays of the sun. "Lucifer wanted me to leave you to your fate and get back to him," she whispered.

Fear squeezed his heart tightly. She'd told him Lucifer wouldn't let go.

The fallen angel couldn't have her.

He refused to—

"He won't let me go, Torag."

He shook his head. "No. You're safe here. You're safe with us."

She reached for him, fingers against his cheek. He barely registered her touch as he scrambled for the words to convince her to stay.

"As long as I'm with you, this family will be hunted down. I'm probably the only wildfire demon in existence. I'm the weapon he wants more than anything to win over every demonic family. To subdue the archangels he's fighting."

He shook his head and grabbed her shoulders. "He can't have you."

Erisi's sad smile was worse than any tears she shed. "I'm leaving, Torag."

Chapter 30 - Shattered

-Erisi-

"You're not going anywhere."

Erisi fixed her eyes on the rock beneath her feet. She couldn't bear seeing the hurt she'd put on his face. His fingers tightened on her wrist, and she treasured the pain, his desire to hold her close. "I need to go before Lucifer wipes our family from existence. He won't give up. I can give him an advantage beyond anything he currently has in his forces."

"No." Despair tore his voice.

"They still have you. You've led this family for a millennium. Now you finally get the title that comes with the responsibility." She knew they'd be alright in the end. The Arav could rebuild under Torag's rule; they'd thrive again.

She tried not to think about what her life would be like away from them. There was nothing she could do to evade Fate. Maybe she could hide for a couple of years, but in the end…

"I'm coming with you," he said with finality.

"No!" Her stomach cramped at the thought. "You can't!"

His eyes narrowed. "You made your decision. Now I'm making mine. You can't stop me."

"The Arav need you. The young need you. You're the only one who knows how to get to the souls. You can't—"

"All the more reason for us to get back here once we tell Lucifer where he can shove his fucking position of general."

Erisi couldn't help it. She laughed until tears ran over her burning cheeks. A strange kind of madness seemed to take over her limbs, turning her movements erratic. Her chest buzzed with adrenaline. Her mind whirred until she felt faint.

When she caught her breath, she told him, "Even if you forget about everything you mean to this family, you can't go near Lucifer."

Torag crossed his arms over his broad chest and glared at her. "Why the hell not?"

"Because he will use you to break me. In the end, he'll get what he wants, and you will be gone."

The determination in his eyes didn't waver. *He isn't going to give up.*

Erisi felt the knot in her throat swell until she could barely speak. "Torag, please…"

"I'm coming with you, Wildfire."

He still held her wrist. He wouldn't let go.

Erisi knew what she needed to do. There was

only one way to stop him.

She would have to break him.

She had to tear her own heart from her chest.

If it meant keeping him safe—

She choked back a sob.

"You will stay here. That is an order." She straightened to her full height.

Torag scoffed and stared down at her.

"This is your last chance, Torag. Obey or you will feel the consequences." Somehow, she rediscovered the steel that lived in her soul and gathered it in her voice, in her eyes, in the tight line of her mouth. He couldn't see the shaking that started in her core. If he did, he would know and he would never give up.

"Don't do this, Erisi. There is no way you can stop me from coming with you."

Oh yes, there is.

"Get on your knees!" The shrill sound of her voice pained her ears.

The hurt flashing over his face felt like a punch to the gut. Torag stood tall, like she knew he would.

"You. Get. Down. Now." Every word burned like acid on her lips.

She infused hellfire into her chains. Behind her, a heavy silence reigned. She could feel the eyes of their family on her back.

Hoping they would heed her warning, she told them, "If anyone feels the need to intervene, they will be punished alongside their new leader."

Thank hell they couldn't see her face.

Her chains slashed his legs, and the disbelief in his eyes took the last of her breath away. He went down, eyes still locked with hers.

Hearing movement behind her, Erisi warned them once more, "Stay away."

Torag shook his head at whoever wanted to charge her in the back.

Still protecting his family. Always protecting his family.

It was the perfect reminder of why she needed to follow through with the cruelty despite the agony in her soul.

Erisi whipped a chain around one of his wrists, the other one around his upper body. The keening sound coming from his lips echoed in the dark place inside of her that Gyasi had created.

The blood pooling in her mouth told her she'd bitten through her bottom lip. It was the taste of her betrayal.

She was breaking him. Her heel was crushing the fragile trust he'd gifted her with. Still, he was fighting to get up, fighting the inevitable.

"Fuck, Torag. Stay down." Her voice broke. If he looked up, she wouldn't be able to hide the tears streaming down her face.

He didn't. He fought her control, his free hand pulling on the chain around his wrist.

She pleaded, "Stay down. Please."

"No." It was more of a growl than a word. The male turned into a beast.

Erisi closed her eyes. She knelt and put her palm against his chest, pushing her hellfire into him. He convulsed without a sound. The thud of him hitting the rock shook her to the core.

His eyes opened, dark onyx in agony.

Throat tight to the point of pain, she was choking. His black eyes were unfocused despite being locked on hers. Torag had well and truly checked out, and she was to blame. His entire body was taut. The muscles of his neck were corded as he fought the steel chain wrapped around his upper body.

Her hellfire was pulsing, vibrating through her entire body with the need to destroy whatever was hurting the demon she loved.

Except it was her.

She was breaking him, destroying the soul she had come to love, bringing back all the pain he harbored from his past.

The hellfire slowly bled out of her chains until only the smallest of flames remained. But Torag didn't realize he could break free. He was in a world where he was powerless once more, unable to fight back against a greater power.

Her heart shattered.

Without turning, Erisi gave her final orders. "Make sure he doesn't come after me. None of you can follow me, or I will destroy you. Torag will lead this family, like he's always done.

You can't fight the Rohi; they've forged an alliance that makes them unstoppable. Find another place to live. Regroup. Thrive."

She could feel the hatred crashing over her in waves from the family behind her. Her family. It poured salt into the wide-open wound she'd inflicted on herself.

She needed them too resentful to follow her to Lucifer. She needed them all to be safe.

Erisi opened her mouth to say goodbye, then closed it without a sound. None of the demons wanted her last words.

"Erisi..."

Steeling herself against Mei's broken voice, she stepped into the long shadows of dusk, fighting to stay upright. Her chains stayed behind, no longer a symbol of her freedom and strength. She'd used them to break the male she loved. To break whatever good was still left in her.

Without looking back, she took flight.

To Lucifer.

To bind herself once more to a powerful demon who would destroy her.

If it kept her family safe, she was willing to pay the price.

Chapter 31 - Decisions

-Torag-

The air was thick and coppery as he forced it through his parched throat. The darkness around him was only broken by howls of tortured souls and sobs of broken beings chained to the rough wall.

A lash of hellfire tore at his back, ripping the barely healed skin across his shoulder blades. Another one, and another, the rhythm too irregular for him to brace for the pain. His heart pulsed in the raw skin of his chest as the knife peeled his skin. The agony of the flaying, inch by torturous inch, sharpened until—

The hoarse laughter of his slave masters rang in his ears as he went down.

It had taken them a century, but they'd finally broken him. It was his last thought before he lost consciousness at their feet.

When Torag woke, it took him a long time to realize more than a millennium had passed since that day. Sura crouched next to him, her earthy eyes cautious as if she feared he would attack at any moment.

His heart rate slowed to a dull thumping at the back of his skull. Sweat dried in the cool air whispering through the cave opening.

He was safe.

They're safe.

Erisi's voice echoed in his ears, and the agony bloomed again. His heart rate spiked.

Even before he looked around the cave, he knew there would be no small demon with ice in her eyes. She'd left them all behind.

She'd left him.

His chest felt like it was being flayed again.

He needed to be by her side when she faced that bastard lord of hers. He got up on legs that wouldn't stop shaking.

"What are your orders?" Sura's voice wavered.

He couldn't face her. Couldn't face the doubt in her eyes. He looked outside the cave where the shadows of night were being chased by first light.

Erisi had been gone for hours. She wasn't coming back.

He swallowed hard when Sura touched his shoulder. "Your orders?"

He wanted to tell her he didn't know. He wanted to take flight and chase after Erisi. Protect the one demon in this world who needed his protection least. He wasn't supposed to lead this family. He was a slave. He'd always be a slave, no matter how many responsibilities he took. No matter how much time went by.

Sura's hand was still there.

His family still needed him. He was the closest they had to a leader. And he'd die protecting them, if that is what it took. Maybe that was enough.

"Send—" He tried to clear the tightness in his throat. "Send scouts to Dera Rawal. Make sure they remain unseen."

He tore his gaze away from the sky.

Erisi left him. She'd chosen to sacrifice herself for this family.

He needed to respect that decision.

Hell knew he understood the protectiveness that drove her to it.

He pushed his fist against his pounding heart in a desperate attempt to contain the pain and turned to look at his family.

"Post guards on strategic locations in the Kirthar range. We need to see them coming if they discover where we hide," he said. Sura nodded and strode off into the caves.

Torag saw Varun get his blanket and offer it to Khloe, who was shivering in the cave's draft. Mei was watching him, her brown eyes grave.

This was his family.

This was where he belonged.

Even with his soul shredded, that much he knew.

Chapter 32 - Consequences

-Erisi-

By the time Erisi touched down on Mount Roraima, her shattered soul was buried in its steel coffin once more. Her dreams had fled in the wind during her desperate flight.

She was ready to face her leader.

The bronze gates opened, and with it came a blast of the chilled air that whistled over the courtyard.

When she walked into the throne room, she found Lucifer with three elite warriors, all carrying the tattoo of the coiled snake Lucifer had chosen as his mark. Given her luck, it didn't surprise her to find a scowling Beelzebub standing guard near the throne.

"My lord." Erisi knelt.

"Stand." Lucifer's voice could have cut flesh. "Care to explain what happened?"

She went with the truth. "I led the Arav to safety."

"You chose to disobey my orders." He stared at her.

"I did."

"And still you show up here?" Lucifer circled her. She felt his presence looming behind her. The demon inside her bucked against the threat.

"I never intended to run from you. I'm just not willing to give you the Arav."

Lucifer's voice washed over her. "I pegged you right, at the very least. I didn't take you for a coward."

Erisi stood tall and awaited his verdict.

"Normally, I'd kill you, of course. Nice and slow to burn off some of my…disappointment."

She knew he was deliberately stoking her anguish, using his positioning behind her and the slow drawl of his words. And still it worked.

"I have big plans for you though." His breath whispered along the back of her neck while he let the silence linger. "Beelzebub, care to explain what I did to the last demon who failed me and who didn't get the luxury of true death? Skip to the good parts."

Beelzebub's grin gave her chills. "Removal of your warrior tattoo. Flaying. Evisceration. Breaking your bones over, and over, and over again."

Nothing she hadn't imagined during her flight then.

"Obviously, no general position for you." Erisi heard the sneer in Lucifer's voice. "Don't worry, you'll be my greatest weapon, the tool of my wrath. Your legend will rise to unknown heights."

As she felt him move away from behind her, she twisted around, fearing—

The ham-sized fist of the largest elite hit her in the face. The crack of her nose came with a blinding pain shooting up her skull. The world faded into a dizzying blur.

Closing her eyes, Erisi listened. She tried to tune out the buzzing in her ears. There was a movement to her right. Dropping low, she sliced at waist-level with the knife she pulled from her boot. A gurgled groan reached her ears. When hard footfalls sounded in front of her, she pushed her hellfire out around her and ran toward the edge of the room. With her back against the wall, she tried to open her eyes once more.

Her vision still swam, but she could make out three large shapes charging at her. Losing the knife, she pulled both daggers from the scabbards around her thighs. The hellfire-infused blades hit two of the warriors in the chest.

As they crashed to the ground, she focused on the third. A hellfire blast slammed into her stomach right before Beelzebub rammed her against the wall, his forearm pressed against her throat. Struggling to breathe, Erisi pushed both her palms against his chest and shoved all her remaining powers into her hellfire. His grip loosened enough for her to suck in a painful breath and ram her knee in Beelzebub's groin.

He staggered back. "You damn hellhound."

While he was still off-balance, she stepped forward and kicked him hard in the stomach. She only just evaded the sweep of his dagger.

Lucifer's calm voice next to her ear triggered terror in her chest. "Too bad you couldn't just fucking obey me."

The dual power of his hellfire and angelfire seared through the back of her neck where his hand gripped her, burning her skin and spinal cord until her limbs failed to obey her.

She sank to the cold marble, gasping for breath.

"Impressive. You killed one elite, knocked the others out for days, and still won against this useless bastard." Lucifer hefted Beelzebub up by the throat. "I have a mission for you, Beelzebub, to redeem the reputation she single-handedly destroyed. Not once, but twice now. Hunt down the Arav. Deliver them personally to the head of the Rohi family like I promised him."

Powerless, Erisi watched as Beelzebub staggered from the room. With her unable to utter a word or move a muscle, despair sliced her insides with vicious claws.

As Lucifer walked away, she tried to reach for him. To stop him.

Her body didn't obey even the most desperate of attempts. Her skull felt like it'd been split by an axe, while her limbs remained numb.

Wildfire pulsed at the core of her, demanding to be released.

It would heal her, then kill every soul in the throne room. Lucifer wouldn't stand a chance.

But her blood oath as his elite meant killing him would destroy her own soul. At best, she'd die the true death. At worst she'd survive soulless, powerless.

Her life for a world without the fallen angel...

But the Rohi would still hunt her family. Even if she survived, she wouldn't be able to chase down Beelzebub. She wouldn't be able to warn them.

She needed to get away.

Desperately she tried to contain the darkness inside her.

It meant healing took too long.

But there was still a chance.

When she finally regained some basic muscle functioning, she crawled to the bottom of the steps Lucifer's throne rested on. "Plea—Please."

"Speak up if you want to be heard," Lucifer told her from somewhere above her.

Erisi shoved every ounce of strength she'd recovered into her voice. "I beg you." A cough tore through her. "I beg you to le—let them go."

Heavy footfalls were the only answer.

Lucifer crouched next to her, his green eyes cold and calculating as he stared down at her trembling body. "Why would I do that? I made a deal with the Rohi and I'm loath to break my word to an ally."

"I'll do anything," she whispered.

He scoffed. "You'll do anything I want regardless."

Erisi hated the weakness she showed, hated the contempt in his eyes. Still, she tried for the sake of her family. "Please…"

The corner of Lucifer's mouth twitched. "You sure beg pretty." Despair dragged her heart down when she saw his response written all over his face. "The answer is still no."

She'd failed.

She couldn't save them.

The life she'd brought to her three beautiful young would be snuffed out. As would Mei's.

Torag would die, his last memory of her breaking him.

Her existence was death and destruction for anyone she touched, anyone she dared to love.

Lyx's cries echoed in her ears. The darkness in her bloomed and twisted. Pulsed relentlessly as despair slowly stripped her of her control.

Once again, she'd failed to protect the ones she loved.

She gave in to the darkness. Wildfire burned her alive and took what remained of her soul.

At least the damn bastard would finally witness the wildfire legend come to life.

Even if it was the last thing he'd see.

Chapter 33 - Lost

-Torag-

Torag was systematically burning down anything flammable in his vicinity. There was something utterly satisfying about watching his hellfire destroy everything and seeing the ashes spread in the wind.

His mind kept playing tricks on him. He heard her voice in the air whistling through the trees. He thought he heard her cry out. The blue of her eyes was all around him in the clear sky.

He slammed his fist down against the rock. The crack reverberated through his aching arm, but the pain didn't drown out the craving in his soul.

He wanted this madness to end. He wanted his rational mind back.

She made her choice and left. He made his choice and stayed.

They both did what they thought was best for this family.

But he wanted to be fucking selfish. He wanted her. He wanted to forget about his responsibilities and find the missing part of his soul.

At night, he led scouting missions through the mountains and to the stronghold. During the day, he plotted with his chiefs, trying to find a way to take their home back. The hours in between, Torag spent lost. Shouting into the fucking wind like a whining bastard.

He was done.

Taking flight, he pushed himself as high as he could go. When the air grew thin, he dropped in a backward fall, only to be reminded of her warm body in his arms, her laugh on the wind.

His landing was more of a crash, his hellfire setting the dry grass around him alight in a useless display of power.

A sob broke through his whirling thoughts. Slowly, Torag turned to find a terrified child with his wide eyes full of tears.

That's it. I'm an asshole. Somehow, he'd managed to scar a child for life.

He didn't particularly care for humans. They were the source of power and growth for any demonic family, useful beasts with souls roaming the earth, nothing more.

But any young was worth protecting. No matter the species.

Another belief he'd shared with Er—

Torag cut off his thoughts before they could

go there. Before his heart split down the middle once more.

Frozen in place, the child looked like a scared bunny facing a caracal. When Torag took a cautious step back, something snapped in the little one, making him run like the wind down the mountain slope.

Torag cursed.

What was he doing here? He was wasting powers he should be saving for their missions at night, was spending time he should be using for plotting.

His entire flight back to the cave, he berated himself. He had made his choice. He knew his family needed him, and they always, always came first.

When he arrived, Sura was standing at the entrance, looking out over the rocky valley at her feet.

"Burned down enough trees for the day?" Yerle appeared from behind Sura's back, the concern in his eyes belying the playful tone of his voice.

"I graduated from burning forests to scaring little humans," Torag grumbled.

Yerle put his hands over his heart. "You do me proud."

After punching him on the shoulder, Torag turned to his war chief. "Any news from our scouts?"

"Lucifer's warriors haven't returned to Dera

Rawal since two days after Erisi—" She swallowed her words at the look on his face and rushed to the rest of her report. "Nothing's changed except the amount of demons they have in their prison. The Rohi are raiding every demonic stronghold in the area. They feel untouchable behind our walls."

Putting a palm to the rough rock, Torag pondered their options. "Whoever fled from the raids might be willing to join us."

Sura shook her head. "They... It's not as if they let anyone go. Whoever the Rohi didn't slaughter, they've enslaved."

"Let's check to make sure. Are there any abandoned strongholds we can claim as our new home?" It would pain him to give up on Dera Rawal, but there were more important considerations than pride and nostalgia.

"The Rohi have stationed a small part of their horde at the strongholds they raided. We could take one of the forts without too many losses, but they're nowhere near as large or as strong as Dera Rawal. And they'd know where we are."

Torag sighed. "There is one way to get into our stronghold unseen, but I don't want to use it. There is another entrance through the caves that house the souls, but it would mean blowing up the cave opening and giving the Rohi access. If our attack goes wrong, we'd lose the souls."

The souls she'd fed. They'd have her eyes when they turned fledgling.

He swallowed hard and forced himself to focus on the conversation.

"That should only be a last resort," Sura agreed. "If we ever decide to use that route, we'd have to move the souls somewhere else."

He tried to think. "The Rohi are spreading themselves thin though. If they leave a dozen warriors behind at every site, their horde might have already dwindled from two hundred to closer to our numbers."

"True, but they have the stronghold. Even one to one, they have the advantage. Not to mention, all the new slaves they're breaking in for their horde."

Torag flinched and cleared his throat. "What if we thin their ranks even further? We take out the Rohi warriors in each of the other strongholds, moving on to the next fort before the reinforcements arrive. If they send enough warriors to take back the other forts or to chase us, we can battle them out in the open instead of behind the stronghold walls."

"Divide and conquer. Let me talk to Chandra to see if he and his master crafters have the materials to prepare our attacks." Sura's earthy eyes held hope, lifting Torag's spirits a little.

He stayed at the entrance, staring outside. When someone sank down next to him, he expected it to be Yerle. Maybe Chandra.

Instead, he found Mei.

She sat so close to the edge of the cliff that

Torag's hands itched to pull her back to safety. Her legs dangled over the side, swinging back and forth.

"Rumor has it you need anger management." She sounded so much like Erisi that it took his breath away.

Her smaller hand found his. The newly formed calluses on her palm made him realize she was becoming the warrior she'd always wanted to be. He wished he could share the pride that washed over him with Erisi, that he could see her smile at Mei. Choking up, he squeezed Mei's hand.

She leaned into him and sighed. "You know you're an idiot, right?"

His head snapped up. "What the hell, Mei?"

"She needs you. Why are you still here?"

Mei didn't let him pull his hand back. Torag could feel her eyes burning into the side of his face as she waited for his answer.

"She's the strongest demon to walk this earth. She doesn't need me." His voice cracked.

"Everyone needs someone. And she needs you. Even more than we need you." The quiet conviction in her naive words felt like a dagger to the heart.

Torag softly brushed her sleek hair away from her face and tried to find words.

Her sad smile told him she understood.

He stood and walked into the darkness of the cave, looking for a place to hide from the renewed agony in solitude.

Mei's voice rang out behind him. "When I turn out to be right, I'm so going to say, 'I told you so'."

Chapter 34 - Revelation

-Torag-

The flutter of wings got closer to the rocks he and the warriors were crouching behind. He gestured to Sura to get ready for their ambush.

She nodded as she infused hellfire in her sword and beckoned the warriors she'd brought along. "Now!"

Torag charged. He needed the outlet for his unrelenting pain. Every slice of his trusted sword, every drop of blood coating his bare chest silenced the fear that he'd made the wrong decision. Only when Sura threw a dagger into his shoulder did he snap out of his battle rage.

"You damn idiot. Can you stop killing our sources of information now?"

Pulling the dagger from his shoulder, he growled, "Care to not mutilate your leader?"

"I've been shouting at you since you charged. This was the only way I could get through to you."

His shoulders slumped. This was bad. His strength lied in strategic thinking and patience, but both seemed to have vanished along with Erisi.

Not meeting Sura's eyes, he turned and surveyed the damage. One demon was so badly hurt it would take weeks for him to recover to the point of talking. A dozen others laid scattered across the rocks, heads and bodies separated, blood tainting the stone below their mangled bodies. At least they'd ambushed the scouts well away from the family's hiding spot...

"Fuck!" He threw his sword down, disgusted with himself.

"Yep." Sura decapitated the wounded demon with a hack of her blade before sheathing the weapon. "At least Yerle managed to grab one before you got to him. Let's hope he has something to tell us."

Torag looked back and found Yerle kneeling on a demon's chest. By the time the pale-skinned Rohi scout was dragged back to their cave and shackled, Torag's rage had cooled.

Running his dagger over the side of his finger, he watched a bead of crimson well up. The demon's eyes followed the drops of blood down to the ground. The Rohi tattoo circling the scout's neck moved as he swallowed.

"What were you doing here?" Torag asked, creating a thin red trail on the inside of his own arm with the dagger. He remembered all the techniques his slave masters had used on him. Ever since he'd arrived at Dera Rawal, he'd fought to abolish torture as a means of punishment and training in his family. He'd always shown his enemies the mercy of a quick death.

But he was willing to overcome his aversion if it meant getting the truth from the enemy in front of him. If it meant keeping his family safe.

"Looking for you." The demon's green eyes were still locked on the blade as it moved.

It made sense that the Rohi wanted them gone. Revenge was a powerful motivation for war, and while the Rohi were clearly the stronger family at this point, having an enemy with nothing left to lose was dangerous.

"What are your leader's plans if he's able to capture us?" Torag asked.

The demon pressed his lips together.

The bloodlust still coursing through Torag's veins reignited. "Make sure I don't kill him," he growled.

Sura sounded more than a tad amused. "Of course. Should he still be able to talk after, or do we have time to get the truth out of him?"

"I guess he should still be able to talk." Torag crouched down next to his prisoner. "Maybe I should start with the legs. Don't need those for talking."

Sura chuckled. The demon turned even paler, a ghostly white against the darkness of the stone behind him.

One quick movement and the cotton pant leg was sliced open, from ankle to thigh. A few red drops tinged the gray fabric.

Tracing the dagger up the demon's left leg, Torag reached the outside of a shaking knee. Slowly, he pushed the blade into the soft tissue. With every inch, the keening sound coming from the demon increased in volume. When the full length of his dagger was embedded in the joint, Torag gave a vicious twist as he pulled it out. The shackled male broke with a high-pitched scream that echoed around the cave.

By now, his family had gathered to watch the spectacle. They'd never seen Torag lose control over his rage. They didn't know the darkness inside of him born from his masters' cruelty. If it got his family back in the safety of their home...

"Keep the young away," Torag growled. Yerle nodded and left to intercept them before they arrived.

Pulling his dagger out, he laid the bloodied blade against the top of the male's shin. Terrified green eyes found his. While the demon trembled in fear, Torag angled the knife, digging the sharp edge into his skin. Nice and slow, Torag peeled the scout's skin from his knee to the bridge of his foot.

Torag stood and waited until the screams died out. He dangled the skin he'd stripped from the male in front of his wide eyes. "Ready to talk now? You must realize you're dead anyway. The difference will be how slow and painful your death will be."

The demon hung his head. "What do you want to know?"

"What are your leader's plans for us? With the stronghold?" He dropped the skin in the dirt and stared the scout down.

"I—" The shackles around his wrists clanged as the demon twisted in pain. "I don't know everything."

Torag's blade had reached the male's abdomen. Evisceration was the torture technique he abhorred most, but it was effective enough for him to consider it if the scout didn't talk soon.

"W—wait. I'll tell you what I do know." The words came out fast, falling one over another. "Ishan has his eye on the Arav young. The prison has already been prepared, the drill masters are raring to go, and Ishan is furious we still haven't found a trace of you."

Torag saw red. Like hell they'd ever get their hands on the young.

The male was still rattling on. "Lucifer made us a promise, and Ishan is furious that he's pulled back his warriors ever since the wildfire bitch fled. At least that bastard vowed to destroy her for her betrayal. And—"

The words sunk in. His heart stopped beating.

Torag slammed his palm next to the male's face and leaned in closely. "What did you just say?" he bit out.

The male cowered and whispered, "Lucifer promised to break that wildf—"

The rest of the male's words drowned in the storm of thoughts crashing through him. Struggling to stay sane, he turned to face Sura. She needed to get the male away from him before he killed—

Instead of his chief's face, the first demon he saw was Mei. She didn't say '*I told you so*', but the tears in her eyes as she stared at the enemy scout slew him. Her fear echoed in his chest.

Torag went down to his knees. The air became so thin he could no longer breathe. Sura crouched next to him, but he couldn't understand a word she was saying.

"Everyone out. Out. Now!" He slammed his palms on the rock below his knees, relishing the pain shooting up his arms, using it to feed the fury. Wings ripped from him. Hellfire flared bright on his hands. He saw the world through a haze of red.

Torag looked at the shackled male thrashing against his restraints, trying to get away. One blow of Torag's sword broke the chains on the male's wrists; the second broke the chains between his ankles. He threw his sword to the enemy scout before pulling out his daggers.

"Fight me."

The enemy turned demon, black spikes covering ivory scales. Pale orange infused the sword, and Torag lamented how short the fight would be.

He dropped his daggers to even the stakes a little. Killing a powerless target would take every ounce of satisfaction from it.

The pain slicing his side when the sword hit fueled his hellfire. Closing his hands around the male's throat, he pushed half his power along his arm. The male struggled against his hold. The whites of his eyes became bloodshot. Rancid breath hit Torag in the face until his enemy could no longer breathe at all. In the end, only vertebrae remained between his hands, the scales and flesh burned away by his fire. Ripping the head clean off its spine, Torag crashed the scout's skull against the rock.

It wasn't enough.

The fire consumed him.

Roaring, Torag slammed his body against the cave wall. This entire place was wrong. He wanted to tear it apart with his bare hands. If the rock caved in on him, it would be a fitting death for the fucking idiot who'd had it all wrong.

He had made the wrong decision.

Splinters of stone embedded in his fists and arms as he kept pounding, charging. He needed the pain. He needed—

Despair filled his lungs, making every breath toxic agony.

He'd left her in Lucifer's hands for weeks. She hadn't been the fallen angel's warrior. She hadn't been his right hand on his quest for power, like he'd imagined all along.

The bastard intended to break her.

Or worse. What if—

What if Lucifer had killed her for her betrayal?

He roared.

A demon charged him. He slammed the earthy form against the wall, only to get hit by another demon. And another. And then the next. Until several held him down.

Torag fought them all. His body bucked against the steel grip of their hands. None of the words they shouted at him registered.

Wrong. He'd gotten it so fucking wrong.

And she'd suffered for it.

Chapter 35 - Into the darkness

-Torag-

It was time to use his fury for something useful.

Torag strapped his sword to his back and sheathed his daggers. His fingers ran over her chains, which were wrapped around his waist. For a beat, Torag considered taking them, but they'd get in his way.

Fate knew he'd need his reflexes, skill, and wits to survive what he was about to do.

Already, he'd lost too much time due to his mindless rage. He'd spent hours shackled to the wall until Sura had felt it was safe to release him. He didn't blame her. He would have brought down the entire cave if she'd let him.

He couldn't bear the thought of her broken at the feet of the bastard she served.

He struggled not to think about other scenarios before he lost it again.

There was only one being who knew enough

about Lucifer to prepare him for what he was about to do. And she wouldn't give the information willingly.

It was time to face his worst fears.

"So when are we going?" Yerle popped up next to him with his crossbow on his back.

Torag froze. "Oh, hell no, you're not coming with me."

"You can try to stop me, but it won't help."

Three more warriors showed up, and Torag's jaw dropped. "What are you doing here?"

"Sura told us the only reason we shouldn't follow you was if we were dead. Are you going to kill us or can we come?" the archer asked.

"Suraaaaa!" Torag's voice thundered through the cave.

His war chief grinned as she appeared from one of the galleries. "You called, my lord?"

Her insolence only stoked his temper. "What the hell do you think you're doing?" he fumed.

Sura tapped her finger against her chin. "I guess I'm trying to make sure my leader doesn't kill himself. Seemed like a good plan."

"Sending more demons along to die is not going to help."

Yerle spoke up. "Do you honestly think I'm letting you face Lucifer alone?" His narrowed amber eyes sparked with rage, an emotion he rarely showed.

"I can't let—"

"You're not letting me do anything, Torag. I'm

choosing to come with you so you don't have to face Lucifer by yourself." Yerle's voice rose until it broke through Torag's daze. "If I wish to join you in death, that is my choice. Suggesting anything else is an insult to my name, contempt for the power I have. Do you understand?"

Torag stared at his shaking friend. The heavy burden he'd carried for over a millennium—to keep his family safe—lightened at the realization that he wasn't carrying it alone. He never had.

He swallowed the knot away. "We're not going to Lucifer yet."

Yerle frowned.

"We need to find out what we'll walk into at Lucifer's base. How to get in unseen. And what Lucifer values more than his revenge on Erisi. I only know one being who might tell us."

Realization dawned on his friend's face. "All the more reason to take us along. Because you sure as fuck won't be facing Nakwatha alone."

Torag held out his hand. Yerle grabbed his forearm and pulled Torag in his embrace. "You're not alone," he whispered for only Torag to hear. "I'm with you every step of the way."

* * *

After a day and a half flight west, ocean silt coated Torag's skin. The jagged rocks lining the coastline far below him bit into the waves crashing on moonlit shores.

Soon, he'd face the demon who had made him

into what he was. Torag wondered if she'd recognize his face.

She should. Nakwatha had personally forced each of the bronze rings into his skin. His worst punishments had been at her hands.

He hoped she hadn't changed her rituals in the past millennium. She'd always been adamant about performing her morning ceremony in the temple on Huaca de los Sacrificios.

Heading further inland, Torag landed on the rocky surface of the mountain overlooking the valley. Nakwatha's palace, temples, and courts sprawled along the earthen platforms and terraces towering over the green of the river valley. Underneath it all, the slaves suffered in the dark.

"Caral Supe," Yerle murmured, his voice holding the same memories churning in Torag's mind. "They really made something of the place. Most of these buildings weren't here when we were around."

Torag couldn't hold back the bitter laugh burning in his tight throat. "Building her legacy one stone and one sacrifice at a time."

"How about we end it today?"

Torag nodded once, heart thundering at the thought of destroying the root of Caral's evil.

Nakwatha's adherence to her rituals showed. The sentries were in the same location as they used to be, their eyes still turned inward toward the palace and temples. Their duty had always been more about catching those trying to escape than about intruders.

Torag and Yerle led their warriors on foot from the mountains to the east along shrubs and reeds lining the river bed, circumventing the north-eastern watchtower.

A well-aimed crossbow bolt dispatched the guard at the entry to the slave tunnel underneath the northern mound. Torag dragged the female behind a few rocks, hoping she'd stay undetected long enough for them to cross the complex to the morning temple.

The Arav warriors took out the two guards posted inside. The rest of the long corridor was dark and deserted at this time of night. The slaves and mercenaries trained by Nakwatha required rest to recover from the torture and abuse they suffered during the day. Sweat rolled down Torag's back at the memory of the quarters they slept in, shackled, pressed together in the hot damp air.

Even a millennium later, he could walk the tunnel in the dark. His fingers trailed along the earthen wall for guidance, occasionally interrupted by a passage to the slave quarters and the maze-like shortcuts underneath the buildings.

His chest ached at the sameness of it all. Nothing had changed.

He shook his pounding head.

He had changed. Yerle had too.

She no longer had power over them.

Beneath the morning temple, they stopped.

Torag motioned for the three warriors to stay down and guard their backs. Yerle followed him up the earth steps to the upper level. They took their positions in the shadows just inside the temple.

An hour before dawn, flute music drifted from the flat roof as the musicians took their place to announce Nakwatha's grand entrance. The haunting tones filtered in through the square lighting holes in the ceiling, and Torag's stomach cramped at the sound. He raised his sword slowly, taking strength from the solid weight in his hand.

A lithe female holding a still form in her arms stepped through the stone archway, followed by three large demons. Torag brought down his sword, hacking into the shoulder of the guard closest to him. Before the male could draw his weapon, Torag sliced his throat with his dagger.

He staggered back when a blast of hellfire hit him in the chest, but the male who'd attacked him crumbled with Yerle's sword in his back. The third guard was writhing on the floor with a knife in his eye. Torag cut his head off.

It rolled along the polished floor before Nakwatha's feet who had simply turned to watch their fight, a cruel smile hugging the corners of her lush mouth. She dropped the sacrifice she was carrying. The small body hit the ground, blood still streaming from the child's slit throat and cracked-open ribcage. Red splattered on

Nakwatha's white tunic, and the smell of copper mixed with the sickly-sweet scent of incense wafting from the braziers.

She stood tall, her glossy black braid touching the shining floor. Her hard eyes locked on his face. "You returned. I could have sworn you were smarter."

If not for Erisi, Torag didn't know if he would have.

"Still praying to gods you don't believe in, I see." He gestured to the black floor dripping with the blood of her young sacrifice, trying to hide how much the sight affected him.

"Still upset over a little spilled blood. You haven't changed." Her soft voice was filled with contempt.

Nakwatha stepped over her victim to approach him, her bare feet slick with blood. "Don't you see what I'm doing? I strengthen myself with the blood of those who have raw power singing in their veins. I can sense it." The midnight black of her eyes sparked with zeal. "I can sense the power under their skin. Taking their blood gives me more. If anything, I pray to myself in the morning. I'm the only goddess around these parts, *slave*."

The word still cut deep.

Torag almost felt the lash of her metal-studded whip in the bite of her voice. The flute music still floating around the temple triggered too many memories. It had been the sound to which every punishment at her hands had taken place.

"Get on your knees." For a beat, Nakwatha's voice merged with the memory of Erisi's, and Torag felt the cracks in his soul widen.

Yerle's light tone cut through the darkness invading his mind. "Still delusional, I see."

Turning her head, she sneered at Yerle. "Still following him around like a lost wolf pup. Aren't you tired of living in his shadow yet?"

His friend stared at her in silence, his smile unaffected by her words.

No longer fixed by Nakwatha's cruel gaze, Torag regained his strength. "Your era ends today," he whispered as he took a step forward.

Crouching next to her sacrifice, the child's blood further soaking into the flowing tunic, she reached into the cracked cavity of his chest. Her bloody hands emerged with his heart. "I've experimented. Blood and death always drew me in. They feed this hunger in me, the power lurking in my soul."

Dark red flames raced from her hands, over her arms and to her chest, until she was alight.

Torag stared. Her hellfire was supposed to be a pale orange. And she hadn't even turned demon.

His heart clenched, as if her cold fingers had reached into his chest and squeezed the power from him. How was he supposed to win and force the truth out of her?

His mouth went dry. She was too powerful.

Someone with less power but better training

than you can still win.

As Erisi's words came back to him, he pushed down his fears. Nakwatha had never relied on her own powers. She'd never had to, surrounded by her guards. Just because she possessed the strength of dark red hellfire didn't mean she had Erisi's prowess. He could still win.

He would win.

"Yerle, make sure no guards come to her rescue." His hellfire flamed red on the metal of his sword.

"On it. Shout if you need my help."

Torag kept his eyes on the female in front of him. He caught the moment she drew hellfire into her palm and dodged it easily. She moved slowly. Her tells were obvious.

Hope surged in his chest.

"You can't win, slave. Give up. Fall to your knees and I might forgive your insolence."

Never would he kneel for her again.

Torag charged, only to change direction at the last moment. Nakwatha howled when his sword cut into her thigh. This close, he couldn't avoid the blast of fire burning his side. Or the one that hit his shoulder. His sword fell to the stone floor.

Outside, metal clanged. It sounded like Yerle was in a fight of his own.

Shaking with the agony of his injuries, he tried to breathe through the bursts of fear.

Close. He needed her close. He'd use her damn arrogance against her.

He huddled in a crouch, slumped forward, hand pressed to his injured shoulder. His other hand inched toward the sheath strapped to his side. He didn't have to fake the whimper as his fingers touched his raw flesh and the bloody blisters.

With a wide smile and hellfire on her palms, Nakwatha approached to finish the job.

His grip on the hilt of his dagger tightened.

A little closer.

Her nails dug into his shoulder. Her hellfire destroyed the scales and muscle underneath her palm. He bit through the pain and shot up. With one hand, he grabbed her chin; the other slammed the dagger through her ear, into her skull.

Her shrill scream made his ears ring. He forced his hellfire through the dagger, straight into her brain. She slumped forward without another sound.

He hoped he hadn't truly killed her.

For so long, he'd wanted nothing more than to face her. Slay her for the agony she'd put him and Yerle and so many others through.

Now all he wanted was to get to Erisi.

First, they needed to get out of here with Nakwatha's lifeless body.

Torag charged outside and found a grinning Yerle, who sliced a warrior's throat and kicked the female's lifeless body toward a few other bodies. "All done. I ran into a small patrol. Is she dead yet?"

"Can't. I haven't been able to interrogate her yet, but we need to get out of here before we have her entire horde on our tails."

Torag retrieved Nakwatha, slinging her limp form over his shoulder. They descended to the slave tunnel and found the Arav warriors on guard, unharmed.

Torag thanked Fate that the darkened corridor was still deserted. In the distance, the faint light told him morning was coming fast.

We need to move.

They didn't get far before the drums started. Low, insistent thrums that echoed around the tunnel. The shouts and howls followed soon after. Gut roiling, Torag drew his sword.

"Run!" Yerle shouted at him. "Get her out of here. If they get her back…"

Torag looked at his friend, at their warriors. "I can't—"

"You fucking can and you will. She needs to die today. And you need to get Erisi back. Go!"

Their enemies came from the southern end of the corridor. Others thundered down the stairs from the temple. Torag turned toward the faint light at the northern end and ran. An arrow whistled past his head, and he ran harder.

There was no time to scout the outside, so he launched himself in the air. The next bolt from somewhere on the ground hit him in the thigh.

He groaned and tightened his hold on the burden on his shoulder.

He had left his best friend to die.

His wings jerked at the thought. He needed to turn back. He couldn't—

A twitch of the female's fingers dangling against his chest reminded him he couldn't return. If the Caral got their leader back, Yerle's fate would be worse than death.

I'll return. I'll get the most powerful demon on earth and come for you, my friend.

He pushed his wings harder, battled the winds to move faster. He didn't dare look back.

By the time he reached Lucifer's territory, his heart was pumping hard enough for his ribs to hurt. His lungs strained, and every muscle in his body burned.

He crash-landed amid the golden grasses of the Gran Sabana. When he looked up at the bright blue sky, he expected a horde to crash down on him. He couldn't even lift his arm to defend himself. They'd slaughter—

The skies were empty as far as the eye could see. No Caral warriors. None of Lucifer's elites. *Yet.*

He tossed the limp female to the side and slumped on his back. Chest heaving, he tried to think. The outline of a plan formed in his mind.

He sat up and pulled the dagger from Nakwatha's skull. Rolling her over, he planted the blade in the knot at the back of her neck. He couldn't help his smile at the irony of using the same technique Erisi had used to subdue him when he still wanted her gone.

Now he'd use it to get her back.

Sitting back, he waited for Nakwatha to wake.

He was ready to trade his past for the future. Hatred for love.

Chapter 36 - The deal

-Torag-

Nakwatha's eyes widened. She gasped for air, her mouth opening and closing like a fish.

For the briefest of moments, she looked helpless.

He watched the cold creep back in her eyes as soon as she'd processed what was happening.

"Such initiative you show, *slave*. Clearly, your new owner didn't know how to break you of that awful habit."

His hands clenched.

He couldn't kill her. And he couldn't walk away from her poison.

He had a demon to find and a fallen angel to trick.

"You're going to tell me about Lucifer," he told her.

Even in her helpless state, she managed to look at him in contempt. "Now, why would I do that?"

The smile on his face felt thin and hard. "Because I will bury you alive with that dagger in your spine and leave you to rot if you don't."

Her silence said it all. He waited.

"What happens once I'm done talking?" she asked.

"I will kill you. Quickly."

She closed her eyes.

When she opened them again, she smiled. "I should have drunk your blood when I had the chance. You'd have made me the most powerful of all."

He tasted bile in his mouth. Without words, he stared at her.

"I got greedy when that Indus bastard offered for you and your wolf pup. And now look at me."

"Talk," he choked out. "How do I get into Lucifer's palace?"

She laughed until a coughing fit tore through her. "You land in front of his palace and you pretend you're more than a slave unworthy to kiss the ground he walks on."

When he didn't move or speak, she continued. "You demand an audience. You make sure you have something he wants. And then you pray to whatever gods you believe in that he doesn't tear you to pieces before you even open your mouth."

"And what does he want?" he asked.

"What we all want. Power." She closed her eyes. "Now kill me. I have nothing more to say."

Torag walked away. He didn't get far before

her screams started.

He sank down to his haunches, hands over his ears, heart pounding.

Everything in him revolted at the thought of killing her.

He had thought that revenge would set him free. That he'd be stronger for vanquishing the female who represented all the bad in his past.

In the end, it wasn't revenge that allowed him to put one foot in front of the other until he reached the screeching female.

It wasn't revenge that got him to pull her up and put his arm around her throat.

It was the thought of the child she'd stepped over this morning. The thought of her slaves huddling in the dark, waiting for bronze rings to be forced into their skin.

Nobody would kneel for her again.

The crack of her neck had bile rise in his throat. In the sudden silence, he put his hand on her still heart and forced all his power through his palms.

Again.

And again.

And again, until bones were all that was left of her chest.

He staggered back. Huddled in a ball, he waited for relief to come. Instead, unshed tears burned his eyes. A pounding void in his chest threatened to swallow him whole.

The thought of Erisi, of Yerle, of the demons

he loved, all those who needed him, gave him the strength to rise. He took a step to the north. Another. And another. He ran, ran until he had no breath left in his body. When he turned demon and took flight, he kept his eyes on the tabletop mountain looming on the darkening horizon.

He landed on the plateau of Mount Roraima, far enough from the palace not to get skewered by Lucifer's guards. Unfortunately, it only granted him a short reprieve.

A dozen warriors surrounded him within moments, swords pointed at his chest.

He held his hands up. "I need an audience with Lucifer."

The female demon with dark-brown scales scoffed. "You all do. I have great alternative accommodation for you."

Two warriors stripped him of all weapons. The nudge of a spear in his back forced him to follow her lead toward the palace. Before they got to the high walls, the spear forced him down rough-hewn stairs descending in a hole in the black sandstone. The haunting cries and smell of damp earth made him shiver with the force of unbidden memories.

Was she here too? Did that bastard keep her in the dark, caged?

He swallowed down his fury. "I'm Torag, leader of the Arav family. I have something Lucifer wants."

"Nice try," the leading female said as she

opened the cell door surrounded by rock. Two males grabbed a hold of his shoulders and threw him in. The door clanged shut behind him.

As soon as the hellfire on the warriors' palms faded and the darkness closed in, Torag set to explore the cell. His fingers found rough rock and slippery bits of something slimy. Water sloshed beneath his boots as he moved along the walls.

They hadn't killed him. There was a small chance that the news of his arrival would reach Lucifer's ears. And if the fallen angel really wanted power and control above all else, maybe he'd want to find out where the family that evaded him was hiding.

He reached the cell door and set about exploring the hinges and metal bars as thick as his wrist.

In the end, he found nothing that would help him escape or prepare for whatever Lucifer or his guards could do to him. He sank down against the wall and waited.

The clang of metal against the cell door woke him from the fitful sleep he'd managed. Hell knew he'd need all of his powers to deal with what was coming for him.

"I'm not sure you can call yourself a leader when you have no stronghold or family left," came a harsh voice from the other side of the bars.

Fear squeezed tight around Torag's heart.

They lived. They had to live. If they'd captured

his family already, he'd be dead by now.

"The Arav are more than their stronghold. You wouldn't have chosen us for your plans otherwise." He stayed at the back of the cell, wary of the male's intentions.

"Except I chose the Rohi," the fallen angel said. A flare lit up Lucifer's face, the bright blue angelfire mixing in with his red hellfire unmistakable.

"Not that it worked out for you," Torag said.

The male smirked. "I control the stronghold and the region."

"But Erisi didn't do your bidding. And we are still at large."

The cold smile on Lucifer's face filled Torag with a sense of foreboding. "Not for much longer."

Torag clenched his fists and forced out the only proposal he'd come up with. "You can control Erisi and the Arav without the Rohi."

"I know," Lucifer said. "I think I have the solution right in front of me."

Torag swallowed. Erisi was right; Lucifer would break him to get to her. "She needs the Arav."

Lucifer scoffed. "The Arav are her greatest weakness."

"We're the only reason she'll fight for."

Fate, he hated bartering with her freedom and the freedom of his family, but it was the only way he could see to protect them all.

When Lucifer stayed silent, Torag continued, "I'll make a deal that binds every Arav soul to her. As her leader, those souls will effectively be yours to command. Erisi can still execute missions as your warrior, even while she leads the Arav."

"Pledge those souls to me, and I will consider your proposal."

Torag stiffened. "No."

"I don't think you understand how a negotiation works," Lucifer sneered. "If you're not going to counter my offer, this is pointless." The male lowered his fire and turned away.

"I don't trust you with our souls. There is no counter-offer to make," Torag told the fallen angel.

"Fine." Lucifer turned to face him again. "If you can get her to agree, you have a deal. You pledge every Arav soul to Erisi. She strengthens her bond with me by renewing her blood oath, just as a little life insurance on my part."

There was a lightness in Lucifer's voice that Torag didn't trust. "Will you call off the Rohi?"

"No. Deal with them yourself. Do we have an agreement?"

Frantically, Torag tried to think through the consequences of this deal. There was no other way. Nothing else he could think of to save them all. "Yes."

Lucifer motioned at the cell door, and a guard stepped forward. As soon as she opened the cell, two tall warriors marched in and dragged him out.

Lucifer led the way along the narrow dungeon corridors. With every step they took, Torag's apprehension grew. He cast a look at the warriors surrounding him, their drawn blades, and tried to come up with a plan for the moment everything went awry. He couldn't think of anything that wouldn't end in his true death.

The farther they walked, the staler the air got. It was tinged with the coppery scent of spilled blood. Occasionally, chains clanged somewhere deep in the dark cells. That and the low groans were the only indication that there were living beings down here.

When they reached the metal bars at the end of a long tunnel, Lucifer turned to Torag. "There's one slight problem."

At Lucifer's nod, two of the warriors slammed him against the wall, tearing his cheek against the rough stone. One of them twisted his wrist behind his back.

Lucifer's whisper sent shivers down his spine. "If you want to get a deal out of Erisi, you'll need to find a way to talk to her."

A female guard opened the cell door, and the others shoved him inside.

"Erisi!" His voice trembled. Terror raked its claws over his clammy skin when she didn't respond.

Please don't let her be dead. Please.

A low growl from the dark had the hairs on

his skin rise.

"Good luck getting her to agree to our deal." Lucifer's chuckle echoed against the stone.

The growl behind Torag stopped.

He turned.

Chapter 37 - Struggle

-Torag-

Wildfire flared. The ice-blue demon charged him.

Instinctively, he reared back against the metal bars behind him. With a loud clank, the chains stopped her mid-attack. She hissed and retreated to the farthest wall, black eyes locked on his face. In the light of the fire haphazardly flaring on her skin, he saw the deep wound the chain had torn into the scales of her right wrist. She crouched with her back to the wall, hunched forward with her wounded arm pressed against her stomach.

"Erisi," he whispered.

She was beyond his reach. His heart squeezed.

Behind his back, Lucifer spoke up. "She's useless to me the way she is now. Get her to turn and agree to our deal. Or die."

Torag heard her labored breath, occasionally broken by a whimper. Rage thundered through him as he considered the agony she was in.

He didn't take his eyes off her. Behind him, fading footsteps and the silence that remained told him Lucifer and his warriors had gone.

She wouldn't turn back while she was chained. He needed to free her. But even with her powers weakened, he didn't stand a chance against her wildfire.

Desperate, he murmured her name. The wildfire demon curled up and whimpered in response, and the ache in his chest magnified. He couldn't leave her like this.

Carefully, he inched closer. Remembering the words Mei had whispered, he said, "I'll take care of you, Wildfire. I promise—"

She tackled him, clawed fingers on his chest, scales under his hands. His stomach dropped. He rolled them over, his weight on hers, and pinned her shoulders to the cold rock. Even in her demonic form, she didn't have the strength to pull free.

He wondered how long and hard she'd been fighting.

"Erisi..." His voice came out as broken as he felt.

Wildfire surged on her skin, burning his fingers and the muscles of his stomach where he held her down. He strained against the agony. "My love, please. Please come back to me."

She bucked under him, fighting to get free.

"Erisi..."

The wildfire demon slammed her hands against Torag's chest and blasted enough fire into him to rip a hoarse cry from his throat.

She snarled at him, her features twisted and teeth bared. The terror of a cornered beast.

The realization hit him. He was once more restraining her.

He let go of her shoulders.

She headbutted him and shoved him off her, before charging again. Her claws raked over the blistered flesh of his chest, ripping through the muscle.

He cried out, but he didn't fight back.

He couldn't subdue her.

Even if he survived until her powers ran dry, he refused to kill her.

So he submitted to Fate and her mercy, knowing it wasn't fair.

Knowing she wouldn't even realize she was killing the male who loved her beyond anything in this world and the next. She would never recover from the guilt.

He didn't know what else to do.

Wildfire poured into his flesh. Her claws raked down, reached his guts. He howled in agony.

He needed to—

The pain overwhelmed him.

The world blurred. He fought to hold on for one more beat.

He needed to tell her.

"I'm sorry, Erisi." Agony took his breath away. He struggled to get air into his lungs, to get out the words. "Whatever happens…"

Wildfire ate into his chest when she shoved her palms against the torn up muscles. He wondered how long he had until it reached his heart. Black dots bloomed before his eyes. "Forgive yourself, my love. I forgive you whatever happ—"

The demon's wildfire hit his heart.

The world ceased to exist.

Chapter 38 - Grief

-Erisi-

Soul-deep sadness coursed through her veins.

Her battered body pressed against wet rough rock, surrounded by pitch-black silence. Erisi knew what the distinct pain in her muscles meant. She'd succumbed to the darkness when she'd realized her failure to protect her family. Was that why her body was wracked by grief?

She fought to remember. Why was she surrounded by the scent of blood and burnt flesh?

Had she killed Lucifer's warriors? In the end, she must have failed because the distant sounds occasionally breaking through the darkness told her she was stuck in his dungeons.

It took all of her remaining strength to raise her arm and call a tiny flame of hellfire to her palm. In the few moments of flickering light, Erisi caught the outline of a body a few feet away, and with the image came more grief.

The flame died out, the effort too great.

Did she kill whoever was laying there? Was her demon grieving for what she'd done in the throes of wildfire?

Hot tears ran over her cheeks.

Why was she crying when she couldn't even remember?

Fear surged, twisting her gut. What if she'd killed another innocent? She wasn't sure she'd survive the guilt.

Trembling, Erisi dragged herself toward the body until her reaching hand encountered warm skin. Blistered skin. It stuck to her fingers.

She swallowed and followed the arm up to a broad shoulder.

Male.

His chest was in a horrendous state, slashed open and burned. Still, it moved under her hand with every shallow breath he took.

Whoever this was, she hadn't killed him yet. A cold solace... He wouldn't survive much longer with injuries liked these. If her fire was still ravaging his heart... She sobbed.

Driven by an urge she couldn't explain, her fingers traced the burnt skin of his throat until she touched the stubble on his face.

Memories fell over her, one by one, until she nearly drowned. His warm mouth capturing her breath. The whisper of her name on his lips.

"No!" Erisi rasped. Desperate, her fingers sought and found the small scar next to his right eye.

Her soul shattered in a million pieces.

She didn't even try to breathe under the pressure building in her lungs. There was no more reason to breathe.

She'd killed the male she loved.

Her cry echoed around the dungeon in a song of grief. The familiar darkness crept over her skin, through her veins, as wildfire took over.

She would not come back this time.

No more.

She wondered if the grief obliterating her soul would kill her. Knew she didn't deserve the mercy of death.

Guilt petrified her insides. Erisi couldn't move under the weight of Torag's dying body against her.

"Wi—"

The sound was barely there, and still it stopped the world in its tracks.

"Wildfi—"

Hot tears dripped on her hands as they cradled his face. "I'm so sorry," she choked out. "I can't—"

"Don't—" Torag groaned in pain as his fingers dug into her forearm. "Don't blame yourself."

"How can I not? I did this to you."

"No." His fingers found her jaw in a soft caress, wiping the tears away. "My love, t-this is not your fault."

Erisi couldn't stop crying. She didn't want to

fight him despite knowing the harsh truth. She did this. When he died, she'd be the one to blame.

"Don't believe me, do you?" Torag's laugh cut off in a grunt of pain. "I guess I'll just need to s... stay alive then."

Always protecting others. Even with his dying breath.

Erisi crawled against his body, careful of the burns and wounds she'd inflicted.

She had nothing left to give. The pain and grief dissolved in a suffocating layer of numbness settling over her body and mind.

His hand rested against her face, his thumb on her lips.

"We will rest," he whispered, "and t-tomorrow will be a better day."

There was no *better* without him. The only thing standing between her and madness were the moments she could still share with him.

But tomorrow...

Tomorrow, when he was no longer...

Her tears fell faster.

Chapter 39 - Hers

-Torag-

Every breath was a fight to be won. Every beat of his heart, the sound of victory.

Torag refused to die.

Not when Erisi was giving up.

Crushed under her guilt, he could feel her slipping away from him. If he died, Erisi would be no more.

He refused to let that happen.

Whenever he found breath, Torag told her he loved her. The heat of her tears on his skin was her only response.

Maybe it was cruel to remind her of his love, knowing there was a good chance he would die. But he needed to break through her apathy. He needed her fight, her fire.

He needed her to understand what was at stake.

How much he needed her.

Erisi used her body to protect him from the

chill of the dungeon, but even her skin had lost its warmth. He feared she would die before he did.

With broken voice, he tried again, "I love you."

She shivered against him, her fingers digging into his side. A single trail of heat dripped down his shoulder.

So he told her again.

And again.

* * *

Male voices drifted along the corridor, slowly growing in volume until he recognized Lucifer's voice. Lights flickered near the entrance of the cell, not quite reaching the farthest wall they were laying against.

"They can't know I live," Torag whispered in her ear. "I refuse to be the reason Lucifer forces you into submission."

He needed to tell her about the deal he'd made, but there was no time, not enough breath. Unless both of them survived, it didn't matter anyway.

Erisi didn't move. Fear worked its way through his ravaged chest until it choked him.

"My love," he murmured against her matted hair. "Stay with me."

"Nothing is moving in there, my lord," he heard a deep voice.

Torag's body tensed, and fresh agony hit him. He swallowed the groan trying to escape his parched mouth.

Finally, Erisi stirred. Her fingers followed the line of his jaw to his mouth. Cold lips touched his in a featherlight caress.

She moved in front of him, shielding his body.

"I wonder if they're both dead." Lucifer was silent for a beat. "Get in there and check."

The other male stuttered, "M-my lord, the Wildfire Warrior—"

"I will not repeat my orders, *warrior*."

The metal clanged as someone thrust the cell door open.

"Of course, my lord." The voice came nearer, trembling in the dark. Torchlight closed in on their hiding spot.

The low growl breaking through the dark made his heart drop. The torch fell as a body slammed on the ground. Wildfire flared up, and the male shouted in anguish.

Torag bit his hand, his heart thundering. Was she coming back to him? Even now, he didn't know...

He didn't dare to hope.

"S-Should we help?" came a female voice from the corridor.

"Leave him. She's already killed plenty of my warriors as it stands." Lucifer cursed, his voice already fading as he moved away. "Of course, the bloody Arav bastard didn't stand a chance."

Torag flinched when something dropped next to him. He braced himself for a flare of wildfire.

"Are you alright?" Her whisper was the most beautiful sound he'd ever heard.

"Erisi…" Torag was surprised at the humidity on his cheeks.

Strong fingers clasped his hand. Her lips brushed over his knuckles.

He caressed her face, needing to feel her, and pulled her down to him. He took her lips in a kiss that made his chest ache. He could barely breathe by the time he let go.

"I didn't know if…"

She softly kissed the corner of his mouth. "For you. I'll always come back for you." Her small body nestled against his side, her arm around his waist. "I'm still terrified of what my demon might do. But she finally understands."

Torag closed his eyes to stop the slow-falling tears. His fingers laced into her short hair to hold her even closer. He wished he had the strength to fold himself around her. "Tell me, Wildfire."

"My demon only understands her instincts. Rage. Grief. But also trust." Erisi's fingers slid up his arm and over his shoulder. "The urge to protect." Her thumb traced the curve of his chin up to his bottom lip. "Love."

Her other hand hovered over his chest, careful not to touch the healing wounds. Torag pressed her hand on his heart, grateful for the pain that told him this was real.

"You're mine. And you're hers too."

He closed his eyes and held her.

Chapter 40 - Retaliation

-Erisi-

He rested in her lap, the even sound of his breath almost enough to calm her inner turmoil. Her fingertips caressed through his hair. The urge to touch him, to feel that he was alive and close hadn't diminished these past weeks.

She'd watched him heal. Watched the wounds marring his chest and stomach scar. As his strength returned, her guilt and grief mingled and morphed into seething fury.

Once more a powerful being had bent her to his wishes and used the ones she loved against her. This time, she'd walked into it with eyes wide open. It only stoked her fury hotter.

He stirred in her lap. The warmth of his lips touched the inside of her wrist, and she was barely able to swallow her sob of relief. He had survived. Somehow, he'd forgiven her for the atrocious acts she had inflicted on him.

"I think it's time we made our move," he told her, voice still hoarse with sleep.

She drew a shaky breath. "I can't bear the thought of you anywhere near Lucifer."

He got up from her lap, and she mourned the loss of his warmth until he took her hands in his. "I hope we both learned from our mistakes. You're not doing this alone."

She had learned. And she knew her wildfire demon was liable to burn the fallen angel to ashes, even if it meant she'd also die the true death.

"I know," she whispered. "And I still don't like it."

His hand tightened around hers. "I understand. You're the most powerful demon alive and I can't stand the thought of you near him. But we need to move. I hate knowing Yerle and our family are under threat while I was healing."

She squeezed his hand softly. "One thing at a time. Lucifer. Yerle. The rest of our family. We can do this, Torag. Together."

He pulled her in his arms and held her close to his pounding heart. "Together."

* * *

Erisi traced her fingertips over her new chain as she waited for the torchlight to come closer. Another chain used to restrain her. Another one she'd broken. And she'd damn well use it to take revenge.

She pressed her body against the rock as the footsteps of the guard got louder. When he passed the cell door, she whipped her chain around his wrist. The torch he'd held fell to the ground, flickering violently. She slammed him face first against the thick cell door bars. Before the grunt of surprise turned into a call for help, her claws raked over his throat, ripping his vocal chords.

Within moments, she had the cell door open using the key chained to the guard's belt.

She stepped over his motionless body to check the corridor and found it empty.

"We're good," she whispered.

Torag stepped into the light with the sword they'd taken from Lucifer's guard weeks ago. It had amused Erisi to ponder how rattled the leader of all demons had been to make a mistake that grave.

"We should be alright until we get to the central hall where the guards convene." She couldn't help but look at the angry red scars on Torag's chest and stomach. "Are you sure—"

"I'm—" He took a deep breath. "I'm good to fight. I just... Maybe we should get out of here and get back to Yerle and our family. Leave the bastard be. Don't make the deal."

Her chest ached. She took a step forward and caressed his cheek. "Lucifer will never let us go, Torag. He'll hunt us down. Worse, he'll hunt every Arav demon to draw us out. We'll never be free of him."

He put his hand over hers and leaned his face into her palm with a shaky sigh. "Together," he whispered.

She locked eyes with him. "Together."

When he let go of her hand, she led the way, following the markers engraved in the rock. The closer they got to the central chambers, the more torches lit their path. When hard voices and a scratchy laugh reached them, they crept forward along the wall. Even the air felt warm against her skin. Not much later she saw the shadows cast by the bonfire at the center of the hall.

"Sounds like there's about five," Torag whispered close behind her. "I'll take the left."

She nodded once and held up three fingers.

By the time they were down, she burst into the hall with her chain sizzling. Five of the guards were awake; the sixth woke up with a snarl. With a practiced flick of her wrist, she wrapped the chain around the ankles of the demon closest to her. A hard tug had him crash to the floor. She dodged the swords of the two demons attacking her. Tried not to turn and look at the commotion behind her back.

He can handle himself. You know he can.

The moment of distraction cost her. She didn't twist away fast enough. The female's blade sliced her upper arm. Erisi threw her chain infused with hellfire into the female's face, then blasted a fiery bolt into her stomach.

She rolled away from the battle axe the male brought down on her, only to be kicked in the shoulder by the other male whose ankles had clearly recovered. His blade came down, only to be blocked by another sword.

Torag pulled back his blade, then hacked at the male's side and shoulder in short, powerful movements that took the warrior all his focus to block. Erisi scrambled up. She retrieved her chain and wrapped it around the throat of the battle axe warrior.

Both their adversaries slumped to the rock.

"We need to move," Torag said, wiping his sword on the tunic of his last adversary.

The tightness in her chest had loosened a little after seeing him fight. She'd never get used to this overwhelming fear that came with the depth of love, but she knew he was a warrior, a survivor through and through.

They ascended the stairs to the plateau and crouched behind a rock to observe the well-guarded palace gates and the thick quartzite walls half a mile away.

"We'll need to fly," she whispered. "I-I'll need to turn to keep us both shielded."

He tipped up her chin, forcing her to meet his dark eyes full of trust. "You'll come back to me."

Closing her eyes, she tried to find that same trust in herself and her demon. Recalled the surge of protectiveness and love that had triggered her demon the last time she turned. It hadn't been darkness then. It wouldn't be darkness now.

She opened her eyes and met his gaze. "I will. I'll always come back to you."

He turned first. His hands trembled with the power it cost his still-healing body.

Seeing his strength fueled the fire inside of her.

Her love for him, this all-consuming need to keep him safe meant she let it happen without a fight.

Her wildfire rose up through her body, bloomed inside her chest, and filled her veins.

She felt her consciousness fade and smiled.

Closing her eyes, she became wildfire once more.

Chapter 41 - The fight

-Torag-

He followed the ice-blue demon into the sky. Flying took every last bit of strength and power he had in him. Trying to keep up with her had him panting, and not for the fun kind of reason.

Her wildfire blasted out and shielded them both when the first hellfire-infused arrows reached them from the archers on the allures. A sound not unlike the ram horn, but higher in pitch, sounded. On the ground, more warriors assembled.

His heart raced when a group took flight. Another blast of fiery arrows whistled past them, narrowly missing their bodies. Foregoing a shield, the Wildfire Warrior's attention was on the attackers in the air. She blasted black fire bolts into the group in rapid succession. Two winged warriors fell. One of them clawed at the hole in his chest as he went down.

The group dispersed and attacked from two sides.

Torag fought to stay airborne while he unsheathed his sword. They were in this together, even if he wouldn't be much support.

His heart seized when the wildfire demon wrapped around him. The heat of her fire surrounded them, encompassing them in a ball of wildfire. He closed his eyes and tried to breathe. His lungs were burning.

Nothing permeated the shield she'd surrounded them with. Her fire didn't even waver as she pushed her wings hard, pulling him along.

They landed on the courtyard, surrounded by warriors. When the warning sound echoed through the air again, Erisi pushed her wildfire farther out. Black flames hindering his view, he could hear the screams. Her shield sizzled where arrows hit, but none broke through.

Once more, Torag stood in awe of her power and the seeming ease with which she handled it.

"Torag!"

Erisi's head snapped around to the source of the sound.

Torag stilled in disbelief. "Yerle?"

"Told you I wouldn't let you do this alone," Yerle shouted, before he cursed loud enough to draw a growl from Erisi. "I think we need to move this party elsewhere before we get skewered and roasted."

Throat tight, Torag fought his emotion. "We

need to get to Lucifer," he shouted at his friend.

As if she'd understood, the wildfire demon started pulling him along in the direction of what looked like a double door leading to the palace. He fought her hold. "Not a wolf pup, Wildfire. Put me the hell down."

She didn't hear him. Still surrounded by the blaze of her fire, she dragged him up a few stairs. Then she dropped the shield and all hell broke loose again.

Seeing a dozen warriors charge with hellfire-infused swords drawn, he tried to pull up his own shield. It flared and faded to nothingness.

The wildfire demon pulled him behind her, his back against the bronze doors, her black wings spread and shielding him from the incoming blasts.

He flinched as hellfire and arrows pierced her wings. She roared. The screams told him she'd served her reply.

His stomach clenched hard at the thought of his friend out there on the courtyard. "Yerle!"

"All good as long as I stay out of her range. Go! Get Lucifer."

"Wildfire," he pleaded, unsure if her demon remembered where they needed to be or only reacted to the threats surrounding them.

The doors were pulled open. He twisted around. Barely blocked the sword that came down on him with his own. The warrior parried his blow aimed at the male's shoulder and—

—got hit in the chest with a ball of wildfire. The male's eyes widened. His mouth opened without a sound and he dropped.

Relief warred with a shimmer of annoyance at Erisi's interference.

She strode inside, wildfire flaring on her palms. Torag shook his head at himself and followed her. He had no fucking powers to speak of. Yes, she was slightly overprotective, but he'd be a pile of ash if not for her.

The long corridor before them was deserted. When Torag glanced back, he found Yerle and a dozen Arav warriors defending the entrance to the hallway. Knowing his friend had survived Caral, had flown home, and came back with reinforcements—

Torag swallowed hard and tried to focus. It looked like the final stand would take place in Lucifer's throne room, just as Erisi had predicted. He wondered how many warriors Lucifer had holed up with.

The Wildfire Warrior kicked open the bronze doors at the end of the hallway and shielded. Beyond her shield, a dozen warriors stood in front of the stairs to a golden throne Lucifer lounged on.

"And once more, you ruin my plans," the male said. He stood with languid movements.. "Subdue her. Do not kill her for real, or you'll be wishing for true death for the coming century."

Torag bit back his growl. His fingers clenched

around the hilt of his sword, wishing he had the use of his powers.

As the warriors inched forward, swords, spears, and battle axes infused with all shades of red hellfire, Erisi stayed in the doorway. The first pure hellfire bolt skimmed her shoulder and hit Torag on the arm. He hissed at the ball of agony that exploded.

The wildfire demon roared and charged into the group of warriors.

"Erisi!"

Fuck! He should have borne the pain quietly.

Her small form disappeared in a mass of tall powerful bodies.

He wanted to throw himself in, but he'd be a liability to her.

Crouched and ready to fight, he waited for the inevitable strike, the next bolt of hellfire.

None of the warriors even looked at him. They threw themselves on the demon their lord wanted alive.

Wildfire blasted from the center of the room. They screamed, but only for a few moments. The second blast left only a small ice-blue demon standing.

Torag couldn't keep his eyes from—

The sharp tip of a knife pressed against the knot at the back of his neck. A hand was buried in his hair, pulling to the point of pain. Torag didn't move. One twist and he'd be unable to lose the use of his limbs. If the bastard infused the blade with his fire, he would not survive at all.

"It looks like you are the key after all," Lucifer drawled from behind him. "Too bad it took me weeks to figure that out."

Torag's heart thundered in his chest.

Wildfire...

The wildfire demon turned to face them.

And turned human.

Chapter 42 - Blood oath

-Erisi-

Erisi refused to go down.

Surrounded by ashes, blood, and the stench of burnt flesh, her body felt like it would shatter now that it'd been purged of its wildfire. She clenched her muscles to stay standing.

Fought to stay conscious and face the bastard.

Maybe her demon had retreated because she was afraid Torag would be hit in the cross fire. Maybe she wanted Erisi to be fully aware when she finished the fallen angel.

Because she would fucking finish him for threatening Torag.

"Let him go," she hissed.

The fallen angel smirked and tightened his grip on Torag's hair, forcing the male's neck further back. He'd made sure she could see the knife dig deeper into Torag's skin.

She couldn't tear her eyes away from Torag's

face. The wild despair in his dark eyes faded into calm resignation.

No. No!

She moved forward, just as he dropped himself onto Lucifer's blade.

His body slumped to the ground.

Lucifer cursed loudly. He turned angel, smooth golden skin marred by black spikes, his spread crimson wings smudged black.

Tears blurred her vision and the darkness rose. Frozen at the very core of her, her fire erupted all over her skin nonetheless.

She charged into the fallen angel. Clawing, kicking and screaming. He staggered back as she bit his shoulder, through the thickened golden skin, blood filling her mouth. A punch to her temple had her see stars, but she didn't let go.

She forced her fire into him. Dug her claws deeper into his flesh and poured pure hellfire into the wound.

Two large hands closed around her neck. Lucifer's fire melted her flesh, unprotected by scales.

She couldn't die before him.

He would fucking go down with her.

She closed her eyes and welcomed the fury of her wildfire.

* * *

"Wildfire."

She keened at the memory of his voice, so

vivid it tore her to pieces.

A hand cupped her face. "Erisi, please come back to me."

She opened her eyes and burst into tears when she saw the worry on his face.

"How..." She melted into his arms, wrapping tight around him.

"He didn't hit the nerves and he hadn't infused the blade with fire yet. I was lucky."

The fury flared again. She slammed her fists on his chest, hard, ignoring the blasts of pain throughout her body. "You damn bastard. Why the fuck would you—"

He caught her hands in his, pulling her closer to him. "I couldn't be the reason he restrained and used you."

The tears wouldn't stop falling. "We said *'together'*." Her voice broke.

Torag closed his eyes and leaned his forehead to hers. "I'm sorry. I'm so sorry, Wildfire. I never wanted to leave you."

Someone groaned.

Erisi turned and found Lucifer, broken, burned and writhing in a growing pool of blood. "She didn't kill him."

Torag still held her hands. "I called for you when I woke."

She took a deep, shivery breath. "We need to finish this before the rest of his horde gets through."

Torag nodded. "Our warriors outside are

holding off what's left of his defenses, but it's only a matter of time before we get overwhelmed."

Our warriors? How—

She didn't have time to question what had happened. Reluctantly, she let go of Torag's hands and crouched next to the fallen angel. She dug her fingers into the wound on his shoulder. Lucifer shouted. His green eyes snapped open.

"I believe we had a deal," she said.

His eyes narrowed.

"I'll renew my blood oath and tie my soul even closer to yours. The Arav will be bound to me. And you stay away from my family."

"I w-will not personally hunt your family. And y-you will obey my c-commands," he hissed through gritted teeth.

"As long as those commands do not harm my family. And not just you," she said. "None of your warriors will attack the Arav or help their enemies."

He tried to sit up, then hissed in pain with the movement and fell back. His chest and stomach were bloody and blistered, but his lower body had gotten the worst of her fury it seemed. Only bone and strips of flesh remained in some places. His groin was burned beyond recognition.

She forced her eyes back to the fallen angel's face. The rage in his green eyes was burning brightly. She had no doubt he'd survive and take the worst kind of revenge.

This deal needed to make sure he couldn't do it through the Arav.

She stared at him, waiting for his answer.

"Fine," he barked. "You have a deal." He raised his bleeding arm. "Drink."

The taste of his blood had her stomach roil. She swallowed a mouthful, forcing herself to keep it down.

"Do you have any fire left for the mark?" she asked.

Lucifer bared his teeth. "You better hope so, or there is no deal."

He was shaking hard, his muscles seizing. The fallen angel pressed his fingers against the roots of the tree tattooed on her stomach. At first nothing happened. Then the smallest flare of his fire touched her skin. It set his blood in her aflame, until it felt like a blazing inferno tore through her stomach, then her veins and every cell of her body.

She reared back. Torag caught her.

Her soul fought against the tightening restraints binding it. She pushed her palm against her sternum in an attempt to lessen the agony.

Torag's arms around her were the only reason she stayed conscious.

"His blood oath," Lucifer demanded, his voice fading.

Erisi looked up at Torag. His eyes were soft, but a deep groove cut between his brows. She pulled him down and kissed him.

When they broke free, she whispered against his lips, "Take my blood."

Her chest ached at the way he caressed her wrist before he opened a vein with his claw. When he put his mouth on her, she shivered.

After a few pulls, he looked up, licked his lips, and put her hand over his pounding heart. "Right here, my love."

Erisi swallowed. Her eyes stung with unshed tears as she pushed her hellfire into him. He tensed under her, then groaned.

It hit her. A surge of power that took her breath and left her weak-legged and shaking. Lightning struck her, the sheer light of it mixing with the darkness of the wildfire at her core. She held onto Torag's hand. Held onto his strength.

"Torag."

He shivered in response, his eyes falling shut.

"Now can I wither in peace, you fuckers? Get the hell out of here." Only a hoarse whisper remained of Lucifer's voice.

The doors of the throne room slammed open, and Erisi turned.

Black dots danced before her eyes at the sudden movement. A bloodied, banged up demon fell in and slammed the doors shut behind him.

Yerle.

"Hi Erisi," Yerle said with a little wave.

She would have dropped to her knees if not for Torag's hold on her.

"He's..." Her throat was too tight to say anything else.

Torag's voice was thick with emotion. "He arrived while we were fighting on the courtyard. Are they—"

Yerle straightened, panting. "They're still holding them back. We need to leave though, because I'm not sure how much longer—" His eyes widened as he caught sight of Lucifer. "Fuck!"

Erisi didn't even have the energy left to laugh. She leaned into Torag's strength.

"Do you think it will grow back?" Yerle asked.

Torag barked out a laugh. "I don't even want to think about it. Let's get out."

He took her hand. The hope she'd pushed down for so long nearly overwhelmed her as they walked away. *Together*.

Lucifer's faint voice barely reached them. "Don't think I will forget this. You will pay. I have eternity to figure out how I can hurt you most."

Erisi didn't turn. Her hand tightened around Torag's fingers as she spoke. "I don't expect you to forget. I want you to remember who did this to you and why you will never break your promise to the Arav."

Once outside the throne room, Erisi looked up at Torag. "Let's find our family."

Chapter 43 - Forgiven

-Erisi-

She was home.

Mei's hug-tackle had her tearing up. So did Sura's blunt apology for not getting her back sooner, for not realizing how much danger she'd been in.

She had a hard time facing the undeserved awe in everyone's eyes when Torag was done telling their story around the fire. He'd told a version that made her seem so much better than she'd been.

"If Sura apologizes one more time, I'm going to scream," she told Torag while they walked to their new sparring spot outside of the caves.

Torag smiled at her. "She feels like she failed you, Wildfire."

"I didn't want her to follow. Then she was fighting off the Rohi and evading Beelzebub. How the hell was she supposed to rescue us? It would only have given Lucifer more leverage. Besides,

Yerle arrived just in time with reinforcements."

He stilled. She knew how heavy the guilt weighed on him for leaving Yerle behind at Caral-Supe, even though he got away.

"We both know guilt isn't rational." Torag looked up at the night sky as they reached the top of the mountain.

Oh, yes, I know.

Torag hadn't forgiven himself. Erisi could see it in his eyes, feel it in his touch. He still felt like he'd failed her even though she'd been the one to walk away. Still believed he hadn't been enough.

Her own guilt only made it worse. She kept seeing the empty look in his onyx eyes when she'd forced him to his knees. She still felt his blistered skin sticking to her fingers after she'd almost killed him.

Grief crashed over her every time she traced the scars she'd etched into his chest. Her mark right over his heart filled her with bittersweet agony.

Tonight, all of it would change.

She fell into a fighting stance and smiled at him. "Ready when you are."

"Never, when it comes to you," he told her with a grin.

He proved ready enough. She found herself distracted by his beauty and power, by the thought of what tonight would bring. Wondering if it would take away some of the pain that filled his eyes at times.

She was slammed with her back to the rock, sporting a few new bruises and a burn on her upper arm. When he helped her up, his large hand engulfing hers, she smiled up at him. "I have a challenge for you."

His eyes lit up at her words. He liked the challenges she threw at him. They tended to end with him buried deep inside her.

Torag's large frame backed her up, one step at a time, until she hit the rocks behind her. His arms rested on either side of her face, his mouth close and enticing.

"I'm listening, Wildfire," he whispered.

His lips explored the side of her throat, making it hard to focus. "Are you really?" She tried to swallow the moan locked inside.

Torag hummed against her skin.

She could do this. Even if the sly bast—

"Fuck!" His fingers in her hair forced her head back. His teeth grazed her earlobe with just the right amount of sting. "Torag!"

"Still listening, Wildfire," he said, amused.

"Each of us has one night—" She swallowed hard when his lips moved over her collarbone and lower still. "One night when the other submits to their every wish."

Torag raised his head, his onyx eyes sparkling. "Mhm, go on."

"Only two rules. One, obedience to whoever rules that night."

A languid smile curled around Torag's lips,

and Erisi's legs went weak.

"Two, the moment either of us says *'Lucifer'*, the fun stops immediately. Doesn't matter why."

"Fuck, couldn't choose a better word, could you?" Torag rested his forehead against hers.

Erisi grinned. "It's guaranteed to kill the mood, so it works perfectly."

"You're on, my love," Torag told her before his lips came down on hers.

He nearly had her forget everything.

It took all her strength to break away and take his hand. She led him back down to the caves.

"Are you sure this is the best place?" Torag looked as nervous as Erisi felt.

His gaze lingered around their shared cave, deep in the mountain. The carved-out gully with tar was alight with hellfire, casting light and shadows onto the rock. In the middle, their *'welcome home'* present from Yerle and Chandra took up most of the space. The large sturdy bed had made Erisi laugh so hard tears had rolled down her cheeks. Torag had just punched his friends, but he'd made use of the gift nonetheless. At least those few times they'd made it to the bed.

"Unless you want to get interrupted outside by Rohi scouts or a young who followed us like last time, I think here is perfect." Erisi kicked her chains in a corner of the room and leaned against the wall. She watched as Torag paced the cave.

"I'm—" He took a deep breath. "I don't know what you have planned. What if I can't... shut up?" He came to a halt in front of her.

"Sura has dragged everyone away for an impromptu celebration. They won't hear you." She took a step toward him. "Afraid you won't be silent?"

Torag closed his eyes when her fingers touched the mark on his chest.

"It's not too late to tell me no, Torag," she whispered. "It's never too late. One word from you, and we join the others for that celebration. You know that, right?"

He opened his eyes. "I want this," he said, his hand closing over her fingers.

The nervousness faded from his features. Her heart stuttered when he sank to his knees in front of her and looked up with those onyx eyes. "Tell me what to do."

Her throat tightened. She wasn't sure she could do this. She—

"My love, it's alright. Anything. I'll do anything you tell me to do."

Erisi sank to her knees next to him, unable to look down at him. The trust in his eyes both ratcheted up the fear living deep inside her and the desire to clear every obstacle standing between them.

They needed this. They needed to get rid of the guilt haunting their minds.

"Tonight—" She swallowed. "Tonight, you're going to earn your own forgiveness."

The groove between his eyes deepened as his

eyelids dropped.

"No, look at me. Your eyes will be on me at all times. I want you to know exactly who's here with you. I want you to see what you mean to me."

Torchlight reflected in the onyx in front of her. Erisi took both of his hands in hers. "I can see it eating away at you. No matter how many times I tell you that you didn't fail me, that you are enough, that you did more for me than I ever believed possible, you still don't believe it. Tonight, you're letting go."

When he struggled to keep his eyes on her, she added, "Remember rule number one: obedience. Tell me you understand. Tell me you will let go after tonight."

Erisi watched his throat work. Any moment now, he'd tell her it was over. He'd use the word and walk away from her.

"I understand. I will submit to whatever you do to me, and after that, I will forgive myself." His voice came out breathless.

Burying her hands in the silk of his hair, she kissed him. All the while, her eyes were fixed on his face, daring him to look away.

He never did. Her male loved a challenge as much as she did.

Panting, she drew back from him. "Stand. Undress."

Erisi remained on her knees. She wasn't sure if she had the strength to stand while witnessing the perfection Fate had gifted her with.

His golden skin took on the warm shine of the flickering fire around them. The shadows emphasized every line, groove, and ridge of his muscled body.

Every scar. Including the ones she'd left on him.

She swallowed.

She wanted to forget all about her foolish challenge. The urge to go to him, to hide from the world in his strong arms nearly overwhelmed her.

He waited, bare before her. Patience had always been one of his strengths. One she wanted to test the limits of tonight.

She needed to touch him. The hunger gnawing inside her made her weak with longing.

Unable to get a word through her parched throat, she stood and took his hand.

Leading him to the fire pit, Erisi pulled Torag down onto the pelts she'd laid over the rough rock. "On your back," she whispered.

Sitting cross-legged behind him, she pulled his head onto her lap and took the vial of gold liquid Yerle had put next to the pelts, as she'd requested.

"Eyes on my face," Erisi told him as she dripped oil onto his chest.

His breath faltered with every drop that landed on his skin. Her fingers spread the liquid from his clavicle to the lower part of his sternum before tracing the warmth of his skin toward his broad shoulders. She worked every part of his pectoral muscles until his breath became shallow. His eyes were still fixed on her face, his lips parted and his breath warm against her skin as she leaned over him.

"Sit." He obeyed without question, and she knelt behind him. After warming some oil in her hands, she pressed her palms against his shoulder blades. Her thumbs worked their way up, then back down along his spine. "Tell me what you feel. Anything. I want to know it all."

Torag's voice was hoarse when he obeyed. "My skin, it feels like it's on fire. Not just where you touch me. Everywhere."

Her hands worked on his lower back. "More."

"I'm fighting the urge to pick you up, to kiss you, to make you mine, to mark you." The words tumbled out in a frustrated growl that turned her core liquid.

Smiling, she ghosted her fingers over the skin of his arms, wrists to elbows to shoulders and back down. "Keep fighting the urge. Tell me more."

He groaned. "I'm going to come like an inexperienced male if you keep touching me."

She got up and knelt in front of him. Fevered onyx eyes stared at her when she leaned forward. "Oh, my gorgeous male, you'll have to wait a lot longer before you get to come. I'm going to use that damn patience of yours against you, even if it kills me too."

Torag's emotions were splayed on his beautiful face—frustration, desire, and the promise of revenge. She couldn't wait.

"Well, at least you'll get to touch me a little. Get me out of these clothes."

The look on his face warned her a second before he ripped her top from her. His thumbs brushed along her thighs as he slid the leather pants off her, deliberately slow. Goosebumps covered her pale skin, but Erisi held up her hand when he moved to take her in his arms.

"No more touching unless I tell you to," she admonished with a smile.

"You little demon," Torag groaned.

"I thought you knew," Erisi teased while she retrieved the vial from before. Torag's eyes were riveted on the golden drops as they landed on the flat of her stomach. They followed her fingers while she worked the oil into her skin. Her breasts were next. She kneaded the skin until her breathing came in pants, synchronized with his.

The moan escaped her lips unbidden. Torag moved forward, reaching for her with hunger in his eyes. As his hand hovered inches from her glistening skin, he growled and closed it into a fist.

"Please," he begged her. "Please let me touch you."

She took a deep breath. "Hands. Only my upper body."

Torag was on her before she'd uttered the last word. His fingers brushed her own when he cupped her breast, thumb on her hard nipple. The flick of his finger made her arch into his touch.

"How can this be even worse? How can it be worse to touch you?" He groaned with the palm of his other hand splayed on her stomach. "Please, I need to taste you, kiss you. Please, Wildfire, I need you more than I need breath."

She shook her head. If he kissed her, this was all over. She was teetering on the edge already, the longing so great it swallowed all her lofty intentions for this damn torture session.

This was supposed to push him to the brink. How the hell was she close to bursting? If only he knew how little control she had left…

His fingers on her skin brought bliss and longing and so much tenderness, it melted her from the inside out.

"Get on the bed," she choked out. "Now."

She couldn't use the chains. They reminded her too much of the moment she'd broken him. She would never use her chains on him again.

In the end, she decided, "Hands on the head end. You do not move them unless I give you permission, do you hear me?"

Torag glared at her but obeyed.

The muscles of his triceps bulged as he gripped the wood above his head. His chest rose and fell in a rapid rhythm as she kissed her way up from his navel to his sternum. The oil she'd used on his skin mingled with his essence, smoky and perfect. She reached the pulse in the hollow of his throat.

Her hand found his rock-hard length pressing against her stomach. When her fingers gripped him tight, he bucked against her. "Fuck!"

Before Erisi could move her hand up and down, Torag's fingers on her wrist stopped her. "I need to be inside of you. I can't hold—" He whimpered when she moved. "Can't hold back."

She looked in his eyes and asked a question she knew the answer to. "Why should I let you have me, Torag?"

His body was shaking under her now. "Because I love you more than my own life, Wildfire. All of you. Any form you choose to take."

The words, the look in his eyes made her heart sing. Still, Erisi licked her lips and continued her cruel questions. She needed to. "Are you worthy of being mine?"

He faltered. There it was—the pain she'd seen before. The belief that he was not enough. Not worthy.

The longer the silence between them, the larger the crack in her heart got.

Erisi let go of him and lifted his chin so he could meet her eyes. "I'm going to tell you this until you believe me. You are worth more than the entirety of demonkind together. You're strong, honorable, fierce, loyal, intelligent, and fucking mine. You are worthy. Of me, of the leadership of this family, of anything you want to be. You are everything to me."

She watched the tears escape his control.

"Do you hear what I'm telling you? I want you to tell me you're worthy."

Torag closed his eyes.

"Eyes on me," she bit out, desperate.

The broken look on his face when he obeyed sent shivers down her naked body.

"Tell me," she whispered. "Please, Torag." Erisi put her hand on the mark she left on his heart. "Please."

He swallowed. "I'm—"

"Worthy," she murmured against his lips. She drew back and watched him tremble, hand still on his racing heart.

"I'm worthy," Torag told her, his fingers clenching around hers on his chest.

"Again," she told him, ignoring the tears streaming down her face.

"I'm worthy."

"You are. And you're mine. Now and forever. I need you." Moving her hips against his cock, she groaned at the friction. His large hands gripped her waist so hard she'd have bruises if not for her rapid healing. "Now you better fucking make the both of us come before I go up in flames."

His kiss only added fuel to the fire. His mouth worshiped every inch of her skin until she couldn't take it anymore.

His revenge was bliss and torture and sweet, sweet agony.

When Torag finally filled her, he did so completely that she didn't know how she'd existed up to that point. Her world narrowed to the light reflected in the onyx eyes of the male she loved.

Chapter 44 - Catharsis

-Torag-

"What are you doing to her?" Yerle asked Torag. From the cave's entrance, they watched Erisi repeat the same pattern with her chains, over and over and over again. She was drenched in sweat, and she still wasn't stopping. "She is unraveling in front of my eyes."

Torag smiled. "Just being patient. It's driving her insane."

"I can see that."

Torag looked at his grinning friend, grateful that they had this moment. That he hadn't lost him to the darkness of Caral. He wasn't sure if he'd survived the guilt.

Forgiven. He was forgiven.

Yerle had just punched his shoulder and told him there was nothing to forgive.

But he was trying to forgive himself.

Erisi was right. He was worthy of forgiveness.

Of the beautiful moments like these with the beings he loved.

"Are you sure it's a good idea though? We're talking about the most dangerous demon in existence here."

Torag wasn't worried. He knew she'd come back to him even if she turned. The question was how much longer he could keep his hands to himself. Erisi turned out to be very good at teasing him.

His patience was running out. Fast.

Torag stood. "Nobody better disturb us tonight. Nobody. You hear me?"

Yerle grinned up at him. "Not even when the Rohi attack?"

"Not even then." He thrust his sword in Yerle's arms. "Keep this safe. I don't think I'll need it tonight."

"Are you sure? She looks pretty damn angry to me."

Torag could hardly contain his smile.

When he got to the ridge Erisi was training on, he dodged a hellfire bolt directed at his feet.

"Get the fuck out. Unless you plan on telling me tonight is the night, you better stay far away."

He tried hard not to laugh out loud at the furious expression on her face. He was going to have fun breaking the little hellcat.

She shoved him. "What the hell are you smiling at?"

His fingers gripped the cotton fabric of her

top. He brought her close, his other hand capturing her chin to force her eyes on him. "Tonight."

Her breath stuttered before she regained her composure. "Fine. Send them all out of the cave, and we'll get started."

Torag's arm locked around her waist. "I think you're forgetting rule number one for tonight, Wildfire. I call the shots."

She glared at him. "I'm not forgetting anything."

"Every single demon is going to stay in this cave while you and I are having fun," he whispered against her ear. "I want them all to hear."

Erisi bucked against his hold. "Fuck no."

"Fuck yes." He grinned at her.

* * *

She was seething by the time they arrived in their quarters. As soon as they entered, she threw her chains down. "You've got to be kidding me, Torag. I can't do this."

Leaning against the wall, he told her, "You know what you've got to say if you want to stop."

She took a few steps and looked up at him. "Is this your revenge for breaking you in front of the family? I've told you how much I regret that decision. I thought it was the only way to keep you from following me. To make you hate me. To make this entire family hate me so nobody would even consider coming after me."

Her rage was quickly turning into the self-flagellation she'd been practicing for weeks now.

Torag pulled her trembling body against him. "This is not revenge. Let me ask you something."

Shining ice-blue eyes looked up at him.

"What do you think I want from you tonight?"

"You need to punish me for breaking you. For hurting you. For almost killing you," Erisi choked out. "I need to atone for all the horrible things I did to you," she whispered, "but please, I don't want everyone to hear."

She was still fighting her tears. He needed her to let go before the end of the night. She needed to grieve.

"See, you're wrong. While I wished you'd taken me with you, I understand perfectly why you did what you did. I would have done the same." Erisi tried to get away, but her push against his chest was weak enough to ignore. "As to what your demon did in that dungeon, you had no control. I still believe she turned back because she knew me, because she grieved over wounding me. It hurt like hell, but you had no control over any of that."

"Then what?" Erisi whispered. "What do you want?"

Torag whispered his next words against the perfectly formed shell of her ear. "You still haven't said what I see in your eyes when you look at me." His teeth tugged her earlobe. "Before I'm done with you, you'll scream it so loud this entire family will know. Do you understand me?"

Defiance flared in the ice of her eyes. "Bite me."

Torag's teeth grazed her throat. "That can be arranged." The shiver running through her body told him she didn't mind.

He let go of her and stepped back. "Get those clothes off."

Apparently, she wasn't going to fight all of his commands, just most of them.

Every inch of pale skin she unveiled had his pulse kicking up a little. By the time she was naked, his heart was racing.

"My beautiful Wildfire," he told her, his voice hoarse, "get over here."

Erisi narrowed her eyes and crossed her arms over her chest. Torag smiled. He'd been waiting for her to test the limits.

Slowly, he removed his weapons and took off his pants. "You're supposed to obey me tonight, Wildfire."

She scowled. Having her wait a week had clearly left her in a vicious mood, exactly what he'd been counting on.

As he threw down his clothes, he warned her, "If you don't obey me, I reserve the right to punish you."

He knew her well enough to see her swallow her moan at his words. When he got closer, he saw the goosebumps on her skin. Erisi took a step back and braced herself against the cavern wall, arms by her sides.

His palm covered the flat of her stomach and slid up until his fingers collared her throat. "Erisi..."

Her eyes were fixed on his face. The pale pink of her lips parted with a small sigh when his other hand found her breast. She gasped when he pinched her nipple hard enough to sting.

"Eyes on me," Torag murmured as he repeated the movement. She obeyed, her body straining against the hand around her throat.

His other fingers continued the sensuous torture while he tasted her. His tongue breached her lips and took control of her mouth, capturing her moans. His thigh pressed between her legs, and she rocked her hips into him. His hand slipped from her breast to her waist. Lower until he pushed a finger deep inside her slick heat.

"Torag..." She sounded breathless.

"I want you to tell me," he told her. His thumb caressed her clit while he pushed his finger deeper.

"Fuck. Torag, please."

"That's not what I want to hear, my love." he admonished her and withdrew his fingers.

Erisi strained against his hold. "You know how I feel."

Love overwhelmed him when he looked at her exasperated face, the blush tingeing her cheeks. "I do," he told her.

"Then why are you doing this?"

He watched her tears threaten to fall and fought the urge to kiss them away. His thumb brushed her mouth. "When you made me say out loud that I forgave myself, that I'm worthy, it was catharsis. It doesn't solve every problem. It doesn't make all the guilt disappear, but it lightened the darkness." He parted her lips with his thumb. "Maybe I'm selfish, but I need to hear it from your lips. And I think you need to say it."

His eyes followed the tear that escaped.

"I don't know if I can, Torag." Her voice trembled as much as her body did against him.

When he moved his thumb, she bit his finger. His grin grew, and Erisi shivered when she looked up and saw the look in his eyes.

"What did you just do, Wildfire?" Torag whispered in her ear. He knew a distraction when he saw one, but for now he'd allow it. "I wonder what punishment I should mete out for that."

Turning her around, he pushed her against the rough wall, his body plastered against her back.

"Maybe I should fuck you in this tight ass," he growled, driving his cock against her writhing curves.

"Fuck you." She threw her head back against his nose.

Torag pushed her harder against the wall, then slammed his palm down on her ass. The red imprint on those gorgeous curves fed the hunger raging through him. He brought his palm down again, and again, his other hand on the back of her neck to keep her restrained.

Any moment now, she'd turn on him and burn him alive.

Instead, she melted against the wall and moaned. For a beat, he thought he'd come without even touching himself. "Fuck, Wildfire."

Spinning her around, he slammed his mouth on hers. His hands lifted her burning ass so he could sink her heat onto his straining cock. They both groaned at the perfection of coming together.

Instead of slamming into her the way he wanted to, he stilled. "Tell me, my love."

"Please, please." Erisi's lips moved against his skin. "Please, Torag, I need you. Please."

He withdrew and slowly slid back in, torturing himself along with her. "Not enough."

Her nails raked his chest, the scratches stinging with a delicious burn.

Holding her hips still in a steel grip, he asked, "Does not telling me mean you don't love me, Wildfire?"

Her head snapped up, her eyes wide and furious. "No, you bastard, it doesn't mean that!"

He rewarded her with a slow roll of his hips that made her head fall back against the rock. "Then why can't you say it, my love?"

Her lips tightened into a narrow line. He stopped moving.

"Please, don't make me." Tears dripped from

her jaw and meandered down her flushed skin.

"I need to hear you say it, Wildfire," he whispered.

She screamed at him. "Everyone I love is cursed! Doomed to be destroyed by me or my enemies. How can you ask me to tell you? It feels like you're asking me to kill you!"

Pain washed over him at the despair in her eyes. He carried her over to their bed and laid her down. His fingers brushed the tears away, only to be drowned in more.

"I love you. And you love me. Do you think your enemies care whether you tell me out loud?"

"I know it doesn't make sense. I know it doesn't—" she sobbed.

"Trust me." Torag kissed the corner of her mouth, tasting the salt of her agony. "Trust me with your love, Erisi. We'll fight whatever comes for us together."

He filled her again, and her arms came around his neck, holding onto him as if he was her lifeline, the only way for her to keep afloat. They moved together, desperate, frantic with desire.

"Trust me, my love," Torag whispered against her lips before devouring her.

Her entire body tensed against him, her core impossibly tight around his cock. He didn't give her time to recover. He didn't give her time to breathe before kissing her again. Before fucking her harder, drawing her body closer to him with his hands on her ass.

Erisi broke free from his lips and gasped for breath. Torag smiled down at her as he slammed into her heat, making the gasp draw out into a shivering sigh.

"Torag, I—" She closed her eyes.

"No," he commanded. "Eyes open. I need to see it as much as I need to hear it."

She gazed up at him. "I love you, Torag."

Her words shook him to his core. His soul expanded into a blaze of light, and his body followed into the crevice of bliss.

When he came back down to earth, he found Erisi smiling up at him with a tenderness he'd never seen from her before.

His fingers brushed the hair from her forehead before he pressed his lips against her skin. "I love you, Erisi."

He kissed her temple and watched her eyelids drop as he told her again. "I love you, Wildfire," he murmured against her cheek.

"And I love you," she told him. His heart soared as high as before. He wondered how often he could get her to tell him.

His lips traced her cheekbone to her ear. Her fingers clenched around his shoulders when he whispered his next challenge. "Every time I make you come, you will say it louder. Until every fucking demon around knows what you feel for me. Until everyone knows you're mine, and mine alone."

She whimpered in response, her core tightening around his still half-hard cock. "I—"

Kissing his way from the shell of her ear to the corner of her mouth, he rocked into her. Her nails dug into his ass, pulling him closer. He smiled into their kiss and brought her wrists up above her head, pinning her.

"Oh, my love, I'll decide just how deep or fast this is going to be."

He moved his hips slightly, and she groaned. His thrusts were shallow, short. She struggled against his hold, arched her body into him, trying to get him closer. He drew back, slipping from her heat.

"Please. Please, Torag, please."

Her soft whimpers made it near impossible to not give them both what they wanted. With the last bit of strength he possessed, he rolled her on her stomach. Kissed the back of her neck and traced his tongue down her spine. His palms slid along the perfection of her ass to her hips.

He pulled her onto her knees, pulled her into him, sliding back into her heat with one hard thrust. She cried out and pushed back.

He let go.

Hands on her hips, he drove into her, over and over again. She tightened around him, hard, and he almost lost it. When she screamed his name, he fucked her harder. When she whimpered, then shouted, "I love you", he spilled deep inside her.

***

Yerle walked up to Torag and punched him on the shoulder. "Fucker."

"What did I do now?" He was too sated, his limbs too heavy to retaliate.

"I never thought she would say it out loud, let alone scream it for the entire mountain range to hear. I just lost another bet."

Erisi's chains wrapped around Yerle's ankles. When she pulled, Torag grinned as his friend's face hit the ground. "If you know what's good for you, you will. Never. Ever. Mention that again." Her furious face was only an inch away from Yerle's beaming smile.

"He has no inkling of what's good for him, don't bother," Sura sighed.

Surrounded by Erisi's wrath, Yerle's yelp, and Sura's relaxed observation, Torag was filled with happiness.

His existence bloomed into a life he'd never even known he'd missed.

As Erisi settled beside him, the heat of her toned body leaning against him made his blood sing. He kissed the top of her head and pulled her against his side, where she fit perfectly.

Ice blue eyes looked up at him. "I love you."

Torag smiled. "Thank hell. It would have been awkward if I was the only one." He captured her wrist before she could punch him. "I love you too, Wildfire."

The world narrowed into a single flare of exquisite heat captured in their kiss.

THE END

Thank you! You, my reader, are my inspiration.

You may not know this. You, my dear reader, are the inspiration for my stories. You are the one I dream up characters for. You are the one I want to share my stories with.

Without you, there wouldn't have been an Erisi, Torag, or Mei. Without you, I wouldn't have this fire to write the next story. And the next.

THANK YOU.

I hope you loved Erisi and Torag as much as I do. If you did (or even if you didn't), <u>I'd love your review</u> of the book on Amazon and/or Goodreads. For starting indie authors like myself, reviews are the best way to reach more readers.

The Hellfire series will continue in *LUCIFER'S RULE*, expected in January 2022. Do you want to find out how Torag and Erisi are raising their young to be as fierce as they are? Want to see what Mei is up to? Or are you dying to find out how Lucifer will take his revenge, and who might bring a fallen angel to his knees?

You can get a sneak peek of Book 2 on the next few pages! If you want to be kept up to date about the release date of Lucifer's Rule and the next books in the series, join my newsletter at *https://www.subscribepage.com/wildfire_newsletter*. You can also follow me on Amazon and get notified when I publish.

Enjoy!

Lucifer's Rule – A sneak peek

-1620 BC, Indus Valley-

Arren was thankful that the demonic horde was training outside the thick walls of the Dera Rawal stronghold today. At least none of the warriors would witness his humiliation at the hands of his father.

"For hell's sake, I'm two hundred years old. Stop treating me like a fledgling." Arren crossed his arms and glared at Torag. "Attack me! Use your damn power instead of swinging your sword at me from afar."

His throat was parched after an hour of sparring under the midday sun with the male, his body gritty as the reddish sands of the training field stuck to his damp, pale skin.

Torag, who seemed untouched by the heat and exertion, shook his head. "I don't need to slice or burn you to be able to teach you."

At the edge of the training field, Jaslene raised her hand. "Please, please, can I? Can I?"

Arren turned and scowled at his sister. Of course she'd rather watch him suffer than join the horde in the desert. "Keep out of this, Jas. You're not trying to teach me shit, you just want to burn me."

Jas shrugged. "True. Doesn't mean it can't be fun."

Sparring with his family was never fun. Despite being the same age as him, both his sisters could beat him without blinking an eye. The worst thing was that Mahala didn't even want to be a warrior. She spent her days working metal under Chandra's tutelage, and still she beat him whenever she reluctantly sparred with him.

Even his damn parents treated Arren as if he was the weak lamb in the flock. It didn't matter that he could beat any other young warrior. Being the young of Torag and Erisi, the demons who defied Lucifer and lived to thrive, made it impossible to shine. Arren spent his days living in their shadows.

He took a deep breath, gripped his sword tighter, and charged Torag. The male stepped aside and blocked his attack, only to be sliced by the next blow of Arren's weapon.

Instead of using his hellfire powers, Torag simply punched him in the face and watched Arren go down. "Defense, Arren. Always think about your defense."

"Just burn me already," Arren snarled while he pulled himself up and positioned himself for the next attack.

"Give up," Jas told him, lazing on a boulder to his right.

"Never!" Arren charged again.

Torag slammed him on the hot sand and kept his hand on Arren's heaving chest. "You can't win like this, Arren. You need to keep calm and think when you attack. You're too hotheaded."

"Burn!" his sister yelled.

Torag looked up, and Jas shrank into herself. "If taunting your brother is your mission in life, you clearly need more to do. Report to Chandra and see what else he can use help with."

Arren shouldn't find so much pleasure in seeing his sister's face fall. "Can't I check with Sura? She's the war chief and I—"

"Report to Chandra. Now." Torag's voice brooked no argument.

The male got up and offered Arren a hand. Arren ignored his help, scrambling to stand on legs that were trembling from exertion.

"Arren..."

His shoulders tensed at the understanding in Torag's voice. Why couldn't his father be cold and vicious? Why did he need to be so damn supportive and protective? It made his humiliation sting all the more.

"I know. I know. Practice, and I will get better."

Torag's hand landed on his shoulder. "Yes. More than that though, you need patience. Do you think I got powerful in a couple of centuries?

I'm over two thousand years old."

Arren swallowed. "But Jas and Maha are more powerful than I am. It's not fair. I practice more than the two of them combined."

It was just his luck that out of the three souls transformed to fledgling demons at the same time, his sisters had gotten the bulk of Erisi's substantial powers during their creation.

"In the end, it will be your dedication and determination that will make you fearsome. They might have more raw power, but that's not the only thing that matters," Torag told him.

Arren leaned into Torag's side, looking up in onyx eyes. He gave up trying to fight against the love radiating from the male who'd do anything to keep him and the rest of the family safe.

Strong arms wrapped around him in a hug Arren didn't want to admit he needed.

"Your time will come. I promise."

Printed in Great Britain
by Amazon